ems
or befo

### *"Rhea to away team!"*

The urgency in Captain Bazel's voice startled Ryssa out of her reverie.

"Sekmal here."

*"Prepare for emergency beam-out!"* Bazel commanded. *"A ship has just dropped out of warp. Sensors say it's the* Einstein.*"*

Everyone froze. That name had become infamous since the Borg assault on Sector 001 back in June: the science vessel that had been assimilated by what was believed to be a dormant, depopulated Borg cube and had played a key role in its subsequent strike against Earth.

"But the *Einstein* was destroyed," Paul said.

*"Believed destroyed,"* Bazel corrected. *"That belief was wrong. It's not only intact . . . it's gotten bigger."*

992672655 0

# STAR TREK

## THE NEXT GENERATION®

# GREATER
# THAN THE SUM

## CHRISTOPHER L. BENNETT

*Based on Star Trek: The Next Generation*
created by Gene Roddenberry

**POCKET BOOKS**
New York   London   Toronto   Sydney

The sale of this book without its cover is unauthorized. If you purchased this book without a cover, you should be aware that it was reported to the publisher as "unsold and destroyed." Neither the author nor the publisher has received payment for the sale of this "stripped book."

Pocket Books
A Division of Simon & Schuster, Inc.
1230 Avenue of the Americas
New York, NY 10020

This book is a work of fiction. Names, characters, places, and incidents either are products of the author's imagination or are used fictitiously. Any resemblance to actual events or locales or persons, living or dead, is entirely coincidental.

Copyright © 2008 by Paramount Pictures Corporation. All Rights Reserved.

™, ® and © 2008 by CBS Studios Inc. All Rights Reserved. STAR TREK and related marks are trademarks of CBS Studios Inc.

**©CBS** CONSUMER PRODUCTS

CBS, the CBS EYE logo, and related marks are trademarks of CBS Broadcasting Inc.
™ & © CBS Broadcasting Inc. All Rights Reserved.

This book is published by Pocket Books, a division of Simon & Schuster, Inc., under exclusive license from CBS Studios Inc.

All rights reserved, including the right to reproduce this book or portions thereof in any form whatsoever. For information address Pocket Books Subsidiary Rights Department, 1230 Avenue of the Americas, New York, NY 10020

First Pocket Books paperback edition August 2008

POCKET and colophon are registered trademarks of Simon & Schuster, Inc.

For information about special discounts for bulk purchases, please contact Simon & Schuster Special Sales at 1-800-456-6798 or business@simonandschuster.com.

Cover art by Mojo; cover design by Alan Dingman

Manufactured in the United States of America

10  9  8  7  6  5  4  3  2  1

ISBN-13: 978-1-4165-7132-2
ISBN-10:    1-4165-7132-9

*To the dragons*

**Gloucestershire County Council**

QY

992672655  0

| Askews | 16-Oct-2008 |
|--------|-------------|
| AF     | £6.99       |
|        |             |

# HISTORIAN'S NOTE

The main events in this book take place in September 2380 over three months after the *Starship Einstein*'s mission to study the presumed dead Borg cube failed. The resulting assimilating of the crew of the *Einstein* and the assault on Earth have shaken the federation (*Star Trek: The Next Generation—Before Dishonor*). It concludes early in January 2381.

# PROLOGUE

*U.S.S. Rhea*
Star cluster NGC 6281

*Stardate 57717*

**"ARE WE *THERE* YET?"**

Lieutenant Commander Dawn Blair rolled her eyes at the question. "Are you going to ask that question every morning, Trys?"

"At least until we get there," T'Ryssa Chen replied, brushing her shaggy bangs out of her eyes. The gesture briefly revealed one of the elegantly pointed ears that she usually kept hidden under her shoulder-length black hair.

"You're just hoping to annoy me into letting you go on the away team," Blair said.

"Is it working?"

"Mmm . . . no."

"Aw, come on, Dawn!" T'Ryssa moaned. "A whole cluster full of carbon planets, and you expect me to sit up here manning a boring old console?"

"Well, it might help if you remembered to call me 'Commander' when we're on duty, *Lieutenant.*"

T'Ryssa's slanted eyebrows twisted in a way that Blair still sometimes found incongruous. She knew the younger woman had been raised by her human mother and had barely known her Vulcan father, but it was hard to shake off one's expectations of Vulcans. Which was probably why T'Ryssa defied those expectations so aggressively. "Right, I keep forgetting."

"On purpose. You always have to be such a non-conformist, Trys. That's why you're still a jg at twenty-six."

"I don't *have* to be," T'Ryssa countered. "I'm just very good at it. Gotta play to your strengths, you know."

She grew serious, or as close as she ever came. "And I'm not very good at sitting still in a cubby-hole, which is why you've gotta let me go down there and do some science! When we get there," she added. "Come on, Daw—Commander Dawn, sir, ma'am—" At the science officer's glare, she started over. "I mean, this is a *Luna*-class ship, right? All about crew diversity and cross-cultural synergies and exploring new approaches? Which means, in short, we're a ship full of nonconformists, and proud of it. Nonconforming—ity—ism—is how we get the job done around here, right?" T'Ryssa bent her knees and clasped her hands in supplication. "So how about it, O Dawn, commander of my heart? Pleeeeeze?" She actually batted her eyelids.

Blair sighed, knowing T'Ryssa would keep this up until she relented. "Okay! Okay. Janyl can man the console, you can go on the away team and out of my hair."

"Oh, thank you, thank you! And such lovely hair it is, my commandress."

"Don't push it," Blair said. She was self-conscious about her hair, an unruly mass of cinnamon-brown waves that she usually kept confined within a bun or French braid while on duty, though Derek from environmental engineering insisted it was the most gorgeous thing he'd ever seen. Still, she couldn't help smirking at T'Ryssa's antics. Blair was too soft a touch to be any good at keeping her in line, which was probably to T'Ryssa's detriment in the long run. But giving her this away mission could help improve her career prospects. The half-Vulcan woman may not have been very good at practicing Starfleet discipline or respecting the chain of command, but she was a good scientist with a knack for understanding alien behaviors, sentient and otherwise. If the anomalous biosigns coming from the carbon planets of the NGC 6281 star cluster were correct and there was complex life there, she could be genuinely useful.

"Anyway," Blair went on, "we have to get there first."

T'Ryssa sagged. "I am so sick of this. We hit a zone of altered subspace, we get knocked out of warp, we spend five hours recalibrating the warp engines, we make it four hours before the structure of subspace changes, and we drop out of warp again. I swear I'm getting motion sick. Are we getting any closer to figuring out a pattern behind these distortions?"

Blair shook her head. "Only that they seem connected to the energy emissions from the carbon planets. And that those emissions seem to be coming from beneath the planets' surfaces, not localized around any of the biosigns."

"What about the cosmozoans?"

"We can't confirm that the energy readings from them are connected. It could be interference from the subspace distortions."

T'Ryssa sighed, and Blair shared in her disappointment. As their sister ship *Titan* had confirmed half a year back, spacegoing life-forms were prone to inhabit star-formation regions. The open clusters *Rhea* was currently surveying were located between the Orion and Carina Arms, removed from the star-formation zones that defined the arms of the galaxy, but they were still fairly young (as all open clusters were, for eventually their components were scattered by gravitational interactions with other stars and nebulae). NGC 6281 itself, a clump of a hundred or so young stars sharing a volume of space barely fifteen light-years in diameter, was less than a quarter billion years old and still retained a faint remnant of the nebula from which it had formed, so finding spacegoing organisms here was not a complete surprise. But the cosmozoans detected in this particular cluster were as strange as the space they occupied, giving off anomalous energy readings and biosignatures and seeming to appear and disappear unpredictably from sensors. Getting close to any of them, however, would take considerable time unless Blair and chief engineer Lorlinna could devise some way to adjust the warp engines to cope with the inexplicably shifting subspace geometry of this cluster. If they were unable to do so, then Captain Bazel might decide to turn back after the survey of the nearest component of the cluster, NGC 6281-34, and move on to the next open cluster once the *Rhea* slogged its way back to normal space.

It all depended on what they found on System 34's planets and whether it was exciting or mysterious enough to warrant surveying any of the other systems in the cluster. But it would be at least another day before they reached that system, a system they could reach in a few hours under normal circumstances.

Dawn Blair found herself agreeing with her friend's sentiment, if only in the privacy of her thoughts. *Are we there yet?*

T'Ryssa Chen hated going through the transporter. It wasn't that she was afraid of it or anything;

rather, she was ticklish, and being transported felt like being tickled from the inside. People kept telling her she was imagining things, that there was no untoward sensation involved with transporting other than a slight tingling numbness, but she knew what she felt. Maybe it was a side effect of her hybrid nervous system; maybe all human-Vulcan blends had the same reaction but were too disciplined to admit it. Or maybe the transporter gods had just decided to pick on her. She tried to shake it off once she materialized, a convulsive move like she was trying to brush spiders off her body, but the heavy EV suit she wore hampered the movement.

Not that she regretted wearing the suit in this environment. NGC 6281-34 III, like most of the planetary bodies that long-range sensors had detected in the cluster, was a carbon planet: a world where carbon was the most abundant element in its mineral composition. In carbon-rich protoplanetary disks, graphite, carbides, and other carbon compounds tended to solidify sooner than the silicates that made up the bulk of normal planets, producing worlds with iron cores, carbide mantles, and crusts of graphite and diamond. The resultant surface chemistry was oxygen-poor, with tarry hydrocarbon seas and an atmosphere of carbon monoxide and methane.

*And it looks about as inviting as it sounds,* Trys thought as she looked around her through the helmet visor. The rocky ground on which they stood was dark and crumbly, like a carbonaceous asteroid. The depressions in the surface were filled with pools of tar, black against gray-brown. The hazy blue-green sky was smudged with clouds of graphite dust.

As First Officer Sekmal and the rest of the away team deployed their tricorders, T'Ryssa struck a pose as though planting an invisible flag and proclaimed, "I dub this planet Pencilvania!"

Sekmal turned to glare at her, raising an eyebrow in that way that Vulcans seemed to be specially trained for. "Explain."

"Pencil. You know. Old writing implement? Used graphite? It's why graphite's called that? Because people wrote with it?" Sekmal simply continued to glare until Trys sighed. "Never mind," she said, taking out her tricorder. *Vulcans.* For all their claims of emotionlessness, the Vulcans on *Rhea* were consistent in their disdain for Trys herself, as though her biology somehow required her to live up to their cultural standards. She could never see the logic in that.

"I thought it was funny," said Paul Janiss, smiling at her through his helmet. Trys gave him a wan smile of gratitude, knowing it was more likely that he just wanted to flatter her into sleeping with him again. Not that she wouldn't be interested in doing so, at least on a purely physical level, but she preferred more sincerity in her praise, and in her men.

"Anyway," Paul went on, "it's not like we're

going to have any other fun on this dump of a planet. Bleakest hole I ever saw."

"Don't dismiss it so quickly," said Thyyshev zh'Skenat, the Andorian geologist. "As the galaxy ages and supernovae inject more carbon into the interstellar medium, the ratio of carbon planets to oxygen planets will increase. In a billion years or so, all new planets may be carbon worlds."

"Thanks, Thyyshev. You just gave me a reason to be glad I'm not immortal."

"How do you know?" Trys asked.

"Know what?"

"That you're not immortal? I mean, there's only one way to know for sure, isn't there?"

It took Paul a moment. "Oh! Good one."

"On the other hand," Trys went on as if he hadn't spoken, "there's no way to prove anyone really *is* immortal either. Just that they haven't died yet. Kind of a meaningless category, really. Maybe it needs a better name. Like 'mortality challenged.'"

Thyyshev's antennae twisted under his specially designed helmet. "Aren't you supposed to be doing your duty or something?"

"It's been known to happen." She consulted her tricorder, moving out from the group. "I still don't get how there could be any life here, though. The system's only a couple hundred million years old. If this planet weren't made of carbides and graphite, it'd probably still be molten."

"Many planets in young star systems are known to be inhabited," Sekmal pointed out. "Generally this is the result of terraforming and colonization. We may discover signs of an intelligent presence here as well."

"I'm not reading any life, intelligent or stupid," Trys told him. "No plants, no microbes. This reads as a brand-new, sterile planet, right out of the replicator."

Her tricorder naturally chose that moment to begin beeping. "Um. Except for those. New readings coming from somewhere over that ridge," she said, gesturing. "Not sure where they came from; they're well within range."

The tricorder beeped again, denoting a sudden strong signal behind her. T'Ryssa turned around—

And yelped. The life-form was practically right in front of her. It was an oddly amorphous being, pale gray and vaguely bipedal in shape, but with no evident legs, its lower half almost conical, like a long skirt or robe that flared at the bottom. It had upper-body protrusions roughly where a humanoid's arms would be, but they were merely flexible rods with winglike membranes attaching them to the sides of the trunk. The head, if it could be called that, was large and featureless. But it had senses of some sort, for it responded to T'Ryssa's surprised reaction with a similar rearing-back motion of its own, though its was slower and more stately.

"Uhh, Commander?" Paul said. Trys looked around to see that more such creatures had appeared near the other members of the team.

"Make no sudden moves," Sekmal said. Facing

the entity before him, he raised his hand and offered it the Vulcan salute, insofar as his EV suit glove permitted. "Peace and long life," he said. "I am Commander Sekmal of the *U.S.S. Rhea,* representing the United Federation of Planets." The entity raised its arm, or wing, in a similar motion but made no sound. "We are on a mission of peaceful exploration. Can you understand me?"

The creatures gave no verbal response—perhaps not surprising, since they had no mouths. Instead, they simply continued their loose mimicry of the away team's actions. "Great," Trys muttered. "Welcome to Mime World."

"Please limit yourself to *constructive* comments, Lieutenant," Sekmal said.

She glared. "Not much I can tell you, Commander. The readings on these . . . Mime Angels are bizarre. Their molecular composition—it isn't normal living tissue. I'm not sure it's even biological. Carbon based, but not quite a match for this planet's chemistry." She moved in closer to the entity that shadowed her, peering curiously into its lack of a face. "No metabolic readings either. They're a match for ambient temperature. And their internal energy readings . . . I've never seen anything like them before."

"I have," Sekmal said. "They resemble the quantum energy emanations from the interior of this planet. There are faint fluctuations in that quantum field that appear to be synchronized with the entities' appearances and actions."

"Hmm," Trys said. "So maybe they are connected to it af— *Whoa!*" She had turned back to her Mime Angel and been surprised to see that it suddenly had a semblance of a face. Only a semblance, though, a smallish set of contours emulating eyes, nostrils, and mouth, static and unmoving. "Are you guys seeing this too?"

The others confirmed that their Angels had also manifested masklike faces. Trys turned back to hers to see that its eyes were wider, as though mirroring her surprise. And yet she still saw no overt movement in its features. She tried making faces at it, grinning, winking, sticking out her tongue. Its own features transformed subtly as she watched, not through any sort of muscular movement but more by dissolving from one expression to the next, or through a subtle change of aspect she couldn't follow with her eyes. She was reminded of the masks of Japanese Noh theater, the way their static features could seem to transform as the performers changed the angle of their heads, due to the clever way the masks were carved. "I was wrong," T'Ryssa said. "They aren't Mime Angels." Her grin widened at the impending pun. "They're Noh Angels."

"Then what are they?" Paul asked without irony, decisively scuttling his chances of ever seeing her naked again.

Still, his question resonated. "What are you?" T'Ryssa whispered to her Noh Angel. It leaned forward, seeming to ask the same question of her.

*"Rhea to away team!"* The urgency in Captain Bazel's voice startled her out of her reverie.

"Sekmal here."

*"Prepare for emergency beam-out!"* Bazel commanded. *"A ship has just dropped out of warp. Sensors say it's the* Einstein.*"*

Everyone froze. That name had become infamous since the Borg assault on Sector 001 back in June: the science vessel that had been assimilated by what was believed to be a dormant, depopulated Borg cube and had played a key role in its subsequent strike against Earth.

"But the *Einstein* was destroyed," Paul said.

*"Believed destroyed,"* Bazel corrected. *"That belief was wrong. It's not only intact . . . it's gotten bigger."*

Captain Bazel stared goggle-eyed at the image on the screen—not because he was alarmed but because, as a Saurian, he was always goggle-eyed. Certainly the sight of what had once been the *Einstein*—its original contours now obscured under a blocky jumble of ill-matched ship parts grafted together by a network of conduits and structural members in Borg black and green—sent at least two of his cardiac nodes racing. But Bazel had not survived seventy years in Starfleet by losing his cool.

*"Please elaborate, Captain,"* Sekmal said. *"You say it has grown larger?"*

"Affirmative. It seems to have assimilated additional vessels, accreted them to its hull. We're attempting to elude them long enough to drop shields and beam you aboard, but their capabilities are unknown at this point. Stand by." Nuax, the Edoan flight controller, was working controls with all three hands as she tried to keep the planet between *Rhea* and the Borg vessel while still remaining in transporter range of the team.

He turned to Caithlin Tomei at tactical. "Extrapolate from the Borg's last known course and program a spread of torpedoes to arc through the atmosphere, hugging the planet. Keep the Borg from seeing them until the last possible moment." Tomei nodded and executed the order.

"Clean miss, sir," she announced a minute later. "No sign of impact."

"Sir!" Nuax called. But Bazel's wide field of vision already let him see what was on the screen: the former *Einstein* was coming over the curve of the planet on a different, tighter trajectory than before, on an intercept course with *Rhea.* There was no chance to drop shields.

But then the shields proved moot anyway as a green shimmer heralded the arrival of half a dozen Borg drones on the bridge. These drones were different from the standard type, their bionic components sleeker and more compact, their movements faster and more aggressive. As Bazel dove from his command chair to avoid the cutting arm that swung down at him, he recalled the reports that the immense Borg vessel that had taken the *Einstein* had employed a new, evolved form of assimilation technology. He realized that experience would likely no longer apply where these drones were concerned.

Indeed, when the security guards opened fire on the invaders, they found that the Borg's strategy had already changed. Before, it was always possible to take out one or two drones with phaser fire before they adapted and their personal shields kicked in. But these drones' shields went up the moment the first phaser beams were fired. *They aren't just reacting—they're anticipating.*

"General distress signal!" Bazel called. "Alert Starfleet!" As the guards recalibrated their phasers to find a frequency that could penetrate the shields, Bazel went on the offensive, striking out physically at the nearest drone. That was a move they apparently hadn't anticipated, for the drone soon fell to the deck, its neck snapped by Saurian strength. Bazel noted that the drone he'd just killed belonged to no species he recognized, proving that the ship had assimilated new blood over the past few months. He knew it shouldn't make any difference, but he felt a stab of relief that he hadn't killed a fellow Starfleet officer.

But Bazel had no time to reflect. Another drone was approaching from the right, trying to come at him from behind but failing to account for Bazel's wide field of vision. He ducked and whirled, taking out the drone's legs from under it with a spinning kick. He caught its head as it fell and drove it into the deck. A second blow ended its ordeal.

The remaining drones kept up their assault, and reports came in over the comm that more drones were attacking engineering, environmental control, and other key areas of the ship. Bazel saw Nuax and T'Hala fall before the drones, slain rather than assimilated, in keeping with these Borg's new aggressiveness. Moments later, the lights flickered and died. Bazel smiled grimly. *Can drones see in the dark?* he wondered as he popped out the filtered contact lenses that let his nocturnally adapted eyes function in normal Starfleet lighting conditions. Looking around, he saw the rest of the bridge crew floundering in the dark and realized it was up to him.

Bazel ran for the tactical console, where Tomei was under attack by a drone. He tore it free from her and sent it flying, but then he saw the puncture marks in her neck. He blinked his inner eyelids closed, filtering out what humans called the "visible" light so he could concentrate solely on the infrared portion of his visual range. Already, Caithlin's body temperature was dropping, the cold spreading out from her neck as the nanoprobes surged through her bloodstream and self-replicated. *Why assimilate her instead of killing?* he wondered, supposing they wished to gain her tactical knowledge. In any case, he had to end this soon if there was any chance of saving her and the others.

He turned to the tactical console and prepared to trigger a release of anesthezine gas. He wasn't sure it would work on the drones, but it was worth a try. And if it failed, at least he would still be conscious, his natural respiratory filters protecting him. He would still be able to try other options.

Though if this failed, Bazel realized, his only option might be the autodestruct system. At least he could try to take the former *Einstein* with him.

But then a phaser beam struck the tactical console. It exploded in his face, the flare of heat blinding his thermal vision. Ignoring the searing pain, he snapped back the nictitating membranes to let visible light in again—only to see the phaser-wielding drone advancing on him as two more closed in on his flanks.

He struck out again, but he was slowed by his injuries. The drones caught him and he felt cold spikes bite into his neck. With his last free thought, he prayed that the away team could somehow survive this . . . and somehow survive the toxic conditions down on the planet long enough for rescue to come.


T'Ryssa Chen had never taken much interest in her Vulcan heritage, feeling that the repression of emotion would take all the fun out of life. But then she listened to the screams coming over the comm channel from *Rhea*. And then a group of Borg drones materialized around the away team and the Noh Angels, and T'Ryssa had to watch as Thyyshev and Paul drew their phasers and were promptly cut down. And for the first time in her life, she wished she knew how to stop herself from feeling.

Sekmal ordered a tactical retreat, firing uselessly at the shielded drones and barking, *"Move!"* with un-Vulcan intensity to break T'Ryssa from her paralysis. It was too late for him; a drone caught up to him and impaled him on a blade that extended from its arm. *"Go!"* he ordered with his last breath.

Weeping equally for her two friends and the commander she couldn't stand, T'Ryssa started to run . . . but paused, turning to the Noh Angel nearest her.

"If you can understand me, please run," she urged it, knowing it was futile. It simply mimicked the grief and horror on her face, a mere mask over an unknowable interior. As Trys ran, she looked back to see a drone closing on it. The Angel changed, its face disappearing from her view and presumably manifesting on its far side to regard the drone. *"No!"* she cried as the drone plunged assimilation tubules into its hide . . .

And then removed them and tried again. And again. The Noh Angel regarded it curiously, bending its wing to nudge the drone's shoulder in mimickry, but showed no other change. Trys came to a halt, amazed by the scene.

And so she was taken by surprise by the drone that came up behind her. She felt the tubules pierce her suit and her skin before she could even reach for her phaser.

*Why me?* she wondered. The others had been killed; why was she being assimilated?

*Because you didn't fight back in time. Because you froze, and you ran. Just like you always run.*

T'Ryssa felt the chill surging through her veins, felt her consciousness slipping away, and longed for a place she could run to. A place where she could be safe . . .

As awareness gradually returned, T'Ryssa didn't much like what she was becoming aware of. Her head was spinning, and half of her body was tingling like it did in the transporter, only worse, while the other half simply ached. She gradually realized she was lying in something that felt like damp grass against her skin. Groggily, she opened her eyes, blinking against the bright daylight. A dark shape moved in front of her, shading her from the light. "Thanks, I . . ."

Her eyes focused, and she saw a dragon peering down at her.

Yelping, T'Ryssa leaped off the ground, startling the large purplish creature into emitting a piercing, ascending shriek. Not wanting to risk the dragon's ire, Trys jogged back from the shoreline of the lake, knowing the legless creature could not easily travel on land. If it tried to use its wings and fly at her, she could retreat to the nearby tree line and—

"Wait a minute. What the hell am I doing on Maravel?" She looked down at herself. "And why am I naked?" The dragon merely opened its jagged beak and cawed again, offering no answer.

She remembered *Rhea,* the carbon planet, the Borg attack. She remembered the tubules piercing her shoulder. Looking at it, she saw two small puncture marks, still a livid green. *So it was real! Was it?* "How could I be here?" she went on aloud. "Wait a minute," she said, still talking to the dragon, which apparently no longer felt threatened, for it had folded its batlike wings and settled down to float at the edge of the lake, watching her with a stony gaze. In her childhood, during that all-too-brief year her mother had been posted here at the Starfleet research station, she had often come out to talk to the relatively docile lake dragons that lived near the colony, the ones that had learned they had nothing to fear from humanoids so long as they posed no threat. She had imagined that their stern demeanor masked an intelligence greater than what the scientists claimed, that they had cosmic wisdom to offer her if only she asked the right question in the right way. They had always made her feel oddly safe. Maybe because, unlike Lieutenant Commander Antigone Chen, they had always taken the time to listen to the musings and complaints of a ten-year-old human-Vulcan girl.

"Wait a minute," she repeated. "Unimatrix Zero. I read about this. Some people who get assimilated, they have a mutation, they can create a virtual dreamworld when they regenerate." The dragon cocked its angular head with seeming skepticism. "No, you're right," she told it. "That's right, the queen shut that down. Or Janeway did, I forget. Same difference.

"So could this be some kind of private Unimatrix Zero? My own little regenerative dreamworld between shifts killing and assimilating people?" She looked down again at the welts on her shoulder. "Then why am I in so much pain?" She tried to will it away, with no luck. She tried to will herself into the forest elf garb she'd imagined herself wearing as she'd played in these woods as a child, green and brown skins with a bow and quiver strapped to her back. But her lithe body stayed resolutely nude.

She sighed. "So either I've got a worse imagination than I thought," she told the dragon, "or I'm really here on Maravel. But how is that possible? I was a hundred sectors away! With a terminal case of Borgdom!"

The dragon let out another shriek, rearing back its spiny neck, and wriggled its boat-shaped lower body to turn itself around, using its wings as paddles. Then it flapped its wings forcefully and rose from the water. "Aww, c'mon, it wasn't that bad!" Trys called.

But then she heard the sound of air car engines closing in on her, along with transporter whines as people materialized in a perimeter around her, just beyond the giant sequoialike trees. Remembering she was naked, Trys moved to cover herself . . . but then stopped. *Okay, either I'm dreaming, or there's something really big going on here and I'm the only one who can tell them about it. Either way, I might as well do it with style.*

So she strode forward casually, naked and unashamed, to greet the Starfleet security contingent as it burst from the trees. "Hi, guys!" she called. "Have you seen my boyfriend? Middle Eastern guy, goes by Adam? You can't miss him . . ."

# 1

———◆———

*U.S.S. Enterprise*
*Stardate 57725*

**JEAN-LUC PICARD WOKE UP ALONE.**

For a long time, that had been a routine event for him. But that had been in another life. His new life, he reminded himself, was only just beginning. But already, what had come before seemed like a life that had been led by a different man. Not that it would be the first time, he thought wryly.

These days, in this life, he usually woke up to find Beverly by his side. Even with her doctor's hours, he was usually the first one to rise. Now, though, she was absent. She couldn't have gotten an emergency call from sickbay; his captain's reflexes would have awakened him as soon as the call came. No, there was something else amiss.

*Can you be so sure?* he asked himself as he

climbed out of bed and donned a robe. *This is still so new. You can't assume you've learned her every quirk.* But intuitively, he was certain. He had known Beverly for nearly half his life, and so the novelty of his current existence was balanced with a sense of familiarity, as though it had been waiting for him all along.

And so he found her in the first place he looked, standing in the main living area of their quarters, gazing out at the star trails that streaked by at warp like horizontal rain. He knew she sensed his approach, felt her openness to him, and so he came up behind her and cradled her gently in his arms, kissing her head. "Good morning . . . Mrs. Picard."

She chuckled. "Good morning, Mister Crusher. Or is it Howard?" she added, holding out her hand to study the gold band adorning her left ring finger. "I still haven't decided."

"Either would be an honor," he told her, though of course they were both teasing. Upon returning from their recent honeymoon in Labarre, they had agreed that they would continue to go by their usual names, to avoid the confusion of two Picards (or Howard-Picards or Picard-Crushers) on the same ship.

Besides, neither of them wished to make a public fuss about their marital status, any more than they had about their wedding. After Lwaxana Troi had turned Will and Deanna's marriage ceremony on Betazed into the most enormous social event since the end of the Dominion War (Picard had never seen so many nude people in the same place and hoped he never would again), they had both agreed they would prefer a small, understated ceremony, just their immediate friends and family, in order to dodge the publicity that would inevitably attend the wedding of Jean-Luc Picard.

A part of Picard, though, almost wished it had been a grand ceremony to reflect the significance of this transition. For so long, he'd been certain he would never marry—because Beverly was the only one he would have chosen to wed, and he'd always considered her unattainable. Besides, the one time he'd ever contemplated marriage before, twenty years ago, it had been thanks to the undue influence of an immortal alien woman who had manipulated his emotions to make him love her. That had rather soured him on the idea of matrimony.

And then there had been Eline . . . but that had truly been another life.

Yet after he almost lost her on Kevratas, he and Beverly had finally acknowledged their feelings for each other. Perhaps they had been inspired by seeing Will and Deanna finally wed, or perhaps Data's death, sacrificing himself to stop Shinzon of Remus from destroying the *Enterprise,* had made them both aware of the finite time they had to find happiness. In any case, they had finally become a couple, and in the ensuing months, Picard had found himself contemplating a proposal.

But then, five months ago, he had heard the voices of the Borg in his head again, and he had known the Federation was not safe. He had taken the

*Enterprise* to the moon where they were constructing a gigantic supercube, destroyed their new queen aborning, and neutralized the immediate threat. But he knew the Borg; it was their nature to adapt, and they always seemed to have an extra trick up their sleeves. After Kathryn Janeway and *Voyager* had collapsed their transwarp network two years before, denying them a quick route to Federation space, their remaining debris from past battles proved to be a Trojan horse, hosting an assimilation virus that awaited only an activation command from a Borg queen—or in this case a psychologically damaged Starfleet admiral who tried to become one. A nanite antidote to the virus had been developed, and again Starfleet had assumed it was safe, leaving them dangerously unprepared for the supercube attack.

After that cube's defeat and the removal of all its drones, Starfleet had again believed itself safe. But less than two months later, the vessel itself had adapted, its technology coming alive and assimilating Admiral Janeway herself to make her its new queen. It had then led the most devastating Borg attack yet on the Sol system, defeated only by the sacrifice of many of Starfleet's finest, including Kathryn Janeway herself.

Picard had thus kept his guard up in the weeks that followed. Although *Enterprise* had resumed its primary mission of exploration, Picard had not been ready to return fully to peacetime status in his own mind. He knew that the destruction of the *Einstein,* the science vessel that had ferried Janeway to her doom and been assimilated along with her, had not been conclusively verified. He had not been able to relax until debris from the ship had been confirmed among the wreckage from the battle—only a small amount, true, but it was likely the small craft had been mostly vaporized in the cataclysmic destruction of its mother ship. Picard had not been willing to take that on faith, but as more time had passed with no reports of Borg activity and no sign of the *Einstein* or any unaccounted ion trails leaving the Sol system, he had finally begun to let himself lower his guard. As he held Beverly in his arms each night, he had found himself more and more unwilling to defer the possibilities of their life together due to his lingering fear of the Borg. After all, there were other threats his crew faced all the time. Indeed, between the last two Borg incidents, Picard had faced the possible destruction of the entire universe from a threat beyond his comprehension, one that had been overcome only because Q, of all people, had made sure that Picard, of all people, was in the right place at the right time.

So finally, last month, in an idyllic glade on a habitable Jovian moon the ship had surveyed, with the giant ringed planet above them painting the night sky in vivid red-gold hues, he had popped the question and been equally surprised and relieved when she had readily said yes. And his new life had begun soon thereafter. Being a newlywed was a giddy, unprecedented thing for him. He had some experience with married life, of a sort, thanks to the memory download imparted to him by the Kataan probe eleven years ago, the legacy of a race extinct for a thousand years. Rather than preserving their science or history, the probe had contained the life experience of an ordinary man named Kamin. Picard had relived Kamin's memories of marriage to his wife Eline, of fatherhood to Batai and Meribor. But the download had not included the first three years of Kamin and Eline's marriage, so his wedding and honeymoon with Beverly had been—fittingly, he felt—a unique experience for him. And the thrill of it was far from wearing off. These were no borrowed memories, but his own real life—even though it still felt too good to be true. For the first time in two decades, maybe longer, he was truly happy.

So the air of melancholy he sensed from his wife troubled him. "What brings you out here to stare at the stars?" he asked.

Beverly sighed. "Do you know what day it is?"

He paused. "I assume you don't mean the stardate."

She turned to him. "It's been ten years to the day since Wesley left to become a Traveler."

Picard nodded, comprehending. Young Wesley Crusher had always been a wunderkind, atypically brilliant, impatient with the slow pace of his growth and the lowered expectations others had of him. It had made the boy something of a nuisance when he had first come aboard the previous *Enterprise* more than sixteen years ago, contemptuous of limits and filled with arrogant certainty of his own rightness, even more so than most adolescent boys. But then an advanced alien called the Traveler had told Picard of Wesley's special genius, his exceptional insight into the workings of the universe, and urged him to nurture the boy. Four years as a brevet ensign had taught Wesley discipline and humility, and he had eventually gone on to Starfleet Academy, expecting and expected to follow in his late father's footsteps.

But in time he had found himself chafing at those expectations, questioning the path everyone else had laid out for him. A decade ago, on Dorvan V, he had met the Traveler again and found where his true path lay. Far from being merely a human prodigy, Wesley was the first evolutionary step toward a more powerful, complex form of life. The path to achieving his full potential had lain not with Starfleet but with the Traveler and his kind. But this had meant leaving behind the life he'd known . . . and the mother who loved him.

"Well," Picard said slowly, "it's not as if we never see him."

"Oh, yes, he was at Will and Deanna's wedding, and our wedding too. He even remembered to manifest clothes this time, thank God." Picard suppressed a smirk. "I'm sure he'll find ways to stay in touch occasionally—whatever 'occasionally' means to someone who exists outside time and space as we know it.

"But that's just it," she went on. "It's not only about missing him, or wishing he'd write more often, or wondering if he's getting enough to eat or if there are any nice girl Travelers out there." She began pacing the room, her filmy robe wafting around her long dancer's legs as she moved. Picard chastised himself for noticing that when he should be focusing on her feelings. Though it heartened him that marriage had apparently restored his libido to that of a twenty-year-old man. He wondered how long that would last.

"Then what is it about?" he asked, to get his mind back on topic.

"It's about being his mother. I don't know if I can anymore. He's evolved so far beyond our level. He's gained insights I can't imagine, and he faces problems I couldn't begin to define. How can I offer him any guidance, any support? Will he ever need me again?"

Picard came over and clasped her shoulders. "Of course he will. He loves his mother. If there's one thing I've learned this past year, it's how precious the ties of family can be. I'm certain Wesley will always value his ties with you."

"I know he will, Jean-Luc. I just don't know if he'll ever really *need* them." She smiled wryly. "I guess I'm suffering from empty nest syndrome. I miss having someone to take care of. Someone dependent on me. I miss being a mom."

Picard's pulse accelerated as he realized where this was going. But the timing was fortuitous. Marriage had opened his eyes to new possibilities that he'd felt were closed off. Ever since his brother

Robert and his nephew René had died in a fire nine years ago, he had feared that the Picard line, the rich family heritage that his father had taught him to cherish, would end with him. But now he was a husband, and although he'd been busy enjoying the more immediate benefits of that state, he had been giving much thought to the opportunities it provided for the future.

"Beverly," he began, very gingerly, "there's something I've been wanting to—"

*"Bridge to Captain Picard."*

He winced. So much for fortuitous timing. "What is it, Number One?" he asked, perhaps more harshly than he should have.

But his first officer was a Klingon and had no problem with harshness. *"We have received an emergency transmission,"* Worf told him. *"Priority One. Admiral Nechayev has summoned us to return to Starfleet Headquarters and will meet with you upon arrival."*

Picard's heart sank. He had a horrible feeling he knew what this was about. *Please, no—not again.*


Starfleet Headquarters
San Francisco
Stardate 57734


Picard tried with limited success to ease the knot in his shoulders before stepping into Admiral Nechayev's office. He and the admiral had not been on the best of terms in recent months, and he expected tensions to run high in this meeting.

So he reacted with some surprise when he entered her office and saw the items laid out upon her desk. "Are those . . ."

Standing beside the desk, Alynna Nechayev gave Picard a smile that softened her severe features. "Bularian canapés, watercress sandwiches, and Earl Grey tea," she told him, coming forward to shake his hand with unexpected warmth. "Welcome back to Earth, Captain Picard. And congratulations on your wedding. I'm sorry I missed it."

"Thank you, Admiral," he said, a bit nonplussed. "But we wanted a small ceremony, and . . ."

"I understand. It was the same way with my wedding. We practically had to elope to get away from my mother and her carefully orchestrated plans. We Nechayevs can be rather . . . controlling."

"I, um, I hadn't noticed."

"You'll have to improve your skill at white lies if you want a successful marriage," she advised with a self-deprecating smile.

"May I ask, Admiral, what the occasion is for . . ." He gestured at the appetizers and the tea.

"Oh, allow me," she said, taking the pot and pouring him a cup. "A decade ago," she explained, "you prepared Bularian canapés, watercress sandwiches, and tea for me as a peace offering, to make me feel welcome at a time when relations between us were less than cordial. I've always remembered that gesture fondly. But I'm afraid that recent events have renewed the tension between us, and I decided it was time to do something about it."

She sighed and gestured him over to the couch, where they sat together. "Twice in the past five months, Captain, Starfleet has faced attack from the Borg. Twice, you have formulated what proved to be the correct strategy for fighting them. And twice, we in Starfleet Command have ignored you, imposed restrictive orders on you, and sought to penalize you for defying them and doing the right thing anyway." She shook her head, and Picard saw that her pale blond hair had taken on more gray in recent months. "We let ourselves forget the thing we all understood implicitly when we were captains: that the commander on the scene is usually better qualified to assess a situation than the desk jockeys back home.

"Frankly, Captain, we were scared. These have been hard years for the Federation. For the first time in generations, the very survival of our civilization has been under threat, whether from the Dominion or the Borg. And just when we thought things had finally settled down, the Borg invaded again. It made us frightened and defensive. And that fear has made it harder for us to trust one another. Kept us from listening to one another. At a time when we should have been united against a common enemy, we've almost jeopardized our own survival with squabbling over jurisdiction and the chain of command. I'm ashamed of my part in that, and I want to apologize."

Picard was truly moved by her words. In the same spirit, he said, "Thank you, Admiral. But the fault lies partly with me as well. I'm sure I could have found a better way to deal with matters than turning into a rogue agent. I've made too much of a habit of that in recent years."

Truth be told, Nechayev's words echoed the concerns Picard had felt about his own crew in the wake of the Borg attack on Earth. Matters had grown so tense that his crew had been split down the middle, with his new second officer, security chief, and counselor staging what was effectively a mutiny in order to carry out Starfleet's orders. Picard had been willing to forgive them, understanding that all parties involved had been trying to do what was right—and perhaps, as Nechayev had said, too frightened to think entirely clearly. But Counselor T'Lana had left the ship in the wake of the incident, and Lieutenant Leybenzon's relationship with the the crew whose security he oversaw remained tenuous at best. The incident had led him to reconsider his own actions carefully and search for ways to improve relations within his new crew. His former command crew had meshed into an amazingly effective team over the years, but what with the personnel losses, transfers, and tensions in recent months, he sometimes wondered if he would ever recapture that magic again.

"I'm glad to hear you say that, Captain," Nechayev said. "We need to be able to move past the fears that isolate us, to reach out and have faith in one another, if we wish to preserve the Federation."

Picard frowned. "Admiral, since you summoned the *Enterprise* all the way to Earth, I assume you aren't speaking in the abstract."

"I wish I were." She put her teacup down and straightened her shoulders. "I have a mission for you, Captain Picard. It involves the Borg, and we need our best Borg expert on the case. And this time, I truly want us to be on the same page . . . for all our sakes."

A chill ran through Picard, displacing the warmth of the tea. "I am at your disposal, Admiral."

Beverly Crusher tried not to be concerned by her new husband's aloofness toward her when they convened in Headquarters' main briefing room along with Worf, Admiral Nechayev, and Professor Annika Hansen. She knew from long experience that it was Jean-Luc's way to maintain formality while on duty, especially in crisis situations. But Beverly feared there was something more to it this time, a deeper coldness that came with the news of a revived Borg threat. She remembered how hesitant he had been to embrace a permanent commitment with her until he had felt confident that the peril from the Collective had subsided. And now a new Borg menace loomed, barely after they had returned from their honeymoon. The timing for this could not have been worse.

But she was a doctor and a Starfleet officer, so she chided herself lightly for dwelling on personal concerns while a much broader threat loomed. It was time for her to be Commander Crusher, not Mrs. Picard.

Across the table, Worf was still being Worf. "A junior lieutenant with a history of discipline problems walks out of the woods naked and tells us the Borg are coming," the Klingon asked, "and we are supposed to believe her?"

"We would be unwise not to," said Professor Hansen—or Seven of Nine, as Beverly remembered she preferred to be called by everyone except her immediate family. Beverly had had a chance to get acquainted with Seven in the past, first in the wake of *Voyager*'s much-heralded return from the Delta Quadrant two and a half years ago, then later in occasional medical consultation work with the civilian think tank where Seven had been employed until a year ago, when she had agreed to accept a teaching post at Starfleet Academy. The Seven she saw at the head of the table now, like the Seven she had encountered briefly during the Borg incursion in June, was a different person from the one she had met on those occasions. That Seven had been formal, even imposing at times, but had learned to embrace her humanity in the nearly seven years since *Voyager*'s crew had liberated her from the Borg collective. Beverly had found her to be soft-spoken, coolly pleasant, and possessed of a dry, mordant wit. But lately she had been all business, as stern and severe as she had reportedly been in her first years on *Voyager*. Beverly figured that, like Jean-Luc, Seven had raised her guard in response to the Borg situation. No one else in the Federation had such a personal reason to fear and hate the Borg as they did. But it struck Beverly as ironic that they both felt the need to become colder, harder, more Borg-like, in order to counter their fears of the Collective.

"Lieutenant Chen," Seven went on, "was found on Maravel, a planet located nearly two thousand light-years from her starship's last reported position. Her arrival there was accompanied by energy signatures consistent with a quantum slipstream vortex." She worked the controls next to the briefing room's main viewer, bringing up a graphic displaying energy readings Crusher could not interpret, but superimposed on a more familiar map of the Beta Quadrant, focusing on the Orion and Carina Arms. "Those signatures appeared to point in the direction of NGC 6281, the open cluster being surveyed by *U.S.S. Rhea*." A cluster midway between the two arms began to blink.

"And the following day," Nechayev interposed, "we received a distress signal from the *Rhea*. It was cut off quickly, but we got enough to confirm that they were under attack by the *Einstein*—or the Borg vessel it has now been transformed into." She smirked. "Lieutenant Chen has dubbed it the *Frankenstein,* and the name has caught on rather quickly around here. It may be facetious, but we find it preferable to soiling the name of a lost Starfleet vessel, not to mention one of humanity's greatest minds, by using it to describe a Borg ship."

"But why would the Borg be so far away?" Worf asked. "If they survived the assault on Earth, why did they not resume their attempts to assimilate Federation personnel?"

"One small ship against the entire Federation?" Picard asked. "The Borg may not be imaginative, but they are not fools. They knew we could over-power them, so they fled to regroup. Get some distance, rebuild their strength for the next assault."

"Note also," Seven said, "that NGC 6281 is in the direction of the Delta Quadrant. These Borg, or rather the vessel that assimilated them, had developed a new, very powerful form of nanotechnological assimilation. And yet, without a transwarp network to boost interlink communications, they are presumably out of contact with the rest of the Collective, unable to share that new technology. They may therefore have concluded that returning to the Delta Quadrant was a higher priority than attacking the Federation."

"Or perhaps," Picard added as if to himself, "they wanted to lull us into a false sense of security." Beverly looked at him with some concern at that, but he did not meet her eyes.

"I agree, the Borg can be devious," Worf said. "So is it wise to trust Lieutenant Chen? She claims to have been in the midst of assimilation when she was . . . somehow spirited away. How do we know she is not some kind of Borg agent? A Trojan horse?"

Nechayev gave a tight smile. "Believe me, Commander Worf, that was our first thought as well."

Seven added, "T'Ryssa Chen has been subjected to every scanning method known to Federation science, plus some that were unknown until I was called in to consult. The lieutenant has been scanned down to the subatomic level, and although her body does show the cellular damage characteristic of infestation by Borg nanoprobes, it is completely free of any nanotechnology. It appears that the assimilation process was halted in its early stage, the nanoprobes eradicated.

"In fact," she went on, cocking the eyebrow that wasn't covered by an ocular implant, "the lieutenant's body is completely free of inorganic impurities of any kind."

"That's impossible," Crusher said. "We all accumulate such impurities as we go through life. Metal builds up in the bones, dust accumulates in the lungs . . ."

"Correct. But all of that has been . . . *removed* from the lieutenant along with the nanoprobes."

"How was that done?" Crusher asked. "Borg nanoprobes have proved resistant to removal by transporter."

"That," Nechayev said, "is a very good question. If we could discover the technology that did this—or the means that made the creatures she encountered on the planet apparently immune to assimilation—it could be a powerful defense against the Borg."

"Not to mention the quantum slipstream," Beverly said, looking at Jean-Luc. "To travel two thousand light-years even faster than a subspace signal . . . remarkable."

"Under the circumstances," her husband told her, "I would call it alarming."

"Agreed," Worf said. "If the . . ." He grimaced. "If the *Frankenstein* is able to assimilate that technology and deliver it to the rest of the Borg, it would be disastrous."

"In fact," Seven told him, "the Borg have already assimilated quantum slipstream drive." She worked the controls and an image of a hairless, smooth-featured alien appeared on the screen. "*Voyager* first obtained knowledge of quantum slipstream propulsion from Arturis, a survivor of a race known to the Collective as Species 116. This species had slipstream and other advanced technology that enabled them to resist assimilation for hundreds of years. Eventually, however, they succumbed, and the Borg acquired that technology."

"Then why have they not used it to attack us in force?"

"The slipstream technology possessed by Species 116 requires immensely complex computations to modify the quantum structure of spacetime from one microsecond to the next. The larger the vessel transiting the slipstream, the more exponentially difficult the computations become, and the more inevitable the instability of the vortex becomes. This is why *Voyager* was unable to use it to return home."

"But Starfleet has been working to overcome that problem," Worf said. "I understand the prototype is slated to be deployed aboard the *Aventine* early next year." He spoke with some pride, and Beverly remembered that an old colleague of his from Deep Space 9 was now serving aboard that vessel.

"Remember, Number One," Picard said, "the Borg cannot innovate. They can only assimilate what others have created."

"How is that possible?" Beverly heard herself asking, though it took a moment to develop the thought fully. "I mean, we know they can adapt to new threats. They must have the ability to solve problems. So why can't they fix the flaws in a drive system?"

"The nature of the two problems is different," Seven told her. "The Borg adapt to threats by searching their database of assimilated knowledge for known countermeasures to a given assault. If no known countermeasure is found, trial and error is employed until a partial defense is discovered. Further trial and error along the same lines is attempted until an improved defense is found."

"So they evolve a solution."

"Correct. However, such stochastic methodology does not allow them to innovate new theoretical models from which solutions to basic problems of physics can be derived. Overcoming the limits of Species 116's slipstream drive requires a leap of imagination of which the Borg are incapable."

"But the slipstream technology that sent Lieutenant Chen to Maravel is different, isn't it?" Jean-Luc divined.

"Correct," Seven said. "Our readings are inconclusive as to its precise functioning, but it was capable of sending an individual humanoid two thousand light-years with no ship or life-support capsule of any kind, and targeting the vortex precisely enough to deliver her directly to the surface of an inhabited planet. In order for her to survive the journey without suffering the effects of anoxia and vacuum exposure, either it was made in mere seconds or the environment within the slipstream was altered in such a way as to sustain her life functions. Either way, this suggests a far more robust, stable, and powerful slipstream technology than Species 116 had managed to create. If the so-called *Frankenstein* is able to assimilate it, it will be able to deliver that technology to the Collective. And then . . ."

"And then," Nechayev said, "they will come in force. The supercube may have been acting alone, but we can't allow ourselves to hope that the rest of the Collective doesn't share their goals. After all the damage we've done to them, we have to assume that the Borg consider the Federation too great a threat to tolerate anymore. We've been protected only by our distance from the bulk of their forces in the Delta Quadrant. Give them a way to traverse that distance, and the Federation is unlikely to survive."

"But what can we do about it?" Worf asked.

"That star cluster is more than six weeks away even at *Enterprise*'s best speed. If the *Fran*—the Borg ship is there now . . ."

"Then it may already be too late," Seven said. "However, the *Rhea* reported great difficulty in traversing the shifting subspace distortions within the cluster. Based on analysis of sensor logs from that ship's last few regular updates, we conclude that any form of warp drive would be equally vulnerable to these distortions; it is a matter of physics rather than engineering. Therefore, even if the Borg have managed to enhance the *Frankenstein*'s warp drive using other assimilated technologies, these distortions will still have slowed the Borg's attempts to travel through the cluster and thus their efforts to obtain the slipstream technology."

"Also," Nechayev added, "we don't know who or what teleported Lieutenant Chen so far from the cluster, or why it sent her to Maravel. According to her report, she lived on that planet in her youth and had some of her happiest times there. Perhaps the being or beings who rescued her sent her someplace they sensed in her mind, someplace familiar."

"And we think these creatures she described, these 'Noh Angels,' are responsible?" Beverly asked.

"Possibly, but we can't be sure. In any case, it could be that they sent the Borg packing in much the same way. It may take them time to return to the cluster. Even if it doesn't, the inhabitants of the cluster must have formidable defenses—hopefully formidable enough to stop the Borg on their own or at least hold them off until *Enterprise* can arrive."

"We should only be so lucky," Picard said. "But we can't depend on that."

"Indeed not," Worf agreed. "We must know the fate of the *Einstein,* one way or the other. If these Borg are acting under direction, pursuing a plan, it must mean they have created yet another queen. We must find that queen and destroy her at all costs."

"Are we sure they will return to the cluster at all?" Beverly asked. "Will they really consider it important enough?"

"A technology that could replace or improve upon their transwarp network?" Picard replied. "Oh, yes."

Beverly conceded the point, but she had another concern. "What about the rest of *Rhea*'s crew? Is there any chance—"

Nechayev was already shaking her head. "We've checked every planet, station, and vessel that they've ever been on. There's no sign of them."

"So we are to assume they've fallen to the Borg," Worf said.

"Finding that out will be part of your mission," the admiral told him. "Along with contacting whatever intelligence resides within the cluster, learning whatever you can about its slipstream and anti-nanoprobe technologies, and doing whatever is necessary to keep those technologies out of Borg hands."

"Whatever is necessary?" Beverly challenged.

"Surely that doesn't include attacking this intelligence to keep their knowledge from the Borg?"

"If their knowledge falls into Borg hands," Worf told her, "their destruction is assured already."

"The doctor does have a point," Seven interposed. "While defeating the Borg is a priority for us all, it is imperative that we do not allow ourselves to become like them in the process." Beverly sensed a heavy emotion, perhaps guilt, behind her words. To defeat the last Borg attack, she had needed to merge with a very powerful weapon of destruction, one whose artificial intelligence drew little distinction between destroying the enemy and destroying innocents who got in the way. It must have been a difficult reminder of her years as a drone.

"Quite right," Picard said. "As Admiral Nechayev has recently reminded me, if we wish to defend the civilization we hold so dear, we must not lose sight of the principles it embodies." Beverly relaxed. That was the Jean-Luc she had married.

"Agreed," Worf said. "But defending principles often requires weapons. And the same weapon rarely works twice against the Borg. We cannot assume the Project Endgame virus will work a second time," he said, referring to the invasive computer program that had defeated the Borg in their last attack. "If we are to defeat this foe, we will need a tactical advantage. Something we know the Borg have not yet adapted to."

Nechayev was nodding. "You're talking about transphasic torpedoes."

"I am, Admiral."

"Transphasic torpedoes?" Beverly asked. "Those are one of the advanced technologies brought back by *Voyager,* aren't they?"

"Correct," Seven said. "They proved instrumental in our destruction of the Borg transwarp hub."

"Along with an ablative hull armor, if I recall," Worf said.

"Yes. But the Borg adapted to the armor during the battle in the transwarp network, nullifying its value as a defense."

"So why have they not adapted to the torpedoes as well?"

"A transphasic torpedo delivers a subspace compression pulse existing in an asymmetric superposition of phase states. If one subcomponent of the pulse is blocked by shielding, enough others will still succeed in penetrating to the target to ensure that the majority of the pulse is delivered. Each torpedo's transphasic configuration is different, randomly generated by a dissonant feedback effect, so that there is no way for the Borg to predict the configuration of its phase states in order to shield against them."

"Not yet, anyway," Nechayev said. "These torpedoes are tough for the Borg to adapt to, but given their evolutionary algorithms, they probably get closer to developing an effective defense each time the weapon is used. That's why Starfleet hasn't deployed transphasic torpedoes against the Borg before. They're our ace in the hole, a last-ditch weapon to be used when all else fails."

"Then why didn't we use them when the biggest Borg ship ever seen attacked Earth?" Beverly asked in bewilderment.

Nechayev glared. "Because it was the biggest Borg ship ever seen, Doctor. It would have taken so many torpedoes to destroy it that the Borg would probably have learned to adapt before we could finish the job.

"However," the admiral went on, "the *Frankenstein* is just one ship, and it's out of contact with the rest of the Collective—as far as we know. So I'm prepared to authorize the installation of transphasic torpedoes aboard *Enterprise*—with the proviso that they are to be used only as a last resort. Just in case we're wrong about them still being out of touch."

"You expect us to rely on conventional weapons?" Worf asked.

"Not at all," Seven told him. "Your primary weapon will be a multivector agent we have been developing."

"Multivector agent?" Picard asked.

"Correct. In the past, we have wielded several apparently successful defenses against the Borg, and yet each one has subsequently been surmounted. For example, Doctor Crusher devised a formula that interfered with the hormonal process by which a Borg queen is created from an androgynous drone. Of course, in its original form, it was of only limited effectiveness, as we found two months later"—Seven hesitated—"when Kathryn Janeway was assimilated and transformed into a queen of sorts. Also two years ago when Admiral Covington of Starfleet Intelligence transformed herself into a queen by downloading the Royal Protocol program."

"Yes," Beverly said. "I was wondering how that could happen. Without the 'royal jelly' secreted by the drones . . ."

"The 'royal jelly,' as you call it, is needed only when the drone population is androgynous, as was the case in the supercube you first encountered in Sector 10. That cube was atypical. Only those drones incubated from harvested embryos, rather than assimilated, are truly androgynous. As my own example makes obvious," Seven said with a wry lift to her visible eyebrow, "assimilated drones do possess sexual characteristics."

"But most of the Borg the *Enterprise* has encountered have been like those on the supercube," Beverly said. She thought specifically of Hugh, the captured drone that Geordi La Forge had liberated a dozen years before. He—to use the pronoun loosely—had been a blank slate with no prior identity, ready and able to absorb whatever input was fed to him, which was ironically why he had been so receptive to learning individuality. The same must have been true of the drones who had absorbed that "virus" of individuality from him and broken from the Collective.

"That is because Federation space is so distant from Borg territory," Seven answered. "Assimilated drones often reassert individual memory and initiative when cut off from communication with the Collective. They may defect or revolt as a result. Drones incubated from embryos—or raised from small children," she added, blushing slightly—"are not prone to question their Borg identity. Therefore, incubated drones are preferentially employed in remote regions of the galaxy or other areas where communication loss may occur.

"However, the drone population as a whole was severely depleted seven years ago in the war with Species 8472." Beverly remembered hearing about the extradimensional invaders who had done so much damage to the Borg and threatened the Federation as well before *Voyager*'s crew had achieved détente with them. "All of the adult replacement drones created since then have naturally been assimilatees. Incubated drones are thus far more rare than they once were.

"The Borg who built the supercube were apparently a surviving remnant of that incubated population, escaping attrition in the 8472 war due to their distance from the front. When the transwarp network collapsed, severing their link to the Collective, presumably any assimilated drones among them regained their memories and fled. This is why there were no sexually mature females within that population, requiring the use of estrogenic secretions to produce a suitable queen body. After waiting two years for instructions that never came, the incubated drones finally initiated a fail-safe program to create their own local queen to lead the attack on Earth."

"So Doctor Crusher's formula would be useless against the *Einstein*," Worf said. "Their new queen would no doubt have been created from a female crew member, as the Janeway queen was."

Beverly shook her head. "In its initial form, perhaps. But there are other hormonal changes involved in creating a queen aside from simply feminizing her. Hormones have a major impact on brain development and activity—in this case, altering the drone's brain to enable it to run the Royal Protocol program and function as a queen."

"Indeed," Seven said. "We have been refining Doctor Crusher's formula into a vector that could not only undo those hormonal changes in an assimilated female, but permanently deprive any drones of the capability to create a new queen even when female drones are available."

Worf frowned. "Why must it be a queen? Why not a male or androgynous drone?"

Seven blinked. "I am not sure. It simply is."

"Perhaps," Beverly said, "because the humanoid female brain tends to be more oriented toward socialization and the regulation of interpersonal relationships. Of course, there's a lot of overlap between male and female brains, but it would be just like the Borg to ignore such nuances."

"Or perhaps such differences are due to hormonal variations among individuals in either sex," Seven countered. "Either way, it is as good a hypothesis as any."

"I think we're getting off topic here," Picard said. "Professor, you were speaking of a multivector agent."

"Indeed." Seven worked the viewer controls and called up another graphic. "The multivector agent combines a retroviral delivery system for the hormonal formula with an experimental antiassimilation nanite technology developed by Doctor Jarem Kaz and Commander Data during the Covington crisis. The original nanites were of only limited use; they were able to disrupt Admiral Covington's assimilation virus but would have been insufficient to overcome Borg nanoprobes under the direction of a true queen."

"And you believe this improved version will be effective?" Worf asked.

"We believe it will be able to disrupt the functioning of Borg implants, in conjunction with a software attack. The nanites will also deliver a refined version of the Project Endgame virus we used to defeat the last Borg attack. It is hoped that the modifications will compensate for their efforts to adapt to the original virus program; at the very least, it should disrupt the focus of the Collective mind sufficiently to prevent them from countering the biological and nanotechnological attacks."

"We're hitting them on every front at once," Nechayev said. "Hardware, software, biology. Every time we thought we'd defeated the Borg, they came at us again from another angle. So we decided to stop thinking like the Borg—to stop reacting to the immediate threat—and start anticipating. It's our hope that this multivector agent will cover all the bases and finally let us take them down for good."

"Ironic," Beverly said.

Seven frowned. "Doctor?"

"A weapon that combines biology and technology—it's like the Borg in microcosm."

"We prefer to think of it as fighting fire with fire," Nechayev said. "Doctor Crusher, we'd like you to coordinate with our experts to make sure the multivector agent is as potent as we can make it."

Beverly nodded. "Aye, Admiral."

"Captain Picard, Commander Worf, you will prepare the *Enterprise* for an extended mission at high warp. I'm sure I can count on your engineering department to break one more speed record."

"I will make certain of it," Worf declared in a tone that would make Beverly afraid to make a liar of him if she were an engineer.

"Good."

Picard looked at Seven. "Will you be accompanying us, Professor?"

"Not this time," Nechayev said. "We're sending one of our top Borg experts into harm's way, so we're keeping the other one close just in case. But rest assured, you will have autonomy on this mission. Save the transphasic torpedoes as an absolute last resort . . . but otherwise, do whatever you deem best to neutralize the *Frankenstein*."

Beverly reflected that it was a hollow assurance, since the star cluster was much too distant to allow for real-time consultation. But it was nice to hear in any case.

As the meeting adjourned, Seven came over to Beverly. "If you will accompany me, Doctor, we will begin."

"Just a moment, Professor." She crossed over to Jean-Luc, who appeared lost in thought. She put a hand on his arm, getting his attention. "I'll see you back on board," she said.

He gave an abstracted nod. "I may be a while. And I'll be quite busy once I return."

"I understand," she said, but her expression was wistful. *I guess the honeymoon's really over.*

# 2

---

*U.S.S. Enterprise*

When Zelik Leybenzon opened the door to his quarters, Worf spoke without preliminaries. He knew that Leybenzon shared his preference for getting directly to the point. "What is the meaning of this?" Worf asked, holding out a padd.

Leybenzon's pale eyes briefly darted down to the padd, then back to Worf. "I believe my request was plain enough, Commander," he said in the Russian accent that reminded Worf so much of his foster parents. "I wish an immediate transfer to another post."

"I would like more of an explanation than that, Lieutenant," Worf told the security chief, crossing his arms over the heavy metal baldric he wore atop his uniform tunic. "After the mutiny, you accepted the captain's offer to remain aboard. You seemed to be doing your part to restore trust among the members of this crew. Why leave now?"

Leybenzon straightened, his eyes forward. "Permission to speak freely, sir?" Worf nodded. "It's the Borg, sir."

"The Borg?" Worf narrowed his eyes. "Surely you are not afraid?"

The security chief reacted as though slapped. "No, sir! However . . . I simply do not feel I can trust the captain's judgment where the Borg are concerned."

Worf loomed over him. "Starfleet Command trusts the captain's judgment in this matter. Are you wiser than they?"

He caught a flash of emotion in Leybenzon's eyes reflecting the career soldier's eternal conviction that the surgical excision of wisdom was a necessary prerequisite for officerdom. However, the security chief simply said, "All I know, Commander, is that I don't believe the captain would be receptive to my input in this matter. He would be better served by a different chief of security."

He fell silent, and after a moment, Worf asked, "And that is all you have to say?"

Leybenzon's armored exterior softened marginally. "Only that I regret having to make this decision. I have found you an . . . agreeable commander."

Worf declined to reciprocate his praise. There was a time when he would have done so; he and Leybenzon had had a good working relationship during the latter's first month aboard, and Worf had appreciated his diligence and the unrelenting stan-

dards of excellence he had demanded of his security personnel. But his role in the mutiny had been
difficult for Worf to forgive. He had made every
effort to do so; after all, Worf was not proud of his
own actions during the mutiny. When the Federation embassy on Qo'noS had been occupied by terrorists last year, Worf had resolved the situation
with deliberate, calculated force and strategic planning, befitting his long experience as a Starfleet
officer and Federation ambassador. But when his
own fellow *Enterprise* crew members had turned
on their captain—under orders from the admiralty,
no less—Worf had lost control and reacted like a
berserker, striking out in an uncontrolled way that
had accomplished nothing, rather than bringing his
cunning or his diplomatic skills to bear on the situation. True, an attack by Klingon terrorists was
nowhere near as personally affecting as betrayal by
his own crewmates. But that had been no excuse
for forgetting a decade of personal growth and
experience, for letting his anger rule his intellect
rather than the reverse. During the Borg crisis, for
whatever reasons, it seemed that everyone had
behaved in ways they later came to regret. And so
Worf had done his best to forgive those involved in
the mutiny and move on.

But now he could not help but feel that Leybenzon was showing a pattern of disloyalty to Captain
Picard, and so he was disinclined to say anything
complimentary to the man. Except that loyalty was
a virtue he himself still held dear, and he had taken

an interest in this man's career. "You do realize," he said, "that if you give up your position on the *Enterprise* now, after less than five months, it is unlikely that you will ever be offered promotion again."

Leybenzon nodded, well aware of the negative reputation that had undermined his career as an officer. Nearly all his superiors had found him thoroughly competent but thoroughly unbearable to work with. "I am aware of that, sir, and frankly, I am content with that. I do not belong in officer country. All I want, sir, is to be on the front lines, fighting for the Federation. I want nothing to do with the messy business of making decisions—I only wish to be out there where the action is."

Worf glowered at him. "So long as it does not involve Captain Picard."

"Not where the Borg are concerned, no, sir."

After studying him a moment longer, Worf said, "Very well. I will authorize your transfer, pending the captain's agreement. I expect that agreement will be forthcoming."

Leybenzon came to attention. "Thank you, sir."

Now that it was done, Worf found his anger toward Leybenzon fading. He could certainly approve of the desire to seek honor on the field of battle. If nothing else, the warrior in Zelik Leybenzon deserved his respect. And so Worf struck his fist to his chest in a Klingon salute. "*Qapla'*, Lieutenant Leybenzon. May you die well."

"Thank you, sir," Leybenzon said with total sincerity.

• • •

Picard approved Leybenzon's transfer with mixed feelings. On the one hand, although he had strived to put the mutiny behind him and restore a relationship of trust with his crew, he had never entirely felt that such trust had been restored between himself and Leybenzon, or that the man was comfortable serving under his command. So he believed it would be better for all concerned if the lieutenant found another posting.

On the other hand, it was one more failure in Picard's ongoing attempt to assemble an effective, lasting command crew. Ever since Will Riker and Deanna Troi had left for *Titan* and Data had died, Picard's crew had remained in a state of flux. First, Beverly had left for Starfleet Medical and Picard had struggled to find a chief medical officer worthy to succeed her. Then Beverly had returned, this time as his lover and now his wife, but Worf's status as first officer had been temporary and uncertain. It had taken months for Picard to convince Starfleet that Worf was the ideal choice, since they still had doubts about him following his actions on Soukara during the Dominion War and his years away from Starfleet as an ambassador. Meanwhile, his choice for second officer and ops manager, Miranda Kadohata, had been on maternity leave for several months, and during the same period, Picard had been unable to find a ship's counselor qualified to fill Deanna Troi's shoes. The assistant counselor, Hegol Den of Bajor, was quite capable as a psychologist but lacked the qualifications or the inclination to serve as a bridge officer or participate in command decisions. And so Picard had been forced to operate for several months with an incomplete or temporary command crew.

Finally, it had seemed that his crew was starting to come together when Starfleet had approved Worf as permanent XO and persuaded Picard to accept the appointment of T'Lana, a Vulcan counselor with decades of experience in diplomatic and intelligence work and a qualified command officer as well. True, there was another minor shake-up when his security chief, Sara Nave, had chosen to transfer to the conn; but she had excelled as a flight controller and her successor, Lio Battaglia, had shown every sign of being a fine security chief.

But then Worf himself had almost declined the position of permanent first officer, dismaying Picard just when he had thought things were finally coming together. The Klingon had eventually changed his mind, but only after the Borg encounter in which Picard had lost both Nave and Battaglia, along with a half dozen other security personnel.

But the mission had to go on. Kadohata had returned from maternity leave, Zelik Leybenzon had transferred aboard as security chief with Worf's recommendation, and Joanna Faur had ably taken over the conn. T'Lana had proved less than supportive during the initial Borg incident, but Picard had valued her candor and her willingness to challenge his authority. He had long ago learned the importance of having a check on his own judgment, and it was that same willingness to defy a commanding officer that had led him to choose Will Riker as his XO nearly seventeen years ago. For a while, during the Q encounter and afterward, things had seemed to go well.

But then the Borg supercube had reawakened and attacked Earth, and when Picard and Worf had refused to obey orders from the admiralty that they knew were wrong, Kadohata, Leybenzon, and T'Lana had acted under Nechayev's orders to relieve their superiors of duty, and the second officer had taken command. In time, Kadohata had recognized her mistake and chosen to work with Picard. Leybenzon had only reluctantly cooperated, and T'Lana had remained defiant, demanding a transfer off the *Enterprise.* Her career as the ship's counselor had ended almost before it had begun.

Following the mutiny, Picard had taken a good long look at his own policies to see if there was anything he could have done differently to prevent such tensions among his crew. He had begun to wonder if perhaps he had been trying too hard to re-create the unique dynamic of his old crew, simply recasting new people in the same roles and expecting them to perform equivalently to Riker, Troi, Data, and the rest. He realized that in so doing, he may have placed undue pressure on them. Both Data and Deanna Troi had been uniquely qualified for their roles. Data's android nature had enabled him to juggle the tasks of second officer, ops manager, and de facto science officer easily enough, but it was unfair to demand the same from a human. Miranda Kadohata had performed above and beyond at meeting those expectations, particularly considering that she had to juggle those demands with her commitments to her family back on Cestus III, including her new baby son and daughter. But that had no doubt placed her under considerable strain, which may have contributed to the breakdown of communication that had led to the mutiny.

Also, after the T'Lana debacle, Picard had questioned the wisdom of simply bringing in another counselor as a command-level adviser. He had reminded himself that Deanna Troi had been not just a counselor but a skilled contact specialist as well, an expert in alien psychology and sociology as well as diplomatic protocols. The only reason she had not borne the official title of diplomatic officer, as she now did aboard *Titan,* was that Picard himself normally represented the ship in diplomatic matters.

So he had decided to make a change in the organization of his command crew. Rather than seeking another counselor who could double as a command-level diplomatic and xenological adviser, he had promoted Hegol to senior counselor, in which post he would still be responsible for the crew's welfare and monitor the captain's mental state, but he would not participate in day-to-day command decisions. Meanwhile, Picard intended to fill the third chair on the bridge with a chief science officer who was a trained contact specialist as well, taking over parts of both Data's and Troi's previous duties. This would relieve Kadohata of some of the excessive burden he had placed on her shoulders. He believed this would be a fairer allocation of duties overall and would make it easier for him to accept his new crew and their own distinctive strengths rather than unconsciously comparing them to his old crew. It was his hope that this would enable him to bond more effectively with his new team.

But Picard's choice for chief science officer, a Rhaandarite lieutenant commander named Gaanth, had not worked out as he had hoped. He had chosen Gaanth in part because Rhaandarites possessed an uncanny ability to read humanoid body language, giving them insights almost as effective as Deanna Troi's Betazoid empathy. They also had keen memories and problem-solving skills and tended to have much more emotional balance than most humanoids, which Picard had expected to be a boon in delicate negotiations or first-contact situations. But Gaanth had proved too hidebound and lacking in initiative, expert in the theory of alien cultural interactions but less than adept at dealing with the unexpected or interpreting the behavior of species not already thoroughly documented.

Moreover, Gaanth's strongly developed sense of social hierarchy had made him uncomfortable with the intensifying romance between the vessel's commanding officer and chief medical officer, and upon their decision to marry, he had requested a transfer.

So now Picard had to find a new science officer and contact specialist—if he was lucky, in the same individual—and on top of that he had to select yet another new security chief (and another deputy, since Leybenzon's handpicked second, Natasha Stolovitsky, had transferred off with him). But the choice for security chief proved easy enough. Lieutenant Jasminder Choudhury came to him highly recommended by Marien Zimbata, formerly captain of the *Victory,* now the commander of Starbase 103. Zimbata had never steered him wrong before, providing him with both Geordi La Forge and Natasha Yar. And Choudhury's record was commendable, both in war and peace. On the *Timur* during the Dominion War, she had risen to the occasion when her security chief had been killed in the first battle of Chin'toka, employing imaginative tactics to save the ship from destruction despite the loss of all its torpedo tubes and most of its phaser banks and shields. And her record showed that, unlike many veterans of the war (Leybenzon being a textbook example), Choudhury had adapted effectively to peacetime as well. Last year, when a dissident faction of Nosgoh had attacked a diplomatic conference on Starbase 103 and taken hostages, it had been Choudhury's skillful negotiation that had uncovered the cultural misunderstanding behind the incident and led to its resolution with no loss of life. She struck Picard as someone who truly understood that a security officer was not simply a fighter, but a protector as well. People like that were not always easy to find in the wake of the war.

But the science officer choice was proving more difficult. He had received a transfer request from a highly skilled officer, Lieutenant Dina Elfiki, who was more than qualified for the post of senior science officer on a *Sovereign*-class starship but whose specialties lay more in the direction of physics and astrometrics than xenoanthropology and contact protocols. That was not a sufficient basis to deny her request, of course, if he could find a top-notch contact specialist as well. Given the likelihood that this mission would require making contact with an unknown, possibly very alien form of life and persuading it to share its technology, he didn't want to leave spacedock without such a specialist on board. He would still prefer to find one person who could fill both roles, but it was not essential.

And so, for the past two days, Picard had been reviewing the files of every available officer in Starfleet with the qualifications for the post. The list was long and heavy with qualified candidates; as with any opening aboard the *Enterprise,* there was plenty of competition for the job.

Which was why Picard was somewhat surprised to see the name of Lieutenant (jg) T'Ryssa Chen on the list of candidates. He knew she was the one who had survived the attack on the *Rhea* and notified Starfleet of the threat, and he could understand her desire to be involved in the mission. But she stood out from the list of contenders, and not in a positive way. When he interviewed her in his ready room on *Enterprise,* it was more as a courtesy than anything else.

"Your willingness to participate in this mission is commendable, Lieutenant Chen. Or do you prefer Lieutenant T'Ryssa?"

"Chen, please," said the lieutenant, a slender woman with tomboyish Asian features under slanted brows. With her hair worn over her ears, those eyebrows and the greenish flush to her golden skin were the only clear evidence of her Vulcan ancestry. "Uh, sir. Or Trys. I've been known to answer to 'Hey, you.'"

He glared at her. "As you were, Lieutenant."

"Oh! Sorry, sir. Just a little nervous. I mean, you're *Captain Picard,* and . . ."

"Yes, I'm aware of that."

She sighed heavily. "I'm not making a very good first impression, am I, sir?"

"Well, I'll say this much, you're perhaps the most unusual Vulcan I've ever met."

Chen bristled a bit. "I'm not a Vulcan. Sir. With respect. I'm a *person.* I just happen to have human and Vulcan genes."

Picard nodded. "A good point. I apologize, Lieutenant."

"Thank you, Captain."

"As I was saying: I can certainly sympathize with your desire to learn the fate of your compatriots aboard the *Rhea*. But the post you are seeking is a key bridge position. And frankly, Lieutenant, you are a long way from proving that you are qualified for such responsibility. Your performance record is spotty, there are numerous reports of disciplinary problems and insubordination—"

"If this is about the tube grub incident, I swear, I had no way of knowing the ambassador was in the room—"

"I was not finished, Lieutenant," he told her sternly.

"Sorry, sir. I'm not insubordinate, really, I just have a little trouble fitting into the whole hierarchical thing."

"Lieutenant!"

She cleared her throat. "Um. Case in point. Go ahead, sir."

Picard started to speak again, but he had forgotten what he was going to say. He cleared his throat. "In short, Lieutenant, what do you think makes you qualified for this posting?"

"I'm trained in xenoanthropology and xenoethology, sir. I traveled a lot growing up, I've been to a lot of new worlds, met lots of people. I'm good at adapting to new situations and I enjoy the discovery, the thrill of getting to know new cultures, new kinds of life and living. And I'm good at my job, when it's doing science, when it's exploring. It's just the whole military discipline stuff I have to work on."

"Yes, your record shows you've done an entirely competent job when you've applied yourself. But I have fifty entirely competent candidates competing for the same post. What is there that makes you uniquely suited for the role?"

"Well . . . sir . . . I think the fact that I'm the only available person who's actually *been* there before has got to count for something," she said, her nervousness giving way to assertiveness. "I've made actual contact with these beings."

He furrowed his brow. "Are you assuming the, er, 'Noh Angels' you encountered on the planet were responsible for your rescue from the Borg?"

"I'm not assuming anything, sir. I don't know if the Angels were intelligent beings—hell, I don't know if they were even living things. But *somebody* stripped me naked, deloused me on a molecular level, and shot me out of the galaxy's biggest cannon. And I have to say, sir," she went on, all sedateness vanishing from her tone, "if they don't put me in the record books for the galaxy's longest naked spaceflight without a ship, you can bet somebody's going to get an earful. I mean, there should at least be a plaque for that or something, don't you think?"

"Lieutenant—"

"I mean, there's a bunch of space records that people have broken naked, but they usually fall into a whole other category—"

"Lieutenant!"

"Sorry, sir. My mind races when I get nervous, and—" She caught herself. "I'll be quiet now."

Picard shook his head fractionally. "Say what you were going to say."

"And I'm really worried about my friends on *Rhea,* sir," she went on as if she'd never interrupted herself. "If something out there saved me, maybe somehow it saved them too." She lowered her head. "At least some of them. And if it didn't," she said, looking up at him again, "then maybe there's something different about me. Something that got its attention. And maybe you can use that. Maybe you'll have to."

"Do you think your telepathy could be a factor?"

Her cheeks flushed green. "I don't . . . do telepathy, sir. I never studied any Vulcan disciplines . . . whatever I was born with, I've never used. It's probably atrophied. And there were eighteen full Vulcans on board."

Picard thought for a moment. "I would be willing to allow you to accompany the *Enterprise* on this mission as a consultant. If your services prove useful, I will call on you."

"If? But that's not good enough!" He gave her a warning glare. "Sir. I mean . . . I *need* to do this. I need to do everything I can to help find out what happened to *Rhea,* to save them if I can. I can't just sit around waiting. I know I can help you on this mission, and I have to try."

He studied her. "Commendable words, Lieutenant. But your record does not show anywhere near that level of commitment. Your Starfleet career has been unfocused, dilettantish; your superiors have noted your tendency to retreat from difficult situations, to weasel out of unwelcome assignments—"

Picard broke off. Chen was wincing, and he saw moisture glistening in her eyes, astonishing to see in a face that appeared so Vulcan. But it wasn't a sympathy ploy; she was struggling to control it. "Lieutenant. Is there something you wish to tell me?"

"It shouldn't have been me, sir."

"Go on."

"I shouldn't have been the one who got out. I . . . I wasn't supposed to be on the away team. It was supposed to be Ensign Janyl. But I didn't want to sit around manning a boring old console while other people were down on a strange new world having fun. So I talked my superior into letting me go instead. I played on our friendship, I flattered her—hell, I annoyed her into giving in, basically." Picard could certainly believe that. "And . . . and so Janyl and Dawn—Commander Blair probably got . . . while I got stuck here with a clichéd case of survivor's guilt."

She took a shuddering breath. "You're absolutely right about me, Captain Picard. I'm a screwup. I run away from my responsibilities. Growing up, Mom and I were always moving around from posting to posting, so I knew I'd never make any long-term commitments anyway, so I ran away from any situation where things got tense. We were on the *Odyssey* for a few years, but just when I finally started to let myself feel settled, we got left behind when the ship went to the Gamma Quadrant and never came back. Avoidance saved my life." Like everyone in Starfleet, Picard vividly remembered the circumstances of the *Odyssey*'s destruction. When sent through the Bajoran wormhole to confront the Jem'Hadar who had taken Deep Space 9's commander hostage—the Dominion's way of making first contact with the Federation—the *Galaxy*-class vessel had evacuated its civilians and nonessential personnel to DS9 before departure. Hundreds of lives had thus been spared. Chen would have been sixteen at the time.

"Then the Dominion War happened while I was in the Academy, and I screwed up enough there that it took me five years to graduate and the war was over by then. I dodged the whole thing.

"So there you go. All my life, I've been running, retreating, avoiding. It's what made me the woman I am today," she said with ironic pride. "So I ran away from a boring shift on *Rhea,* and then . . . well, look at me. Second time in a row, my ship gets blown up and I get away. And this time . . . this time all my friends on the ship didn't get left behind with me. Every last one of them got killed or Borgified, and I . . . well, just call me Ishmael."

It was a long moment before Picard spoke. "You did not escape by choice this time."

"Didn't I? Whatever saved me, sir, they sent me to Maravel. To the one place in my life where I was happiest. Do you have any idea how many times I wanted to run away from a tough situation and go back there, to be free to play in the woods? They must've read that in my thoughts. Must've sensed that I wanted to run away. Maybe that's why they saved only me—because everyone else wanted to stay and fight the Borg, but I just wanted to run away and hide."

She shot to her feet and began pacing the ready room like a caged tiger. Picard chose to allow it. Finally, she paused by the clear crystal model of the *Enterprise*-E, gazing into its facets for a time before she turned to address him. "I know it's not your job to help me get therapy, sir. I know I'm not giving you any good reason to trust in my objectivity or stability. But I've never been as strongly motivated about any mission as I am about this one. Never been this focused on a goal. I *need* to do this. I need to go out there and do something that will make a difference, that will make my survival mean something for *Rhea*'s crew. Even if it's just helping to screw over the goddamn Borg and avenge their deaths.

"I promise you, Captain Picard, if you put me in a position where I can work toward that goal, you'll find you've never had a more relentless officer." Her resolve faltered a bit. "And yes, I know your first officer's a Klingon. Which was part of the point I was going for, and—" She cleared her throat. "I should quit while I'm ahead, shouldn't I, sir?"

Picard looked her over sternly, but the corner of his mouth was threatening to turn up in a smirk. Clearing his throat to cover it, he rose from the desk. "You've made an eloquent case, Lieutenant, and I assure you I shall give careful consideration to your petition." He shook her hand. "Thank you."

She looked betrayed, starting to object, but then controlled herself. "Very well, sir. Thank you," she said stiffly.

"You're dismissed."

She turned and left, but his sensitive ears caught her muttering, "I mean, baring your soul used to count for something . . ."

He let out a breath and ran his hand over his pate. *If nothing else,* he thought, *I doubt I'll have a more memorable interview for this post.*


"So what do you think?"

Hegol Den gazed placidly at Picard, taking his time before answering the captain's question. "Are you asking me if I think you should appoint Lieutenant Chen to your crew?" the middle-aged Bajoran asked.

Picard smiled, knowing his counselor better than that. Hegol could not have been more different from his predecessor, T'Lana. Rather than telling people what he thought they should do, he merely listened, asked questions, and helped his patients guide themselves to the answers they sought. His approach was not that different from Deanna Troi's, although he was content to see to the psychological well-being of the crew rather than taking an interest in command decisions or contact situations. However, Picard had found it worthwhile to consult him on this decision. "I'm asking if you think she's capable of doing the job. If she can be relied on to let her sense of culpability motivate her in a positive way rather than hampering her."

"I'd have to meet with her myself to make a fair assessment."

"Your impressions, then."

Hegol ran a hand through his close-shorn gray-brown curls. "She sounds volatile, but that's not surprising for a half-Vulcan."

"You mean a half-human."

"Why do you assume that?"

Picard looked at him in confusion. "Vulcans are not known for their volatility."

"But that's cultural, isn't it? Why did the Vulcans adopt emotional control?"

Picard nodded, understanding. "Because their innate emotions are so . . . volatile." Hegol nodded back. "And T'Ryssa Chen has never studied Vulcan disciplines."

"I'm not proposing that she's liable to go berserk, mind you. Merely that she's probably governed by strong passions. Instead of learning to repress them, she chooses to manage them by embracing them, domesticating them, using them as a source of enjoyment for herself and amusement for others. It may not be a Starfleet or Vulcan form of discipline, but it is a form of self-management. At least, that's my secondhand impression. I wouldn't recommend basing your decision on it."

"Whatever self-management she practices, I question its effectiveness," Picard said. "Perhaps it brings her entertainment, but it has not brought out much sense of responsibility."

"From what you told me, she sounds very resolute. Traumatic experiences are often transformative."

"I'm not sure I can rely on that, though."

"What would make you sure?"

Picard gave a rueful grin. "The chance to try her out for a month on a mission that wasn't so urgent."

Hegol furrowed his brow, deepening the ridges on his nose. "It will take at least six weeks to reach the cluster, won't it?" Picard nodded. "That would be an adequate trial period."

"Yes, but who would I replace her with if she didn't work out?"

"It sounds like you have an overabundance of candidates, Captain. In fact," Hegol said, "I find it interesting that you've chosen to consult me specifically about T'Ryssa Chen. Doesn't that suggest that you're already considering her a leading candidate?"

"Well, she certainly stood out from the pack. She's . . . irritating, perhaps, but there's no questioning her sincerity. And I sympathize with her desire to learn the fate of her comrades. But as she herself pointed out, I'm not here to give her therapy."

"I should hope not. I've grown rather fond of the office."

They shared a chuckle. "And there's more," Picard said. "She's just so . . . young. Inexperienced. I don't feel comfortable taking a, a child to confront the Borg."

Hegol leaned forward. "T'Ryssa Chen is twenty-six years old. You were only two years older when you became a captain."

"That was not the same. I didn't have to face anything as . . . as terrible as the Borg. No mere child should be forced to face such a thing."

"Hmm," the counselor said. "You've mentioned children twice now. Have children been on your mind recently?"

Picard fidgeted. "Not particularly."

"Hmm. Tell me, Captain, how are you finding married life?"

That brought a resigned grimace. "All right. Naturally, in the wake of marriage, the prospect of . . . procreation does naturally come to mind, yes."

"Naturally."

Picard winced. It wasn't like him to repeat himself. "You think I'm avoiding the idea of parenthood because of the Borg threat."

"Do you think you are?"

"I think . . . I think that the middle of an urgent crisis is not the best time to contemplate such matters."

Hegol folded his hands. "That's fair. So you simply need to wait until there are no crises occurring in the known galaxy."

The captain had to admire Hegol's methods. Even with his laid-back, nonconfrontational manner, he still had a way of cutting to the heart of a matter. "I don't mean—look, this is why I never believed in having families on starships."

"Is that still the case?"

"Yes."

"Does your wife feel the same way?"

That brought him up short. "That's different," he said after a moment. "Beverly is an experienced officer. She understands the risks."

"So . . . did Commander Nella Daren not understand the risks?"

Hegol had hit on something Picard hadn't thought about in some time. Nella Daren had been a science officer aboard the previous *Enterprise,* and for a brief time, Picard had allowed himself to become romantically involved with her. When a crisis had arisen that had required him to order her into danger, he had found himself nearly paralyzed with fear for her safety. They had agreed that it was best for her to transfer to another ship, so they would not be placed in that position anymore. They had hoped to continue the relationship over a distance, but their attempts had soon tapered off, and Nella had met another man. She was now happily married and expecting her second child. "She did, of course. But . . ."

"But?"

Hegol's simple question left him no recourse but to look inside himself. "All right. This is the first time since marrying Beverly that I've had to take her into danger. It's natural that I'd have concerns about that, isn't it?"

"That sounds reasonable."

"But what does that have to do with my decision about Lieutenant Chen?"

Hegol smiled. "That, Captain Picard, is an excellent question."

And he left it at that, ending the session and leaving Picard to think about it for himself. On the way out of the counselor's office, Picard was again struck by how different he was from Counselor T'Lana—although at the same time, he doubted that T'Lana would disapprove.

He reflected on the day when T'Lana had left the ship, just after Admiral Janeway's funeral. He had been surprised to see her; given her condemnation of his actions in the incident and her eagerness to leave *Enterprise* thereafter, he had assumed she would have no interest in speaking to him again. But she had, and her words had been entirely unexpected.

"I want you to know," T'Lana had told him, "that my transfer request was not a protest against your actions in the crisis."

Picard had been bewildered, for that had certainly been how it appeared. "Then may I ask what your reasons are?"

"During my confinement to quarters, I had much time to reflect on my recent actions," the delicate-featured Vulcan had replied. "I realized that I behaved in a highly illogical fashion. I insisted that I was incapable of error and refused to consider that other points of view might have merit. There is no excuse for such behavior."

"It sounds like simple stubbornness to me," Picard had said, wondering why he felt motivated to speak in her defense.

"You do not understand, sir. My profession is predicated on the importance of self-examination. We help people by encouraging them to question their own assumptions and preconceptions and recognize the psychological issues that may be influencing those preconceptions. For a counselor, for any therapist, to deny the value of questioning oneself is akin to . . . to a biologist denying the existence of evolution." She had looked away. "Counselors must ourselves undergo periodic counseling to ensure our emotional competency. Had I been required to undergo such evaluation during recent events, I would not have been granted clearance to practice. As such, I believe I must remove myself from duty until I have resolved these issues."

"I must say, I'm surprised to hear a Vulcan speak of emotional competency," he had said.

"I am also a therapist, sir. And I let myself forget a fact I related to Commander La Forge mere weeks ago: that Vulcans' intrinsically turbulent emotions can produce neuroses far greater and more complex than those of other species." She had folded her hands before her. "I believe, sir, that I am afflicted with such a neurosis. I believe that my sense of guilt over the death of Captain Wozniak of the *Indefatigable,* which I have believed to be due in part to poor advice I provided to her, has left me so . . . afraid of giving bad advice that I had convinced myself I was incapable of doing so.

"Vulcans value the tenacity that you call 'stubbornness,' sir. But my behavior in the recent crisis went beyond stubbornness, nearly to the point of clinical narcissism. I must therefore conclude that I am not currently competent to perform as a counselor.

"My decision to leave *Enterprise* is thus for your benefit as well as my own. Although I still do not agree with your actions and decisions during the crisis, I recognize that I failed to address that disagreement in a constructive manner. And I wish to apologize for that failure, sir."

Picard had been genuinely moved. "I believe, Counselor, that you underestimate your own effectiveness and insight as a therapist. You have just helped a particularly strong-willed patient to make a major breakthrough."

One of her sleek eyebrows had risen. "Your sentiment is facetiously expressed, but appreciated. I am grateful for your forgiveness, Captain. And it is my hope that someday, when I have resolved my psychological difficulties, I will be able to be of use to you again."

Now, three months later, as he pondered Hegol's words about T'Ryssa Chen, Picard wondered what his former counselor would have made of the young woman. He found it rather likely that T'Lana would have disapproved of her—which probably counted as a point in the lieutenant's favor. Yet there was every chance that Chen might prove as problematical in her own way as T'Lana had.

In the meantime, there was one more personnel issue he had to address. And as he expected, he found her in the ship's lounge, the Happy Bottom Riding Club (leave it to Will Riker to coin such an irreverent name as a parting shot). More specifically, he found her behind the bar, just beneath a large, saucer-shaped hat. "Guinan," he said, smiling in greeting.

"Captain," came that mellow voice he knew so well. "What can I get for you?"

"Just tea, thank you. I must say," he went on as she filled the order, "I'm pleasantly surprised to find you still here."

Ever the Listener, she caught the edge in his voice. "There's still time before you ship out."

He controlled his reaction. On some level, he'd been hoping she'd changed her mind. It had been only a few months since he'd convinced Guinan to come back and tend bar aboard this *Enterprise* as she had aboard its predecessor. Her periodic inter-stellar wanderlust had overtaken her not long after that ship had met its fate at Veridian III, so the *Enterprise*-E had needed to make do without her. But she had returned from parts unknown in time for Will and Deanna's wedding, and Picard had begun plying her to return. She had declined for a time, saying she was reluctant to repeat herself. But after the Borg attack on Earth, she had just shown up one day and asked if the offer was still open. Perhaps she sensed that Picard could use a friend in the wake of that ordeal, or perhaps she had needed one herself. In either case, she had been very welcome and had quickly fallen back into her special rapport with the crew, old and new alike. She had soon helped nudge Picard into finally proposing to Beverly, using anecdotes from several of her twenty-three marriages. Indeed, somewhere in her past few years of traveling, she had earned a title equivalent to a justice of the peace, and Picard had been honored when she had agreed to conduct the wedding herself. ("I also do bar mitzvahs and *kahs-wan*s," she had informed him.)

So he just could not accept that she would jump ship on him now, less than three months after her return. "You still plan to leave before we do so?"

She met his eyes. "It's the Borg, Picard. Don't pre-tend you don't understand my reasons for leaving."

"I understand better than anyone," he said. "But I'm still going."

"You have to. You're under orders. I'm a civilian." She sighed. "It's not that I'm afraid. Well, of course I'm afraid. I'm terrified. But I've faced the Borg with you before, and I've had faith that you'd get us through it."

"Then why not now?"

"Because enough is enough. I've seen enough of the Borg to last a lifetime, even one as long as mine. And you can handle the Borg just fine without me."

Picard held her gaze. "It's not the Borg that I need you here to help me with. It's been such a challenge, trying to assemble a stable command crew. There have been so many losses, so many divisions among us. I've heard mutterings among the crew—all this instability in the command staff is making them concerned."

"I've heard the same mutterings," Guinan confirmed. "But they've been getting quieter."

"No doubt thanks to your sage counsel. Your presence has done much to smooth tensions. But I fear your departure could exacerbate the sense of instability that still lingers among the crew, especially on the heels of Leybenzon's and Gaanth's departures."

Guinan looked at him evenly. "It doesn't suit you to use guilt to make me stay."

"That was not my intention." He winced, shook his head. "That's not true. I suppose it was, and I apologize. But you are needed here, Guinan. I am determined to make it work this time, to find a new team that can be as successful as my old one. And

I see you as an invaluable part of that process."

She was silent for a moment, then asked, "So how's that coming? Found your contact specialist yet?"

It took him some time to choose his words. He told her about T'Ryssa Chen and his ambivalence concerning her. "I don't know. Despite her inexperience, her erratic record, there's just something about her. Perhaps it's her personal stake in the mission, her unique experience with the cluster's inhabitants. Perhaps it's the unusual perspective she offers. I've so rarely encountered anyone of Vulcan parentage who wasn't raised as a Vulcan. She has the same heritage as Ambassador Spock but could not be more his opposite."

"Or maybe you just like her," Guinan said. "I haven't even met her, and I already like her."

Picard harrumphed. "You've always had a fondness for rogues," he said, remembering how she had taken Ro Laren under her wing over a decade ago.

"Well, we rogues have to stick together."

"But my reason tells me I should choose someone with more experience—and someone who brings less personal baggage on the mission."

Guinan raised her hairless brows. "By that standard, *you* should stay behind."

"Hmm. Point taken."

She frowned. "It's not like you to take this long to make a decision."

"It's a key decision, Guinan. I feel I'm so close. The command crew is almost falling into place;

I only need the contact specialist. I have to choose well."

Guinan pondered. "A wise man once told me that it's often more important to make a prompt decision than a perfect one. If you make the wrong choice, at least you'll know that you did and have a chance to fix it. And that's better than not making a choice at all until it's too late."

He furrowed his brow. "Didn't I tell you that?"

She tilted her head. "I suppose you did."

He smiled. "You see why I need you?"

Guinan's expression grew thoughtful. "I think I'm beginning to."

Trys received the call from Captain Picard while she was reenacting her unclothed quantum slipstream journey with help from a cute subspace physicist she'd met at Starfleet HQ, except without the quantum slipstream part. She scrambled to amend the "unclothed" part as quickly as possible, at least partly, while harrying her fellow researcher into the next room.

*"Lieutenant Chen,"* the forbidding captain said, *"you will report aboard* Enterprise *at zero seven hundred tomorrow to begin your duties as contact specialist."*

It was a moment before she found her voice. "Oh, sir, you don't know what this means to me. Thank you."

His eyes registered disapproval at her sloppily

worn tunic and disheveled hair. She was glad he couldn't see her lower half. *"Lieutenant. When your commanding officer gives you an order, you are expected to acknowledge it according to procedure."*

"Oh!" She snapped to attention. "Uhh, zero-seven-hundred tomorrow, aye, aye, sir."

*"Understand this, Lieutenant. A posting on* Enterprise *means that you will be serving with the very finest that Starfleet has to offer. You will be expected to comport yourself in a way that proves you are worthy of that posting. Do I make myself clear?"*

"Yes, sir, crystal clear!" She hated standing at attention, snapping formulaic responses. That kind of regimentation felt so . . . *Vulcan.* But if it was what she had to do to learn the fate of *Rhea's* crew, then she would do it or kill herself trying. Besides, this was *Captain Picard.* If anyone in Starfleet deserved her wholehearted respect, not for his rank or position but for who he was, it was this man. "I swear, I will not let you down, sir."

*"I will hold you to that. Picard out."*

Trys sent her companion home early, determined to get a good night's sleep and make a good first impression. But she spent the entire night staring at the ceiling.

# 3

———

*U.S.S. Enterprise*
En route to NGC 6281
Stardate 57758

"Do not see yourselves as instigators of force," Jasminder Choudhury told her security trainees in a soft, contemplative voice as they moved through their exercises. A fit, fortyish woman with South Asian features and nut-brown skin, she stood before them in loose workout clothes, her unruly black hair bound in a tight ponytail behind her. "Forces are intrinsic to the universe. We do not create them, merely channel them. The attacker's force and the defender's force are part of the same continuum. Understanding that oneness is the key to achieving your goals."

Worf grimaced as he listened to her lecture from the doorway, watched the sedate, yogalike exercises the security personnel were performing. This was her idea of grooming an effective fighting force?

"Let me show you what I mean," Choudhury said in a gently lilting alto with a slight Denevan accent. "Mister Konya, if you will assist me?"

A Betazoid man with large, dark eyes and sandy blond hair stepped forward and stood loosely, not assuming any particular defensive stance. Choudhury moved behind him and, a moment later, moved to attack him. Konya anticipated her motion and stepped aside, grabbing her and using her momentum to send her to the mat. She turned the fall into a roll and arose smoothly from it, not even breathing hard. "You see? By understanding your opponent— feeling what he feels—you gain the key to success."

"But that isn't really fair," said Ensign Balidemaj, waving her hand in Rennan Konya's direction. "We can't all read people's minds."

"Read their motor cortices, actually," Konya corrected. Worf was aware of the man's record; a fairly weak telepath by Betazoid standards, Konya had compensated by training himself to tune into the motor functions of the brain rather than its more complex cognitive functions. He could tap into other people's sensory awareness of their own bodies from the inside and could thus anticipate their movements by directly sensing their muscles tensing, their weight shifting, and so on, as well as gaining an intimate knowledge of exactly where and how an opponent was most vulnerable at any moment. This ability gave him a considerable edge in personal combat—but his Betazoid sensitivity to others' pain made him reluctant to inflict it. Apparently that philosophy had not hampered him unduly aboard his previous posting, the *U.S.S. da Vinci* attached to the Starfleet Corps of Engineers; his record there had impressed Lieutenant Choudhury enough that she had requested him as her second in command, a posting that had earned the enlisted man a brevet promotion to ensign (for *Enterprise*'s crew, security staff included, was more officer-heavy than that of a *Saber*-class vessel). But Worf questioned whether his borderline pacifistic approach would cut it against the level of threats that *Enterprise* often faced—and what Choudhury's choice of him as her second said about her own judgment.

Choudhury smiled serenely in response to Abby Balidemaj's objection. "Rennan?" she asked. Planting her long, strong legs in a basic wide stance, she waited for Konya to attack her. Though it took slightly longer, in the end, he was on the mat and she stood calmly over him. "Empathy is not merely a function of telepathic perception," she said. "It is a thing of the spirit. An understanding of the oneness that we are but facets of." She glanced over at Worf. "Meditate on this as you conduct your exercises."

Leaving them to it, she strolled over to him. He couldn't help but notice the uncanny grace of her movements. "Commander Worf," she greeted.

"Lieutenant." Unlike many humanoid women,

her eyes fell at a comfortable height for him to meet. She was nearly as tall as Jadzia had been . . . as K'Ehleyr had been. He looked away, repressing the thought.

"You seem troubled, sir. Is there a problem?"

He crossed his arms. "Yes, there is. I find your methods . . . unconventional."

She nodded. "You fear I'm making them weak."

She spoke calmly but still faced the issue overtly. He therefore did the same. "Yes."

"My predecessor did a fine job of honing these men and women into warriors. But we are security."

"They are much the same."

"Not entirely. Do you know the etymology of the word 'security'?"

"I have always considered it more an action than a word."

"Interesting," she replied. "Well, it comes from the Latin *cura*, meaning 'to care.' Our job is to take care of people, Commander. We're responsible for protecting others. It takes more than physical force to achieve that. It takes perceptiveness, sensitivity, judgment. It takes the ability to understand the sources of conflict and resolve them—ideally before they erupt. I believe it is not enough for us to be myrmidons or cannon fodder. We need to be not only first on the scene but also capable of applying the necessary skills to resolve a conflict, whether that be with combat or with diplomacy."

"The captain," Worf said with pride, "is a formidable diplomat. I have . . . some experience in that field myself."

"Indeed. But my job is to minimize the need for my superior officers to place themselves in harm's way. We are the first responders to danger, and that makes it our responsibility to resolve it if we can—not merely to point phasers and hope our superiors can talk their way out of our having to use them."

As Worf pondered her words, she went on. "Besides, starship security is not merely about confronting external threats. The skills of a warrior are of little use at maintaining the peace within one's own community."

The Klingon bristled. "This is the *Enterprise.* We do not fight among ourselves."

"Aside from the occasional alien force influencing the crew." She paused. "Or the occasional mutiny," she added without rancor or accusation.

But Worf was stung nonetheless. Choudhury had reminded him of his own failure to wield his diplomatic skills to avert the conflict that had broken out among the crew—*his* crew, whose unity and cooperation were his duty as first officer to ensure.

"In general," he conceded for now, "your goals are laudable. But I question their appropriateness for the current mission. We are going to confront the Borg. They do not negotiate. They do not take hostages," he added, alluding to her noted achievements in the Nosgoh incident.

Choudhury pursed her full lips. "With respect,

sir, isn't that precisely what they do? Isn't every drone a hostage of sorts?"

He had to give her credit. She debated as well as any diplomat or politician he had battled against in his four years as an ambassador—and more intelligently than most of them. "In principle, yes. However, the danger they pose is so great that all other concerns must be secondary. It is regrettable, but necessary. When you have faced the Borg, you will understand. If," he added, lowering his voice to a growl, "you survive."

The corners of her mouth turned up slightly. "Whether I survive, die, or am assimilated, I believe that I will gain much more understanding, sir."

He stared at Choudhury, but she did not elaborate on her digression. "But I would submit, Commander," she went on, "that liberating Borg drones has been an effective tactical move on multiple occasions. The liberation of Captain Picard from the Collective proved instrumental to defeating their first attack on Earth. The liberation of the drone called Hugh enabled a 'virus' of individuality to spread through an entire cube, perhaps more, and deprived the Collective of many potential fighters. The liberation of Seven of Nine by the crew of *Voyager* gave them access to vital Borg intelligence and technology and proved instrumental in multiple victories over the Collective. Seven of Nine and *Voyager* later assisted the drones of Unimatrix Zero to rebel against the Borg and launch a resistance movement."

Worf recalled hearing of how *Voyager*'s crew had

helped the drones of Unimatrix Zero to retain their personalities and memories upon awakening in the real world and rebel against their oppressors. Of course, Worf had firsthand memory of the Hugh incident, for it had happened on *Enterprise* during his own tenure as security chief.

"Sir," Choudhury said, "the drones we're going up against—they were the crew of *Einstein*. And probably the crew of *Rhea* as well. They're Starfleet, sir. They're family," she said, her tone gaining in intensity and conviction. "Don't we have a duty to them as well?"

Again, Choudhury's words resonated with Worf's own recent thoughts. "I, too, entertained such notions during our initial assault on the Borg cube in Sector 10," he said. "But circumstances did not allow us to pursue such options, either then or when the vessel subsequently attacked Earth. These Borg, Lieutenant, are different from those encountered in the past. They are more ruthless, more aggressive. It is doubtful that we will have the luxury to work on their liberation.

"I need to know, Lieutenant, that I can count on you to do what must be done."

She met his gaze evenly, that same conviction shining in her dark eyes. "That is what I always do, sir."

"So how are the new people working out?" Beverly asked Picard over dinner in their quarters.

"Quite well, for the most part," he replied. "Lieutenant Choudhury is extremely capable, organized, methodical."

"She's a little unusual for a security chief. Very . . . peaceful."

"It's a change, to be sure. I think her team simply needs a little more time to adjust to her style." He smiled wryly. "And so does Worf, to be honest. I think he still needs some convincing."

Privately, Beverly felt that Choudhury was a vast improvement over Leybenzon. From her perspective, the last thing this ship needed was a security chief who was too gung-ho about fighting and dying in battle. As much as she respected Worf, she felt that he had indulged Leybenzon's Spartan approach a bit too much. She hoped that Choudhury would be a better balance to his more Klingon tendencies.

"But you and Jasminder seem to have hit it off marvelously," Beverly said.

"Oh, she's an intriguing person. Just this morning, after her routine security report, we had the most fascinating conversation about the principle of the circle of states as defined in the *Artha Shastra* and how it illuminates the ongoing political interplay among Romulan factions, Klingons, and Remans."

She quirked an eyebrow at his enthusiasm. "Should I be jealous?"

Picard stared, somehow managing to look like a thoroughly indignant deer in a groundcar's headlights. "Certainly not! My interest is purely intellectual."

After staring for another moment, Beverly laughed and let him off the hook. "I'm only teasing. Call it a wife's prerogative. Seriously, she sounds charming. We should have her over for dinner sometime."

"I'll talk to her about it."

"And how about our new chief science officer?"

"Lieutenant Elfiki is working out quite well. She's already managed to enhance the resolution of our long-range scans of NGC 6281 and has offered some theories, based on *Rhea*'s reports, on how we might be able to tune the engines to compensate for the subspace distortions within the cluster." He grimaced. "We will need every bit of extra speed we can get. We're at maximum sustainable warp already, and it feels like we're moving at a crawl."

Beverly gave him a wistful look. "Hurry up and wait—literally. It's the life of an officer, Jean-Luc."

"I know. Nothing we can do until we get there, so no sense wasting energy on worrying about it."

"Exactly."

"Still . . . I worry."

She placed her hand on his. "So do I."

He smiled and nodded in thanks. Beverly took another bite and changed the subject. "So how about Trys Chen?"

Picard sank back in his chair. "Well. I haven't had to put her on report yet, at least."

"Yet?"

He sighed. "I do believe she's making a sincere effort. But discipline does not come easily to her. And she enjoys being the class clown. She's always interrupting with jokes, or chatting with bridge officers when she and they should be focusing on their work."

Beverly tilted her head. "I seem to remember a certain first officer of the *Enterprise* who was known for his sense of humor and gregarious manner."

"Yes, but Will knew how to save it for the appropriate time." He softened. "Still, Lieutenant Chen has shown some signs of improvement. She did a good job today with her presentation offering hypotheses on the creatures she encountered in the cluster. True, it was little more than guesswork with only her memories to go on, but she presented it with minimal digressions and offered some imaginative proposals."

Beverly smiled. "What is it?" Picard asked.

"The look on your face just now," she said. "It reminded me of how Jack would look when he was talking about Wesley saying his first full sentence or solving his first equation."

Picard fell silent, looking away. Beverly felt his shields going up between them. She'd said it without premeditation, but she didn't regret having brought it up now. "Jean-Luc, why won't you just talk about it?"

"About what?"

"About the thing you and I both know you were

on the verge of bringing up when this Borg business interrupted. About starting a family." His stony silence continued, and her tone grew more pleading. "We don't have to commit to anything right now, Jean-Luc. Can't we just have an open, adult discussion about the possibility?"

Picard gave a heavy sigh. As was his way, he pondered for a time before he spoke. "You know how I feel about you, Beverly." She nodded. "And you know how I feel about . . . the Picard legacy. You understand that I do truly cherish the opportunity you have given me to know a kind of happiness I had long since lost hope of ever knowing. To be a husband and a father.

"But now is not the time. Not while we remain under imminent threat from the Borg. Not while it is my responsibility to cope with that threat. I cannot afford the distraction. Not until the crisis is resolved."

"Jean-Luc, there are always crises and threats out there. That's no reason to back away from bringing new lives into the world. That's what life does. It creates new life in defiance of death. Otherwise, death wins."

"The Borg are no ordinary danger, Beverly! They are an entirely different level of threat. No matter what we think we do to defeat them, they come back. We cannot relax our guard, even for a moment, until they are beaten once and for all!"

She didn't like what she heard in his words. "If you had felt that way two months ago, you never would have proposed to me. Are you saying you regret that choice? That trying to move ahead with your life was a mistake?"

He sobered. "No," he said after a moment, speaking gently. "Of course not. I am saying that I will do whatever it takes to preserve what we have now. To ensure that it does not end in tragedy."

"And how long will it be until you're sure? After we deal with the *Frankenstein* and the *Rhea,* will you keep us going all the way to the Delta Quadrant, make sure you've wiped out every last cube and drone and Royal Protocol before you even consider starting a family?"

Picard continued in what he thought was a reassuring tone. "I promise you, Beverly, we will have a serious discussion about the matter as soon as the immediate threat is resolved. All right?" He rose and clasped her shoulder.

Sensing the futility of pressing him further, she nodded and placed her hand on his. Satisfied, he kissed her brow and proceeded to clear the table. *But what then, Jean-Luc?* she thought. *Will you just find another reason to put it off?*

Miranda Kadohata thought of herself as an easygoing person. Years of hard work as a starship officer and parent had taught her the value of staying loose and relaxed, of focusing her energy on the tasks she needed to perform rather than wasting it on tension or frustration. She also thought of herself as someone who got on well with others—sometimes too well, at least in her single years, when she had tended to get involved with the wrong men over and over. But eventually she'd gotten it right with Vicenzo. And her nonromantic relationships tended to go pretty smoothly as a rule.

But T'Ryssa Chen was proving to be an exception. Miranda had found the young contact specialist annoying from the moment they'd been introduced, when Chen's first words to her had been, "Miranda, huh? So you're the one they named all those ships after!"—as if there had actually been something original or amusing about such an observation. She'd shaken it off, hoping it would be a minor bump in the course of establishing a good working relationship. But Chen had continued to be irreverent to the point of disrespect, forgetting to address her by rank or "sir," neglecting to make adequate reports to her or clear plans with her before acting on them, and so forth. She hadn't crossed the line into insubordination, but Miranda felt it was only a matter of time.

If anything, Miranda had been trying to go easy on her. She was self-aware enough to recognize that she felt a little envy toward the lieutenant. Miranda was a lifelong research junkie, and science was her passion. When she had taken over Data's position as second officer and ops manager, she had also inherited his role of de facto science officer, a post he had groomed her to fill. She felt she had performed well, particularly during the Q incident and the subsequent survey of Gorsach IX, and she had enjoyed the scientific side of her work more than her other duties.

But then, after the Borg attacks and the mutiny, Picard had done his personnel restructuring, and Miranda had found her scientific duties reassigned to a separate science officer. At first, she had perceived it as punishment for her participation in the mutiny. The captain had explained his reasoning for the change, his belief that no mere mortal should be required to do three distinct jobs at the same time while juggling the responsibilities of a three-time mother as well. But that had felt to Miranda more like a judgment on the quality of her performance than an act of kindness.

Over time, though, she had come to realize that Picard had been right. The lighter workload had relieved her of a strain she hadn't even noticed being under—a strain that had not only affected her judgment in the Borg crisis but had caused some tensions with her husband back on Cestus III as well. They'd had a few fights over subspace, and Miranda had started to fall back into her old patterns of getting interested in the wrong men, specifically Zelik Leybenzon. Nothing had happened between them, but she'd quickly gone from being unable to stand the hard-nosed, bellicose security chief to finding him strangely compelling and striking up a flirtatious friendship. That relationship had been nipped in the bud once she'd backed out

of the mutiny and freed Picard, earning Leybenzon's resentment, and in retrospect she couldn't
be happier about that. She'd patched things up
with Vicenzo, and things had been smooth ever
since.

So although Miranda still missed the hands-on
science work, she was satisfied with her job as it
now stood. As second officer and ops manager, she
still got to supervise the efforts of the science staff
and coordinate with them in allocating sensor time
and lab facilities, so she wasn't completely cut out
of the process. And those jobs were largely exercises in problem solving, keeping ship's personnel
and resources organized and figuring out how to
assign them to carry out the many tasks necessary to
keep a *Sovereign*-class starship running smoothly.
That was enjoyable work for an analytical mind,
although a touch of compulsiveness helped too.

Still, the new science officers, Dina Elfiki and
T'Ryssa Chen, were getting to do the job Miranda
had enjoyed most. A little jealousy was natural
enough. But she could live with that so long as she
believed her replacements in the job were at least
as skilled and dedicated as she was. Where Elfiki
was concerned, she had no doubts about that. The
Egyptian native may have been frail, soft-spoken,
and girlish in appearance—and annoyingly stun-
ning with those great big dark eyes and holostar
cheekbones—but she was a wholehearted science
geek with an adventurous spirit, and Miranda had
hit it off with her instantly. But Chen was another

matter. Miranda had tried to give her every chance, but in her view, Chen just wasn't shaping up to be *Enterprise* material.

Captain Picard had admitted to doubts of his own but was giving the young lieutenant every chance to prove herself. Chen's first major test came three weeks into the mission, when *Enterprise* reached the space claimed by the Mabrae. They were a prickly, highly territorial people that Picard had made first contact with more than twenty years ago, and the fastest route to NGC 6281 passed directly through their space. It was thus necessary to negotiate passage, and to do so quickly, lest the negotiations eat up the time they would save by cutting through Mabrae territory. Picard chose to include Chen in his negotiations to see what insights she could gain into Mabrae culture and psychology. Since Picard was himself an expert on this race, having lived and worked alongside them for months on an archaeological dig, he was in a good position to assess the validity of Chen's conclusions.

And so Chen got to go over to the Mabrae ship that met *Enterprise* at their border while Miranda had to stay behind manning ops. Miranda had hoped to meet the Mabrae, an intriguing humanoid species that had evolved in a complex symbiosis with epiphytic plants that grew on their bodies. Instead of clothing, they wore plants of assorted types, bred to perform various practical and aesthetic functions. Their close personal connection to plants and the soil was at the root (so to speak) of their territorial nature.

When Picard and Chen returned from the first negotiating session, assembling with Miranda and the rest of the command crew in the observation lounge, Picard looked disheartened, but Chen brightened considerably when asked for her impressions of the Mabrae. "I'd heard their diplomatic types wore vines with colorful flowers," she said, grinning, "but I didn't know just how skimpy those vines could be. Their main negotiator, Beron—he's not wearing much more than a fig leaf, and he wears it well," she told her crewmates with a leer.

"Lieutenant," Miranda said, "I don't think that's the kind of impression we're waiting to hear from you."

"Hey, it's a cultural observation," Chen said, her slanted eyebrows rising in the middle. "They like their negotiators to be seductive. People who look good and smell good. They're flowers for luring in the insects. These guys learned everything they know from plants. Okay?" she asked, staring challengingly at Miranda.

"That's nothing more than you can find in the computer file on them."

"Maybe, but I said it better."

"Lieutenant," Picard said, and Chen subsided. Picard was the only one whose authority she submitted to readily.

The captain went on to discuss the failure of the first negotiating session. "Beron knows how urgent this is to us," he finished, "and that puts us at a disadvantage." He turned to Chen. "We need to improve our strategy, find some angle that will help us get what we need from them. And soon."

"That's just the problem," Chen said. "We need it fast. They've got all the time in the world. Like I said, they got it all from plants. They know that plants are slow and soft and flimsy, but just by being patient and methodical they can burrow through stone or grow through a metal fence and trap it inside their wood. That's their model. We can be as stubborn and stony as we want and they'll just keep nibbling away at us for as long as it takes to overwhelm us."

Picard seemed pleased by her insight, and Miranda was a little impressed herself. "Go on," the captain said. "What would you propose we do in response to this?"

Chen frowned. "We need to stop being stone. We need to be water."

"Meaning?" Worf asked.

"Water doesn't push up against plants' resistance, it flows around them. It . . . it seeps inside them, nourishes them. So . . ." She faltered. "I'm not sure where this metaphor's going. Um . . . I guess I'm saying we need to come at the negotiations from another angle. Don't resist what they're demanding, just come around and hit them from a direction they weren't expecting. Offer them something too good to resist. Show them we can flow like water. I think they'll respect that."

"Intriguing," Picard said. "Specifically, how would you propose we do that?"

"Um . . ." She shook her head, growing dejected. "I have no idea, sir. Sorry."

"That's all right," Picard said. "Your training is in alien psychology, not negotiating strategy. You've started us in a promising direction, at least."

"No, wait, I think I have something!" Chen said. "They're asking for Starfleet technology, right? Well, let's offer them something better. Say we'll give them the quantum slipstream tech from the cluster once we get it."

Picard shook his head. "Out of the question. The Mabrae haven't even reached warp 5. They're nowhere near advanced enough to be able to handle that technology safely. We don't even know if we'll be able to obtain the cluster's technology for ourselves."

"Well, I didn't say we'd actually *give* it to them, sir."

Miranda leaned forward. "You want us to lie to them?"

"If it gets us through their space. Or—here's a thought—if they can't go warp 5, let's just outrun them. We'll be through their space before they can stop us."

Picard was shaking his head. "Neither option is acceptable. The last time the Mabrae even suspected the Federation of not dealing fairly with them, they broke off relations for more than a decade."

"If it's a choice between making the Mabrae mad and letting the Borg get slipstream, I'd go with option one!"

Worf opened his mouth to chastise her, but Miranda beat him to it. "Lieutenant!" she barked. "Remember who you're speaking to!"

Chen clamped down on her intensity. "Sorry, sir," she said, but she pointedly directed it only at Picard, not Miranda, who distinctly heard her mutter, "And it's 'whom.' "

After a moment, Worf spoke. "She does have a point, Captain. Given the urgency of the threat—"

"If the negotiations drag on too long," Picard said, "we may do exactly as the lieutenant suggests. But that would be a risky move. Their ships may be inferior to ours, but there are many of them in our path and they will all fight tenaciously to defend their territory. We could not be certain of getting through their space without damage that could delay us or weaken us for our confrontation with the Borg. For the moment, a diplomatic solution is still our best option."

He looked around the table. "We're all tired and could use some dinner. All of you, consider the problem. Consult with your respective departments about what we might be able to offer the Mabrae. We'll reconvene at nineteen hundred. Dismissed."

Miranda intercepted Chen before she could leave. "You made a decent observation or two there, but you've got to work on your attitude if you want to be taken seriously."

The lieutenant glared at her. "I think the captain takes me seriously. And you could stand to be a little less serious."

"What's that supposed to mean?"

Chen sighed. "I'd tell you, but I'm sure you'd just tell me how it's wrong. Since apparently everything I do in your presence is wrong."

Miranda strove for calm. "It's part of my job to oversee crew performance. To help people who need improvement learn where they need to improve."

"I'd buy that if you ever said anything positive about me."

Miranda's eyes widened. "I just did!"

" 'A decent observation or two'? Oh, please, can I get that inscribed on my tombstone? And it doesn't count as a compliment if you don't even pause for breath before tacking on a criticism."

"Just what is your problem with me, Lieutenant?"

"My problem with you is your problem with me. You just can't stand that I'm doing the job you wanted, can you?"

"In order for me to feel that way, I'd first have to be convinced you were *doing* the job. And I don't recall giving you permission to speak freely, *Lieutenant*."

Chen reacted as though slapped. Then she just crossed her arms and stood there, staring expectantly. Miranda was tempted to put her on report, but the girl would just take it as proof that she was being persecuted. "Dismissed," she said. Chen strode from the lounge, her body taut with anger and humiliation, and Miranda felt as though she'd just sent Aoki to her room.

"Something bothering you, Worf?" Geordi La Forge asked as they waited for the turbolift after the meeting.

"What do you mean?"

"Well, lately, you've been a little tense in briefings."

Worf repressed a grimace. La Forge's bionic eyes gave him an unfair advantage in reading the reactions of the people around him. Yet he remained oddly clueless in other respects. "Have you not noticed," Worf said in a low growl, "that aside from the captain, you and I are the only males left on the alpha-shift command staff?"

La Forge blinked. "You know, you're right," he said, stroking his sparse goatee. "Well, Doctor Crusher and Deanna were the only women on the staff for quite a while, so I guess turnabout is fair play." His tone was light, unconcerned.

Worf leaned closer. "Do you not feel . . . outnumbered?"

Those pale, cybernetic eyes stared at him. "Worf," the engineer said with a chuckle, "it's not a battle. We're all on the same side."

Worf stared for a moment, then crossed his arms. "It is no wonder you have had so little success with women."

La Forge glowered, but Miranda Kadohata arrived before he could speak. "Geordi," she greeted, then turned to Worf. "Commander, could I have a moment of your time? In private, please," she said apologetically to La Forge as the lift doors opened.

"That's all right," the engineer said, glaring at Worf. "I'll take the next lift."

In the lift, Kadohata told Worf about her clash with T'Ryssa Chen. Worf was gratified that she felt she could come to him with such a problem; it was a sign of how successful they had both been at putting the unfortunate and mutually shameful events of the mutiny behind them. But from the way she spoke of Lieutenant Chen, one might think she feared another mutiny was imminent. "The girl has an attitude problem," she finished. "She's just not *Enterprise* material."

"Hmm," Worf said. "It is true that she has difficulties with authority. I have had my share of clashes with her as well."

"Then you agree with me."

"No, Commander. I do not."

Kadohata stared, and Worf elaborated. "I do not believe she is deliberately insubordinate. She is . . . a 'free spirit.' An iconoclast. I have known such officers before." *Jadzia, my beloved, one day I will join you in* Sto-Vo-Kor. "They have been successful at balancing their . . . exuberance with Starfleet discipline. Lieutenant Chen may simply require more seasoning."

"I don't think an entire spice rack would season her enough." Kadohata winced. "Bollocks, now I'm talking like her."

Worf allowed himself a small smile. "I myself was much more undisciplined in my youth. As were you, I believe. Were you not nearly expelled from Starfleet Academy for your own lack of respect for authority?"

Kadohata winced at the reminder. "Well, yes. But that was just my first year. Or two," she added reluctantly. "Chen's been out of the Academy for four years. She ought to have learned better by now."

"We all learn at our own pace," Worf said. He went on, though his reluctance was greater than Kadohata's. "Over the years, there have been . . . multiple instances where I have acted on impulse and defied authority. I have been fortunate to have commanding officers like Captain Picard and Commander Riker. Officers who gave me license to be true to myself within the bounds of Starfleet discipline—who did not quash my passions but helped teach me to focus them onto my duty."

Kadohata stared up at him. "So you're saying— *you're* saying we should go easy on her?"

"I believe she has the potential to become a good officer—if treated with the same patience and encouragement that you and I received."

The second officer looked embarrassed at her own anger . . . and impressed at Worf. "You've really changed since those old days on the D. You've grown wise."

"I believe," he told her, "that was my point."

The solution to the Mabrae problem ultimately came from the environmental engineering department, at Miranda Kadohata's suggestion. Picard won the right of passage through their space in exchange for sharing techniques that would improve their ability to sustain their arboretumlike shipboard environments for longer voyages or with larger crews. He also managed to acquire Mabrae navigational data that would shave several days off the *Enterprise*'s journey to NGC 6281. The roughly defined border of the Orion Arm lay not far beyond Mabrae space, leaving relatively clear sailing ahead; the interarm gaps were not devoid of stars, of course, but lacked the abundance of nebulae and dust clouds that made up the galactic arms. Still, the Mabrae charts of the region helped Elfiki and the science department plot the gravitational and subspace fields of the interarm gap more precisely, letting them refine their course to minimize delays.

About once a week, the ship dropped out of warp to lay a subspace relay, to shorten the communication lag with Starfleet. Each time, the crew congregated in the forward observation lounges to admire the vista ahead. Stretched out before them, silhouetted against the galaxy's Central Bulge, was the Sagittarius-Carina Arm, one of the largest arms in the galaxy, home to many prominent nebulae and stellar nurseries. Many of the clouds and streamers of interstellar dust that made up the "spine" of the Milky Way as seen from Earth loomed larger now, closer and more distinct, as did the famous nebulae of the great arm. Fifteen degrees to port lay the Sagittarius Triplet, containing the Lagoon and Trifid Nebulae along with NGC 6559, called the Simal Nebula by the Bolians. This was the near end of one of the largest star-formation complexes in the galaxy, a five-thousand-light-year swath that also included the Omega and Eagle Nebulae, and that was appearing more foreshortened as *Enterprise* grew closer to the Carina Arm, the two clusters of bright nebulae now only five or six degrees apart so that they formed the second-most-prominent group of objects in the view ahead. The most prominent was the cluster that was their destination, now close enough to appear as a loose spray of bright blue stars about three degrees across, with a central clump shaped something like a Vulcan lyre from this angle and containing about a third of the cluster's hundred-odd members.

Geordi La Forge had missed the first opportunity to gawk at the Triplet, having been busy overseeing the deployment of the beacon. The second time, though, he chose to leave it in the capable hands of Lieutenant Taurik and take a good look for himself. His bionic eyes gave him a view of the region in a way that no shipboard monitor could. In his view, there weren't five separate nebulae; there was a single vast stream of turbulent matter, seething with energies across the full spectrum: dark streamers of dust and organic matter painted in cool radio wavelengths, warming to infrared as they drew near the litters of newborn stars that asserted themselves in brash visible and ultraviolet hues, while harsh bursts of X-ray light peeked out from inside fields of infrared tinged with red and violet, fierce protostars going through their birth throes within clumps of ionized hydrogen. It was an extraordinary vista. *I can't wait to tell Data about this,* he thought . . . and then remembered. Nearly a year since Data had died, and still he sometimes forgot his friend was no longer with him. But then, Data had been on his mind more than usual lately.

Geordi continued staring out the ports well after the ship had returned to warp, the magnificence of the Triplet blurred to invisibility as the warp field cycled the starlight in prismatic streaks. He stayed that way until a voice asked, "Credit for your thoughts?"

He turned to see Dina Elfiki beside him. "I was just . . . admiring the view."

"The view ended twenty minutes ago. And you've been quiet all day." She tilted her head. "Don't tell me—you're wondering if the Borg have beaten us to the cluster yet."

"Everyone's new favorite pastime," he replied grimly. "But for once, that's not what I'm brooding over." Geordi sighed. "Have you been following the news from back home?"

"We just got the latest updates," Dina said. "But you can't have gotten them already if you've been standing here."

"No, but today was the day that the Federation Judiciary Council heard B-4's case."

"Ahh." Dina nodded. She had never met B-4, the android that Noonien Soong had built as one of his early prototypes for Data—the android whose limited intelligence had allowed Shinzon to co-opt him in the plot that had resulted in Data's death.

"You know we kept him on board the *Enterprise* for a few months," Geordi said. "Data downloaded his memories into B-4 before he died, and we were trying to see if there was any way to . . ."

"Bring Data back?"

"Not that," Geordi said, shaking his head. "We knew it was just knowledge he'd downloaded, not personality. Even if B-4 could've processed all that knowledge, instead of just fragments, he still would've been a different person. But . . ." He paused to choose his words. "Data thought of B-4 as kind of a brother. He really tried to bring out his potential, to help him become more than he was. I guess I was . . . trying to carry out Data's last wish."

"Commendable," Dina said. "So why do you look so guilty?"

"Because I gave up. Eventually, Starfleet ordered us to deactivate B-4, to take him apart and ship him to the Daystrom Institute for dissection. They said he was too much of a security risk. And I didn't fight it. Nobody did. I guess I let myself get convinced that

B-4 was just a mindless machine, that we were wasting our time with him." He lowered his head. "And maybe I resented him for reminding me of the friend I'd lost. For playing a part in the events that got Data killed."

Dina was nodding sagely. "I see. So you gave up on him, shut him down for good . . ."

"And then Bruce Maddox at the Daystrom Institute put him back together and started insisting he had civil rights. He fought for it all the way to the Federation Council, and today they decide whether B-4 has the right to live. Whether what I did to him was . . . attempted murder."

Dina put a slender hand on his shoulder. "You can't look at it that way. You followed an order. And all you did was dismantle him for transport—you knew he could be reactivated again."

"Still, I should've been the one fighting for him. Like Captain Picard fought for Data's right to live fifteen years ago. But I decided B-4 didn't count because I didn't like him. Because he annoyed me. What kind of person does that make me?"

"The same kind we all are, I guess. Imperfect. Heck, given the chance, I would've taken him apart myself unless someone had told me not to. I never could resist taking things apart to see how they worked."

Geordi looked at her and realized she was holding a padd close to her chest. "Is that . . ."

She nodded. "Today's news." She tapped its buttons to call up a headline and read for a moment.

"The council found in favor of B-4. Said he has the right to choose his fate." She shrugged. "I wonder if he even understands what that means. The story just says he had no comment."

Geordi sighed. "I'm not sure whether to feel good or bad about that. B-4 is safe from my mistake, but I did nothing to save him."

Dina clasped his shoulder briefly. "If you want to be a good person, Geordi, maybe the thing to do is to focus on what this means for him rather than how it makes you feel."

Her words helped—but not as much as her brief contact had. He smiled. "You're right. You're pretty smart, you know that?"

She moved back a bit, and he could see discomfort in her EM signature. "Geordi . . . if you're trying to flirt with me . . . I'd really rather keep things professional."

"Oh . . . hey . . . no, I wasn't, really."

"You weren't?"

He chuckled a bit at her surprise. "Don't get me wrong, it's not that I don't think you're . . ." He cleared his throat. "I just figure . . . I've noticed the way the other men on board react to you, and I can see how you react to that. I figure you could use a break from all that."

"Wow. That's . . . I appreciate that, Geordi."

"Besides, we're going to be working closely together, and . . . well, I don't want to try to start anything that could complicate that."

She was blushing now. "I should've known."

"What?"

"That with your special vision, you wouldn't be so easily distracted by what's on the surface. I'm sorry I jumped to conclusions."

He was tempted to refute her assumption. Even if he didn't see her face the same way most did, he was very much aware of her physical elegance and grace, the warmth of her body, the scent of her hair . . . But he quickly shook off that train of thought. That wasn't a place he should be trying to go with her. And if it reassured her to think he wasn't as affected by her beauty as other men, he was content to let her go on believing it. "Don't mention it."

Dina tilted her head thoughtfully. "In fact, I've been dying to ask you how your eyes work, but I wasn't sure I knew you well enough to impose."

"Go right ahead."

"You really can't see things the way we can? Not at all?"

He shook his head. "It's very different for me."

"But they're full spectrum, right? Why can't you just filter out the nonvisible part of the spectrum?"

"Doesn't work that way. My visual cortex can only process so many channels, so the information has to be compressed. Different wavelength bands are combined and . . ."

They spent the next hour talking about his eyes, and he barely gave another thought to the beauty of hers.

# 4

———•———

*U.S.S. Enterprise*
Star cluster NGC 6281
Stardate 57859

*Enterprise* hit the first zone of distorted subspace
about nine light-years out from the heart of the cluster, nearly two light-years from the nearest component stars. They were nowhere near the system
where *Rhea* had been taken, unfortunately; that
ship's survey route had brought it to the cluster from
a different angle. Picard could have taken the ship
around the edge of the cluster and tried to re-create
*Rhea*'s course, but the cold truth was that *Rhea* was
probably a Borg ship now, unless the resident intelligences of the cluster had somehow saved its crew as
they had saved T'Ryssa Chen. Besides, it could be
anywhere in the cluster by now, if it was in the cluster at all (scans revealed no Borg signatures, but the

distortion made their results unreliable). Picard had decided that if their scans continued to produce no evidence of the *Luna*-class starship or the *Frankenstein* itself, the best course of action would be to contact the denizens of the cluster and attempt to win their assistance at locating them—and, if necessary, fighting off what they had become.

Dina Elfiki and Geordi La Forge had spent weeks working with *Rhea*'s sensor logs (transmitted daily to Starfleet before the ship had been lost), trying to devise a means of coping with the odd subspace distortion zones that made warp travel so difficult within the cluster. They had not succeeded in finding a way to detect the discontinuities between one zone and the next, other than running into them and enduring a bumpy drop to sublight as the warp field collapsed. But they had learned from the experience of *Rhea*'s engineers, enabling them to analyze each new zone's subspace topology and recalibrate the engines to match in less than half an hour—although La Forge recommended maintaining warp 3 at most to minimize the impact to the engines when the ship hit a discontinuity. It would still take days to reach the heart of the cluster.

Luckily, the stars here were grouped close together, so there was no shortage of planetary systems to scan. The nearest to *Enterprise* were an arc of three stars less than a light-year apart, listed as Systems 5, 8, and 17 (cataloged roughly in order of brightness as seen from Earth). The ship surveyed each system in turn, finding the same planetary compositions that *Rhea*'s long-range scans had detected elsewhere in the cluster. "Four terrestrial bodies, all carbon planets," Elfiki reported from the bridge science station as they scanned System 5, a blue B9 star orbited by seven major planets. "Three Neptune-mass giants . . . the inner one is $H_2O$-poor, characteristic of a hot carbon planet of its type. Harder to tell with the cooler ones farther out, but that's consistent with what we'd expect, and in context it's reasonable to assume they're carbon worlds too."

Systems 8 and 17 showed similar results, though their proximity to each other had thrown their planets into eccentric orbits and probably ejected some of them altogether. "Odd to find so many carbon planets here," Miranda Kadohata observed from ops. "The stars' abundances of heavy elements are about the same as Sol's."

"The protoplanetary disks could've picked up extra carbon after the stars formed," Elfiki said. "The cluster could have passed through a carbon-rich dust cloud."

"Or, given the subspace anomalies," Worf suggested, "it may be that the laws of physics here are simply abnormal."

Certainly the biology was abnormal. All the terrestrial worlds here, regardless of their surface temperature, showed anomalous life readings consistent with the Noh Angels Chen had encountered in System 34; even the giant planets showed similar biosigns in their atmospheres and liquid-methane mantles. Sensor observations from orbit showed them taking a variety of forms, similar to the Noh Angels but less humanoid. Picard attempted a general hail at each planet they surveyed, hoping to draw the attention of some intelligence or other. The hails evoked no response in System 5. In Systems 8 and 17, some fluctuations were detected in the planets' internal energy fields following the hails, but no recognizable pattern emerged. Chen asked to go down to one of the planets and attempt contact with the creatures on the surface. Normally Picard would have agreed, but the urgency of the mission required him to say no. He doubted these creatures would be any more responsive than the first ones had been, and he had no reason yet to believe they were the intelligences behind the slipstream drive.

Picard suspected, rather, that those intelligences were more likely to be connected with the quantum energy readings that emanated from deep within all the planets they scanned. "But Sekmal said those readings matched the energy readings of the Angels," Chen argued, "and that they seemed to be in sync."

"They may indeed be connected," Picard told her. "But we cannot be sure of that, or know which way the causal relationship goes. We need to gather more information." He looked at the sprinkling of bright blue stars on the viewscreen. "And I suspect that the ones we're looking for are most likely to be found in the heart of the cluster."

"We can't know that," Chen countered. "We

can't assume they think anything like us. They may like being on the periphery."

"We've found the same readings, the same type of life, on all these worlds," Picard told her. "That kind of uniformity suggests a more centripetal psychology, don't you think?" She looked down, conceding the point. "Besides, statistics alone say we're most likely to find something important in the largest concentration of systems."

"Not necessarily," Elfiki put in. "The closer these stars are to each other, the more likely it is that their planets would be jettisoned by their gravitational interactions."

"But the stars on the outskirts could already have lost their planets," Kadohata countered. "They might be that far out because they were flung there by past interactions."

Picard pondered. "The beings we're searching for were able to generate a stable slipstream vortex and target it within a few meters over a distance of two thousand light-years. Clearly they have an advanced mastery over space and subspace, especially if they're the ones responsible for the distortions we've encountered. If they wished their planets to remain in orbit despite gravitational perturbations, I believe they could arrange it. We will proceed to the core of the cluster."

But the core was still days away, and there were more stars to survey along the way. En route to

System 58, one of the few yellow dwarfs within the cluster, they encountered one of the planets ejected from System 8—a world still warmed somewhat by internal heat but too frigid for most humanoid life. It, too, was populated by Noh Angel–type organisms, and it gave off the same quantum energy readings from beneath its crust. Here again, Picard attempted a general hail. This time, the rogue planet sent back a subspace carrier wave on a broad range of frequencies, not unlike the hailing frequencies used by *Enterprise.* However, there was no discernible content within the signal. It was *something,* a sign that they were indeed getting the attention of whatever resided within this cluster, but it was no more than a tantalizing hint at the possibility of communication. On a leisurely survey mission, Picard would have been intrigued by the mystery, but now it was a frustrating obstacle.

The following day, the cosmozoan appeared. It was a sleek, elongated form with a lenticular forward section and a slim, tapering aft section with two gracefully backswept delta wings, vaguely evocative of a Starfleet vessel. As with the Noh Angels, it seemed to materialize out of nowhere, though its appearance was accompanied by quantum energy readings, suggesting that it might have traveled by quantum slipstream. Excited by the possibility that it might be an organic starship, Picard hailed it, but it gave no response, and extensive scans confirmed that it was a single creature with no occupants. Indeed, it didn't even seem to have any internal anatomy, leaving it unclear how it could even be alive. "It's another kind of Noh Angel," Chen declared. "It's the same pattern. We show up, then something that looks a little like us pops out of nowhere, gawks at us, apes our movements, but doesn't say a word. I bet it'll mimic every move the ship makes."

Picard ordered Lieutenant Faur to attempt a few gentle maneuvers to test Chen's hypothesis. Indeed, the creature mimicked *Enterprise*'s movements fairly closely. He even ordered a shuttle launched, and a few moments later, a bud broke off of the main creature and began maneuvering on its own.

The bridge crew spent hours trying to establish some form of communication with the creature, whether by moving the ship in a mathematical progression, blinking the running lights at it in binary code, or launching probes at it to see if it would take hold of them, absorb them somehow, or at least evade them. (It simply ignored them, until one maneuvered close enough to land on its hull. It then manifested a vaguely probe-shaped bud to stare at it.) In desperation, Picard even indulged Chen's suggestion that they bring *Enterprise* in close and see if the creature was interested in mating with it. It remained strictly platonic in its interest, however.

Picard next ordered a warp hop to see if the creature would follow, and if so, by what means. But aft sensors showed it remained where it had been. When *Enterprise* dropped to sublight again, though, another "Noh ship" soon manifested in its vicinity.

"We've got them curious now," Kadohata observed.

"But how did this one detect our presence here?" Worf asked. "We are not in proximity to any planets."

"Maybe they live in subspace," Kadohata suggested, "or another dimensional phase. It might've been here already, just not in a way we could detect."

Picard studied the creature a moment longer, watching as its delta wings swayed gently like the fins of a ray. "Let's proceed to the next system. See how the creatures respond."

It was three light-years to the nearest system, numbered 38 in the catalog and located on the outskirts of the cluster's core. They hit five more subspace discontinuities en route, taking over two days to arrive. Somehow, these abrupt changes in the multidimensional geometry of subspace had much less effect on subspace radio and sensors than on warp drive. There was a certain amount of refractive distortion in subspace signals, but it became significant only when the signals passed through multiple discontinuities, and it did not follow any predictable pattern. This was a mixed blessing, for it let them continue receiving slightly distorted telemetry from the probes they had left in the surveyed systems, but made it impossible to tell when a discontinuity was upcoming or to map the different subspace zones by their refraction patterns. Interestingly, none of the delta-winged creatures manifested near the ship when it dropped out of warp at a discontinuity. Perhaps they preferred to avoid the breaks in subspace.

Which made it a mystery when they finally reached System 38 and were soon joined by another spacegoing creature that read as largely identical to the first two. If they were separated by five such barriers, why would they be the same species?

System 38 had more carbon planets, again giving off the expected quantum energy readings. But Elfiki had something new to report after a few hours of scanning. "I'm comparing the energy patterns here with those being measured by our probes back in the first cluster of systems," she said. "The patterns are too similar to be coincidental. Somehow they're synchronized, even across three to five light-years."

"Why did we not detect this before?" Worf asked.

"I think we did, sir. There were some resonances in the energy patterns of the planets within each system, but they seemed to correspond to variations in the stars' energy output. It seemed most likely that the planets were responding to those fluctuations. And among the first few systems, the patterns weren't aligned as closely as they are now. It's as though they were operating independently before but have now begun working in coordination."

Worf straightened, ever alert to potential threats. "In response to our presence?"

"Perhaps, sir. No way to be sure. But this confirms that the systems must be linked through subspace, or even by quantum entanglement."

"But how?" Kadohata asked. "Our scans have shown no signs of advanced technology—or even primitive technology, come to that. Just these generalized energy readings emanating from everywhere beneath the planetary crusts."

"Beneath the crusts," Chen muttered, frowning.

After a moment, Picard said, "Do you have something to share, Lieutenant?"

She blushed green. "It's a crazy idea."

"At this point, that may be precisely what we need."

"Okay . . . these are carbon planets, right? Their crusts are mostly graphite . . . but down deep, where the pressure's higher, they're diamond."

"That's right," Elfiki said.

"Well, isn't diamond a semiconductor?"

"Only when doped with boron or phosphorus," Kadohata told her.

"Yeah, but the carbon inside those planets isn't pure. Maybe as it turned into diamond, there was enough dopey stuff inside it to make it semiconductive."

Elfiki tilted her head. "Could be. We've detected relatively high abundances of boron and phosphorus in these systems. The diamond could have semiconducting properties."

"Okay," Chen said. "And didn't they used to make computers out of semiconductors?"

"They did," Elfiki replied, seeming unsure of the connection. "Originally they used silicon, but in the early twenty-first century, the increased speed and operating temperature of preoptical computers required switching to more durable diamond chips."

"Wait a minute," Kadohata said, staring at Chen. "You think . . . the *planets* are computers?"

"Pretty much, yeah," the lieutenant replied.

"But where's the current come from?"

"These are mostly big, hot stars, Commander," Elfiki said. "They have very strong magnetic fields that the planets are moving through, rotating within. Many of the planets have large iron cores with strong magnetic fields of their own."

The second officer shook her head. "Even so, just sending current through a semiconductor doesn't make a computer."

"No," Chen said. "Probably there were just random currents running through the diamond layers at first. But shifting geology would've moved things around, created new patterns; maybe, by a fluke, some kind of natural circuit arose. And maybe somehow it . . . I don't know . . . was able to grow and spread." She faltered under Kadohata's skeptical glare.

But Elfiki said, "It's not out of the question, Commander. As the planets accreted more matter on their surfaces, creating more pressure down below, successive layers of graphite could've crystallized into diamond strata, each with its own pattern of impurities. Each layer would've had portions that were semiconductive and ones that were insulating, overlapping with adjacent layers in different ways. Add in the odd deposits of metal and silicon dioxide or layers of graphene to function as conductors and transistors, and you could theoretically get some kind of crude electronic circuit."

"But one that grows and evolves?" Kadohata asked.

Elfiki shrugged. "Junctions between semiconductors create electric fields, and applied electric fields can affect the resistance of semiconductors, change the way current flows through them. So it's possible that one part of the diamond substrate could have had an effect on its surroundings. It sounds unlikely, I know. But as long as you have energy and a mechanism for processing and directing energy, growth and evolution are possible. We've found too many exotic kinds of life to rule out any possibility, sir."

"However it happened," Chen said, "we know there's a lot of energy and activity going on inside those planets. The stuff below the diamond layers is just carbide ceramic and iron. Odds are, it's the diamond layers that are producing this activity. And computers can be made out of diamond semiconductors."

"A naturally evolved computer?" Worf challenged.

Kadohata frowned at his skepticism, even as she began to question her own. "To be fair, sir, that's what the humanoid brain is. I think Data would've said there's not that much difference between our kind of brain and his." Worf appeared chastened. "And we know that programs within computers can evolve intelligence without anyone consciously making them that way. We've seen it happen with Moriarty, *Voyager*'s EMH, and certain other holograms."

"Or maybe it isn't naturally evolved," Elfiki said, "but still a computer. The diamond cores of these planets could've been altered by some colonizing race, maybe Trys's Noh Angels. Didn't you say the planet's internal energy patterns seemed to fluctuate in sync with their behavior?"

Chen frowned. "Yeah, but I don't think the Angels were causing them. It was more like . . . they were controlling the Angels."

"On what do you base that opinion?" Picard asked.

The young lieutenant shook her head. "I don't know, sir. Just a hunch."

"So what you're saying is that you believe these planets to be the intelligences we seek."

"I'm not sure about the plural, sir. Like Dina— Lieutenant Elfiki said, they seem to be linked through subspace. Their patterns are synchronized with each other—just within each system normally, but now something new has come along for them to deal with, namely us, and they're all operating on the same wavelength—thinking about the same thing. Plus we've seen Noh Angels all through the cluster, all behaving the same way.

"Captain, I think it's possible that the planets all make up *one* big mind. A collective mind. The whole cluster may be a single life-form. And the Noh Angels and ships are its appendages."

A chill ran through Picard. "Or . . . its drones." He looked out at the brown-black world on the main viewer, at the shiplike entity that paced *Enterprise* in its orbit. "Convincing the cluster intelligence to side with us over the Borg," he said in a hushed voice, "may be far harder than we had imagined."

"I fold."

Picard's luck with cards was failing him. Even though the game was draw poker, which suited his strengths better because it was more about judging people than judging cards, the hands being dealt to him tonight were giving him little to work with.

*No,* he amended, *that's not entirely fair.* The truth was, he was up against some formidable opponents. Miranda Kadohata, who had revived *Enterprise*'s poker night tradition a few months back, was a strong player. Worf was formidable as well, much more so than in his first *Enterprise* career, his four years as a diplomat having honed his skills at reading people. But Picard knew him well enough to recognize his subtle tells, the way he grew marginally more still and wary when he held something worth defending. Beverly, of course, he could read like a book, and Geordi La Forge was doing no better than usual, even with his good-luck charm, the absurd visor that had been Data's trademark on poker night.

But the real challenge on poker night these days came from Jasminder Choudhury. Even after six weeks, Picard still found her completely inscrutable. She played every hand with the serenity and poise of a bodhisattva, giving away nothing he could use to assess the strength of her hands or the legitimacy of her bluffs. "How do you do it?" Geordi cried after she outbluffed Beverly and Worf and raked in yet another pile of chips. "Even the captain doesn't have a poker face that good. Your heartbeat doesn't even change!" Though Geordi took care not to "peek" at the cards with his cybernetic vision (at least until after a hand was over), it had long ago been agreed that his ability to discern people's metabolic activity was allowable, simply a variation on the people-reading skills that all poker players were expected to employ. Besides, it didn't help his game that much anyway.

"The key," Choudhury said with a friendly smile, "is to cast off desire. From desire comes expectation and attachment, and from expectation and attachment come suffering. Or, in this case, tells."

Picard chuckled. "I'm not certain Gautama Buddha had poker in mind when he formulated the Four Noble Truths."

"And if you're renouncing material gain,"

Beverly asked, "how do you reconcile that with cleaning out the rest of us?"

"I only said I'd renounced the desire for it," Choudhury said. "Surely you've noticed how life tends to give you what you don't want. The deal is to me, I believe," she went on innocently as the joke sank in.

In truth, Picard didn't mind losing so much; whatever the gain or loss in chips (which were purely arbitrary tokens anyway), poker night was a welcome release of tension after the long, slow haul through the cluster's subspace morass and the rather disturbing hypothesis T'Ryssa Chen had proposed this afternoon. (It would have been exciting in any other circumstances. Eight months ago, Will Riker and *Titan* had discovered a whole star system that was a single life-form. *Enterprise* may have just beaten that discovery by a factor of a hundred, and some surviving whimsical impulse within Picard was sorely tempted to contact his former XO and gloat a bit. But the threat of the Borg put a damper on everything.)

To her credit, Kadohata had invited Lieutenant Chen to the game, making an attempt to overcome the tension Picard had sensed between them. Chen had declined, however, citing a prior commitment that Picard could tell she had yet to arrange. He didn't have to see her play to know she had a poor poker face, something she would have to work on if she wished to function well in diplomatic contacts. He also figured he would need to have a talk with her about her ongoing tendency to retreat from difficult situations.

Dina Elfiki had declined as well, saying, "I'm sorry—it's against my religion."

"Gambling?" Kadohata had asked.

"Losing."

Choudhury dealt the cards with the same graceful precision she displayed in combat practice. Unfortunately, the hand she dealt Picard was deadly. He would have to draw the maximum of three new cards to have even a remote chance of getting anything. However, if he kept the king and nine of hearts, he had a slim chance for a king-high straight flush. The smart move was to fold; how much was he willing to rely on his luck and people-reading skills?

He caught Beverly eyeing him, trying to apply her own people-reading skills, and so he made an extra effort to school himself to calm. *Cast off desire; don't worry how you do, just play.*

Beverly, who sat across from Picard so the others wouldn't think they were ganging up (and so she could keep a better eye on him), turned to Kadohata after making her opening bid of three silver chips, and Picard figured he was off the hook. "So how are Vicenzo and the kids, Miranda?"

"Oh, fine. Call." She put three chips of her own into the pot. "Colin and Sylvana are scooting around on their bums all over the house—Vicenzo says he's thinking of sticking numbers on their backs and holding races."

Geordi chuckled but then glanced at his cards and sighed. "Well, I'm not going anywhere with these cards. Fold."

"Aoki, though," Kadohata went on, frowning a bit as she spoke of her five-year-old. "She's going through a phase of some sort."

"A phase?" Beverly asked as Worf called. Picard chose to stay in, calling as well. He had nothing to lose by waiting until he saw the new cards.

"She's become obsessed with wigs. For days, she was ordering all sorts of wigs from the replicator, long, flowing wigs in any color you could imagine. It seemed like she put a different one on every hour. Didn't want to be seen without one."

Choudhury called the bet, which was a relief. Had she raised, it wouldn't have been worth the risk for Picard to stay in. "Two, please," Beverly asked, discarding two. She seemed edgy, cautious; was her hand that good? Except her attention didn't seem to be fully on her cards.

"Vicenzo tried restricting her replicator use," Kadohata went on, "hoping to nip it in the bud. Two for me, thanks, love." She glanced at the new cards. "But Aoki just got creative. Whenever she plays with her friends now, she always drapes a sweater or a towel over her head and says, 'Act like this is my hair.' The same phrase, every time. 'Act like this is my hair.'"

"Mister Worf, the draw is yours," Choudhury said.

"I am aware of that. I will stand."

Worf seemed confident, but his ambassadorship had improved his bluffing skills. Choudhury remained an enigma. But Geordi was already out, Beverly seemed preoccupied, and Kadohata was tapping her chin with her right index finger, a nervous habit. Was it in response to her cards or her family issues? She was normally too good a player to be so obvious in her tells.

Well, he'd come this far. "Three," he said. The new cards offered no hope of a straight flush; all he had was a pair of nines. Beverly would've needed at least a pair of jacks to open, so he had no option but to fold when his next turn came.

"That doesn't sound so bad," Beverly said as Choudhury dealt herself two new cards.

"Maybe," Kadohata replied. "But I'm afraid she's feeling insecure about how she looks. And she's just so beautiful."

"Most likely she feels neglected," Worf observed. "She is jealous of the attention given her siblings and wishes to stand out."

"When did you become an expert on child psychology, Worf?" Geordi asked.

"My brother Nikolai was jealous as well when the Rozhenkos adopted me. We were . . . very competitive."

"Oh, really?" Choudhury asked.

Worf glowered. "That is a story for another time. Commander Kadohata has the floor."

Beverly doubled the bet to six. "I don't think you should worry, Miranda. Of all the things we can want to change about our looks, hair is the most trivial one. I can't even remember how many different shades and styles I've gone through over the years." Picard cocked a brow. He could remember every one.

"Maybe. I just wish I were there to tell her how proud I am of her, and that she doesn't have to doubt herself." Miranda sighed. "I fold."

Worf matched the bet, and Picard promptly folded. Beverly went on, "Well, if you ask me, a little humility can be a good thing. Better than the alternative, anyway. When Wesley was young, he got so impatient with the other children because they couldn't keep up with him. He didn't entirely believe that they couldn't function on his level. Once when he was four, a neighbor of the same age told him she couldn't read, and he called her a liar. He'd been reading almost since before he could walk—he literally couldn't remember a time when he couldn't read. He just figured it was something everyone was born knowing."

"What did you do?"

Beverly sighed. "That was a tough one. I had to help him understand he was special but without feeding his tendency toward arrogance. I tried to explain that everyone developed at their own rate, that our differences don't make us better or worse than each other. I think I ended up using medical metaphors, comparing brain cells to heart cells or some such thing. It was always easier to get an idea across to him if you could science it up. Science came so naturally to him." She smirked. "I imagine it still does."

"I raise," Choudhury said after a moment, "to twelve."

"My, my," Beverly said. "I'm curious enough to call."

"You miss Wes, don't you?" Kadohata asked.

"Every day."

"I raise to twenty-four," Worf said.

"At least you know he's a grown man who can take care of himself. And at least you had eighteen straight years with him."

"Not quite. I spent that year at Starfleet Medical."

"Right. All that time with your son hundreds of light-years away . . . no wonder you came back."

"That's how I saw it."

Choudhury saw Worf's bet, and Beverly sighed, tossing her cards away. "My curiosity has reached its limits."

Worf stared at Choudhury like a hawk. "I will see your bet . . . and your cards."

"Ooh, bad move, Worf," Geordi said. "She hasn't lost yet."

"The patient warrior is rewarded." He laid out his hand, a king-high flush.

"Kahless," Choudhury noted. "He also said, 'Even the most prepared and cunning warrior may die.'" Almost apologetically, she showed him her full house.

As Worf growled and Choudhury raked in the chips, Kadohata went on. "If only Vicenzo were willing to give up his career and bring the kids here, or if only I were willing to stay home." She shook her head. "For all the hardships, all the worry . . . it's like nothing else in the world. The joy of holding a life you created in your arms, watching them grow, seeing a part of yourself become something . . . so familiar yet so incredibly new."

"It's the best, isn't it?" Beverly said.

Picard fidgeted. "It's your deal, Beverly."

"So how about you, Worf?" Kadohata asked as Beverly took the cards and dealt. "Any insights from the other parent in the group?"

"My experience at parenting was . . . undistinguished. My son has grown into a fine man who brings honor to his house, but in many ways he has done so despite me. His mother and my adoptive parents deserve the bulk of the credit."

"So are you glad you didn't raise him?"

It was a moment before he responded. "No. I should have found the courage to carry on, no matter the difficulty. I missed so many years of my son's life. That is not something any man should miss."

*Enough of this,* Picard thought, angry at what he realized was happening. But he kept his poker face engaged, needing to maintain decorum before his crew. "On second thought, deal me out. Good night." He rose and made a dignified exit.

Unsurprisingly, Beverly came close on his heels.

"Jean-Luc?" He kept walking, and her footsteps accelerated until she caught up with him. "What was that about?"

"You know perfectly well," he said after making sure the corridor was empty. "Now I know why Guinan was regaling me with stories about her children yesterday. You put them up to this, didn't you?"

"We were just making conversation." He simply looked at her until she sighed. "All right. It wasn't a conspiracy or anything. We just thought that hearing some stories about parenting might help you consider the issue."

"Beverly, we've discussed this. Now is simply not an appropriate time to consider that issue. Our priority should be the mission."

"I don't think this is only about the mission, Jean-Luc. You just stormed out of a poker game with your friends. Don't you think that's overreacting?"

They had reached the turbolift, and he led her inside, speaking more freely now that they were in private. "If I'm reacting to anything, it's the fact that you tried to ambush me and exploit our friends into helping you. I don't appreciate those kinds of games! If you wish to discuss something with me, then discuss it."

"I've tried that. You just shoot me down. And I'm not content to sit by and do nothing while you let yourself fall into the habit of avoiding this."

"I assure you, we will discuss the issue when the time is right."

"Since when could Jean-Luc Picard only think about one thing at a time? What happened to the master strategist who could plan five moves ahead?" She caught herself, softening her tone. "I'm not asking you to start trying to conceive with me tonight. I just want us to be able to talk about this. To plan for the future."

"I . . . I want to make sure we *have* a future to plan for."

"The way I see it, the more we have to look forward to, the harder we'll fight to protect it. You see this as a distraction from fighting the Borg—I call it an incentive."

He fell silent, and after a moment, she reached out and touched his arm. "Jean-Luc, what are you really afraid of?"

But just then, the lift doors opened. The crewman waiting there caught sight of their intense expressions and blushed a bit. "Uhh . . . I can take the next lift, sir. Doctor."

Picard nodded back, straightening his uniform. When the lift was under way again, he said, "This is really not the time to discuss this, Beverly. And the game is still going on."

She sighed, sensing she'd make no further headway. "All right. We should go back."

He shook his head. "You go. My luck was not with me tonight anyway. I'll see you after."

He leaned in to kiss her, but her response was lukewarm—not angry, but disappointed. She shook her head. "Neither was mine."

• • •

T'Ryssa stared through her suit visor at the creatures arrayed about the away team. "They're Noh Angels," she breathed.

"Then what are they?" asked Paul Janiss, sitting on a rock in a *Thinker* pose but with a clueless expression on his face. *Silly of him,* Trys thought. *Doesn't he know you shouldn't go naked on a carbon planet?*

*"You'll never know,"* Captain Bazel said over her suit comm as the Angels rose from the stage floor, lifted toward the rafters by wires. *"Frankenstein has just dropped out of warp! Prepare for emergency beam-up!"*

"But Frankenstein was destroyed! The castle burned down!" Paul said.

"Indeed," said Sekmal, brandishing his torch and pitchfork. "I was there."

*"Don't any of you watch old movies?"* Bazel cried. *"He always comes back! And this time he's assimilated Dracula and the Wolf Man!"*

Now Borg marionettes were descending from the rafters, swooping down on the away team and entangling them in strings. T'Ryssa fled from the stage, but the curtains engulfed her, impeding her movements. She struggled to get free, the heavy canvas flapping and rustling . . .

. . . her leathery wings flapping and rustling as she broke the lake's surface and flew upward into empty space, bright blue sparkles of starlight dripping off behind her. *No,* she thought. *I have to go back. Find the* Rhea. *Help them.*

She turned away from the starscape, away from the viewscreen, to see the interior of the bridge. "The away team are all dead, sir," Dawn Blair told Captain Bazel. "Except Trys Chen, who ran away when they needed her." Trys wondered how she could see and hear them if she wasn't there. But then, this was the holodeck.

"What?" Bazel exclaimed as Trys worked the arch controls and made a Borg hologram materialize behind him. "She has a job to do! She can't just go wandering off in the middle of a crisis!"

The Borg drone shook its head and sighed. "That is just like her."

"You're telling me," said her mother from the science station. "She always runs away when things get tough." The drone noticed Antigone and began advancing on her. "She runs away from discipline. She misses chances at promotion because she can't confront her own weaknesses. She runs from being the kind of officer she could be."

"Shut *up!*" Trys cried, at once furious at her mother and terrified of the Borg reaching its arm out toward her. "Computer, end program!"

But she faded from the holodeck instead of them. She watched from no particular vantage point as the scene continued to play out. The performers were inside her, acting out their scenes. She beheld them from all directions at once, and they were part of her. She made them all and controlled their destinies. So why could she not affect this scene? She folded an origami dragon and set it upon the puppet Borg, but too late to keep it from injecting the puppet of her mother. "When is she going to learn this kind of resistance is futile?" Antigone Chen said as metal implants burst through her foam-rubber skin.

Trys shot upright, the sheets falling from her body. Beside her, Rennan Konya sat up and put a hand on her bare shoulder. "Another nightmare?" he asked.

She looked into his big, dark Betazoid eyes and wanted to hug him to her, but that impulse was already giving way to embarrassment and annoyance. Having a Betazoid lover, someone who not only sensed her every mood and desire but had an even deeper insight into her physical responses and how to intensify them than she did herself, had undeniable charms. But there were times, especially when her nightmares shocked her awake as they slept together, that his deep well of sensitivity and sympathy felt smothering to her. She didn't feel ready to let him get as close as he wanted.

So she just shrugged. "Yeah, no big deal. At least there was a little variety this time. There were puppets!" she said with a forced grin.

Rennan studied her. "Puppet Borg?" he said with a smirk.

"Yeah, and Noh Angels. And it was all on a holo-deck, or a stage, or . . ."

"Hmm. Maybe that's your mind trying to cope. Getting more detachment from the events."

"Yeah, except in a weird way, I was . . . they were inside me. Part of me. I don't know how to describe it." She looked down, looked inward. "I was . . . not me. I was a dragon for a bit . . . but then I was . . . everywhere. Bigger than I can even imagine."

"Except you did imagine it. You dreamed it."

"Well, I didn't feel like me," she said, turning back to face him.

Then she screamed, because a dragon was peering over his shoulder.

She jumped back and fell off the side of the bed, dragging the sheets with her and landing painfully on her tailbone. As she scrambled to her feet, pulling the sheets up around her nude body, Rennan rolled out of bed far more deftly and called, "Lights!" Illumination revealed it was no mirage: a massive gray-white creature with a featureless, wedge-shaped head and wide, diaphanous wings filled much of her quarters.

"Konya to security! Intruder alert in Lieutenant Chen's quarters!"

Trys thought of her phaser, tucked away in its drawer, but was slow to move. Rennan moved faster, no doubt sensing her muscles straining toward the drawer as she thought of it, and reached it well before she could.

But as she watched the creature, she realized it

was making no belligerent moves, simply watching them curiously. "Wait," she said to Rennan, who brought the phaser to bear but made no further aggressive move.

"Trys, is that—"

She thought of nodding, without actually moving her head more than a fraction. He would be able to sense that as an affirmation. "It's a Noh Angel."

He furrowed his brow, concentrating. "I'm not sensing anything from it."

Trys gaped. "You're serious?"

"Yes—why?"

She turned back to the creature, which cocked its head in response. "Because . . . I think I am."

The door opened and Lieutenant Choudhury rushed in along with Crewman Gonzales. Choudhury quickly sized up the situation, including the calm body language of the room's occupants, and gestured for Gonzales to stand down. "Shall I assume the intruder has made no hostile moves?"

"I think . . . it's an attempt to communicate," Trys told her.

"From the consciousness that you believe to inhabit the cluster?"

"I'm certain of it now." She took a step toward the pseudodragon, slowly. "I was dreaming of dragons. It's mimicking what was in my mind."

"I'd still advise caution," Choudhury said. She glanced over at Konya. "And Ensign, I'd advise getting into uniform. This isn't a wedding."

"Oh! Sorry, ma'am." Trys smirked, even as she

pulled the sheets more tightly around her own body. As a Betazoid, Rennan had not been raised with a nudity taboo.

"So how do you suggest we communicate back, T'Ryssa?" Choudhury asked.

Trys took another step toward the dragonlike creature. *Do you understand me?* she thought at it. *Are you trying to make a connection with me? Come on, you were in my mind, can't you figure out my damn language?*

The dragon thing reared back, slowly, gracefully. It seemed to be mimicking her panicked reaction to its arrival but with no understanding of the emotional subtext behind the physical motion. Then it simply . . . disappeared.

She turned to stare at the others. "Was it something I thought?"

# 5

———

"How did this entity get inside the ship?" Picard demanded from the head of the conference table.

"We think," said Miranda Kadohata, "that it was created there."

"Explain."

Kadohata moved to the large wall screen opposite the windows, working controls on the console beneath it to bring up a display of subspace energy readings. "The quantum signature we detected when the 'dragon' materialized was similar to the ones we've been getting from the spacegoing Noh Angels. Now, we were thinking those might be quantum slipstream signatures, but there was none of the associated spatial distortion inside Lieutenant Chen's quarters."

"So what does that mean?"

"You recall Arturis, that alien *Voyager* got quantum slipstream from? He tried to deceive them with a faked Starfleet vessel, get them to abandon *Voyager* and fall into his trap. He used a technology he called particle synthesis to create the illusion. Like next-generation holodeck technology. *Voyager*'s crew hypothesized that it was related to the slipstream technology, using quantum manipulation to turn virtual particles real and effectively extract matter from quantum energy."

"So the quantum signatures you detected indicate particle synthesis?"

"Yes, sir. But like the slipstream, it seems to be a more robust kind than what Arturis used. He could only create surface shells, form with little substance. The cluster constructs are more solid, which is why we couldn't identify them as products of particle synthesis."

Worf frowned. "These creatures are not living things, then?"

Kadohata hesitated. "They're not ordinary biological matter, Commander," she said. "Which must be why they resisted assimilation."

"But they are alive, Captain," T'Ryssa Chen said. "At least as much as my fingers and toes are alive."

Picard studied her. "You're saying these are appendages of the entity that inhabits the cluster?"

"Yes, sir. I'm certain of it. I realize now, the cluster entity's been trying to communicate with me. I don't know why I can connect with it and other, trained telepaths can't. Maybe because it knows me. Because it studied me down to the atomic level when it cleared the nanoprobes out of my body, so it knows how to make contact with my brain.

"But the images I've been getting in my dreams—the ones that aren't part of my usual nightmares about the Borg attack—I realized there was a pattern to them. Performers on a stage, holodeck characters, puppets, marionettes, origami—the entity was telling me what it is, and what the Noh Angels are. My brain was interpreting the concepts in terms I understand. I think it's so alien it can't communicate in our kind of language.

"But I felt what its existence is like, sir. The more I've tried to filter through my impressions, the clearer they get. I think it's talking to me even now, that these intuitions I've been getting about it are coming from it."

"And what do you sense about its nature, Lieutenant?"

She folded her hands before her, letting her eyes go unfocused. "It . . . pervades the cluster. Every body with a diamond core is part of its mind. That's me interpreting, sir—I'm not sure it's even that aware of its own physical makeup, any more than you can sense your own neurons and ganglia. But its awareness is . . . nonlocal. It's everywhere in the cluster at once.

"And it's . . . creative. It has a vivid imagination, and it can use particle synthesis to make its thoughts real. The Noh Angels are like . . . facets of its mind expressing themselves, interacting. You know those old kid-holos where a person had an angel on one shoulder and a devil on the other? The two halves of a personality given physical form?"

Picard nodded, thinking of the many small sculptures inside his Kurlan *naiskos,* representing the many facets of the personality. "So we are glimpsing its thought processes?"

"Well, an expression of them. It might be more accurate to say we're watching it play. It's like it has a holodeck fifteen light-years across, and it populates it with characters that act out its mental landscape. Because that 'holodeck' is essentially inside its mind, in a literal sense. We're seeing its daydreams, sir."

"So how do we fit into that landscape?" Beverly asked. "Does it know we're not figments of its imagination?"

Chen pondered her question and smiled slightly. "I think it does. It doesn't seem confused by us, just curious. Even amused. I get the sense it's met space travelers before. That it welcomes the company." Her smile widened. "It doesn't mean anybody any harm, Captain. It's as interested in new life as we are."

Picard met her gaze sternly. "That may be so, Lieutenant. But as you say, it is very alien to us, and we to it. We cannot assume the lack of intent to do harm means that no harm will be done."

Worf was nodding. "Indeed. Would it be as *friendly* to the Borg as it has been toward Lieutenant Chen?"

It gratified Picard that his first officer's thought process was coming to mesh so well with his own.

"Quite right. We must attempt to convey to it the danger the Borg pose. But as a collective mind itself, it might be more sympathetic to their point of view."

"If that were so, Captain," Chen asked, "then why did it save me from assimilation?"

"Why," Worf countered, "did it not save *Rhea*'s crew from the same fate?"

That silenced her for a time. "I don't know," she said, lowering her head.

"Sir," Kadohata said, "maybe we should be asking these questions of the cluster entity itself." Her gaze went to Chen.

The young lieutenant fidgeted. "I'm certainly willing to try, Captain," she said. "But I'm not sure how. I know I said I have this intuitive sense of the entity . . . but I've been trying to think at it and I haven't been getting anything. It only really seems to happen in my dreams. And that's not a very reliable form of communication."

Jasminder Choudhury leaned forward. "I think I could help there. I could instruct T'Ryssa in some directed dreaming techniques. Perhaps that would allow her to achieve more lucid communication. And perhaps some meditative training could help her to filter out the noise of conscious thought and perception that is blocking her subconscious rapport with the entity."

Picard looked to Beverly, who nodded. "It wouldn't be the first time that directed dreaming has been used for communication with telepathic aliens. But I'd want T'Ryssa to wear a cortical monitor so I can keep track of her mental state, bring her out of it if something goes wrong."

"Very well." He turned back to Chen. "Lieutenant, your thoughts?"

"I'm willing to try, Captain. It's my job, after all." She smirked. "Although I don't envy Jasminder—teaching me how to meditate is probably going to be the hardest part of this."

*Very possibly*, Picard thought. *But it might do you a world of good.* He nodded. "Make it so."


Jasminder Choudhury's quarters were orderly but aesthetically pleasing as well, as Trys would have expected. There were some tasteful adornments reflecting her ancestral Punjabi culture—a wall hanging embroidered in the *phulkari* style, a holo of the Golden Temple at Amritsar, a Buddhist mandala—but they stood alongside furnishings and artwork from her native Deneva and various items from other cultures, including a Japanese landscape painting, a small Vulcan IDIC mosaic, and an Axanar crystal topiary as a centerpiece on her table. A small shelf bore a few genuine hard copy books, including a Qur'an, a Bible, Surak's *Analects,* Cochrane's *Transformational Relativity and Continuum Distortion Propulsion,* and Galen's *Toward a Prehistory of the Milky Way.* Trys figured it would be as good a place as any to learn to meditate, though she still had her doubts about the results.

She wrinkled her nose as Choudhury prepared to light a stick of incense. "Um, could we skip that part? The curse of Vulcan genes—I have an acute sense of smell."

"Certainly," Choudhury said, dousing the flame. "Our goal is to make you as comfortable as possible." The security chief studied her. "Before we begin, though, there is one thing I'd like to clear up between us."

"What's that?"

"I'd like to know what your intentions are toward my deputy."

Trys's brows went up. "Rennan? Well, I don't know if I have any . . . *intentions* per se. We're just . . . having fun."

"But it is your intention to break things off with him before they get too serious, isn't it?" Her tone was not judging, but not approving either.

Trys fidgeted. "Maybe. I haven't really thought about it."

"Or you've been trying not to confront it."

"Look, where are you going with this?"

Choudhury looked at her thoughtfully. "I'm just saying . . . if you have no long-term plans with him, then it would be best if you ended it promptly, before things got complicated. You need to have your mind clear of distractions if this attempt at communication is going to work. And I need my deputy to be clear-minded as well."

Trys glared at her. "This is how you get someone ready to meditate? By pissing her off?"

"The things that trouble our spirits are within us already. In meditation, we must face them, accept them, and set them aside one by one."

"How do you face something and set it aside at the same time?"

"By detaching yourself from the thing you face. Instead of craving its benefits or fearing its consequences, instead of worrying about how you can affect it or it you, you simply acknowledge it as a thing that exists. You let it be, and you move on."

"Just look at it objectively? No value judgment, no emotional response? Sounds downright Vulcan."

"'Vulcan' is a genome, or a culture. A Vulcan culture may value a principle, as may a human culture, but the principle itself is simply what it is."

Trys shook her head. "I'm just not sure I can do that. Separate myself from all concepts of meaning or feeling, just see everything in the abstract like that."

"Well, you're the contact expert, not me. But aren't we trying to make contact with a being to which all our familiar concepts and standards of meaning are completely alien? Don't we have a better chance of finding common ground if we set aside those preconceptions?"

After a moment, Trys sighed. "Okay. How do we start?"

While Chen and Choudhury worked on communication with the cluster entity, the science staff continued to study it based on the insights Trys had provided so far. They were soon able to confirm that the subspace distortions pervading the cluster were another creation of the entity, produced by the same sort of quantum manipulation of subspace geometry that enabled it to generate slipstream vortices. "But what purpose do the distortions serve?" Picard wondered as he, Elfiki, and La Forge studied the readouts together in main engineering.

"Who can say?" Dina Elfiki replied. "They might be another manifestation of its thought processes, like the constructs," she added, using the more prosaic term that had supplanted Chen's "Noh Angels" now that their true nature was marginally understood. "They might even be an integral part of its brain function, facilitating communication between its planetary components or . . . or subdividing its brain into different regions with different specializations, like the various lobes and cortices of the humanoid brain."

"So asking it to restore subspace to normal to allow easy warp passage might not be possible."

"I don't know, Captain. For all we can tell, it might just be playing cat's cradle with the subspace manifold."

Picard shook his head. "Given the sheer energies it has at its disposal . . . the almost Q-like power it has manifested . . . I sincerely hope its motives are not so frivolous."

Geordi La Forge cocked his head. "I don't know if I'd go that far about its power, Captain. Or at least about its advancement. Sure, it's got a lot of energy to work with, the magnetic field energy of more than a hundred stars and their planets. But it's doing what it does by sheer brute-force computation. Kilo for kilo, its computer hardware is a lot less sophisticated than ours, but there's a mind-boggling amount of it, hundreds of planetary mantles' worth.

"See, that's the key to slipstream drive, too. If warp is analog, slipstream is digital. Warp uses large amounts of energy to reshape spacetime on a macroscopic scale. Quantum slipstream changes the parameters of each little bit of spacetime discretely to create the curvature you want. That greater precision lets you do more with less energy—the trade-off being that you need immensely more computing power and control to pull it off safely. And the cluster entity has that computing power in spades."

"Which still makes it extremely dangerous."

"Yes, sir. But unlike Q, it's a kind of danger that we can comprehend, and maybe cope with if we have to. Plus, the cluster's reaction time tends to be kind of slow, as we've seen. Electrical signals take time to cross entire planets. That could also give us an edge."

Of course, Picard's hope was that conflict with the cluster entity would not become necessary. T'Ryssa Chen was certain it posed no malice. And even with the threat of the Borg foremost in his mind, the explorer in Picard was fascinated by this unique new form of life and wished to achieve amicable relations with it if at all possible.

• • •

But the mission also required persuading it to be less than amicable toward the Borg, and that might not be so easy, as Chen reported in a briefing the following day. "I've managed to let the entity know I want to understand what happened when the *Frankenstein* attacked, and it's been telling me as best it can. It sent me a dream image: I was sitting on a porch watching two neighborhood cats that had come into my yard. One was black and gray and had a white arrowhead on its chest, and the other had a white face with a big splotch of black over one eye and a mostly black body."

"Starfleet and the Borg," Worf interpreted.

T'Ryssa nodded. "I felt curious, amused by their antics as I watched them. But then they got into a fight. So I went over and separated them, as gently as possible. I didn't take sides, didn't feel any preference for either one, but I didn't want either one to get hurt. So I moved them both far away from each other."

"And this is how the entity perceived the Borg attack on *Rhea*?" Picard asked.

"Right, sir. It has nothing against us, but it has nothing against the Borg, either. Once it figured out we were hurting each other, it stepped in to protect both sides. It sent me and the Borg to safe places. For me, it read my memories of Maravel and sent me there. I have no idea where it sent the Borg."

"Maybe back to the Delta Quadrant?" Kadohata asked. "If so, that could be a good thing. If they didn't get the slipstream knowledge, then it would take them decades to get back here."

"I'm not sure it could send them quite that far," T'Ryssa said. "But I get the impression it did send them a distance similar to mine, far enough that it'd take them a while to get back."

Knowing that the *Frankenstein* was far from the cluster and its slipstream knowledge was a relief for Picard—but knowing for certain that it still existed and was most likely on its way back heightened his tension. And who knew what the entity considered a "safe place" to send them? Perhaps another Borg enclave here in the Beta Quadrant? Those Borg would still be cut off from the main Collective, but they could provide powerful reinforcements. It made little difference for the moment; *Enterprise* and its crew were already as prepared as they could be for the Borg's arrival. But would those preparations be enough?

"What of the crew of *Rhea*?" Worf was asking. "Why did it not save them as well?"

T'Ryssa grew uncomfortable. "That part's still kind of confusing. I know that it . . . it sensed my fear of the nanoprobes that had started to assimilate me, so it took them out to protect me. That's why it's been making contact with me—it recognizes me and is a little confused that I came back, so it's following up, checking to make sure its intervention worked and I'm okay.

"But the rest of *Rhea*'s crew . . . what I'm getting from the entity is confusing. Ambivalent. It's like . . . it still hasn't decided yet whether to help them."

"Hasn't decided?" Beverly asked. "By now, they would've been long since assimilated or killed. What's left to decide?"

"I don't understand it any more than you do, Doc. All I know is, as far as the entity's concerned, *Rhea*'s fate is still an open question."


Picard ordered T'Ryssa to pursue the *Rhea* question more aggressively in her next meditation session. The result was unexpected: a quantum slipstream vortex opened up near *Enterprise*. T'Ryssa appeared on the bridge a few moments later. "This is its answer, sir. It's going to take us to *Rhea*."

"Is it safe?" Worf asked.

"It reads as stable," La Forge answered. "And it should work, too. A slipstream vortex is the only thing I know that could cut right through the subspace discontinuities, since they're generated the same way. If the *Rhea*'s still in System 34, we could be there in minutes, instead of the week or two we'd need with warp drive."

"Sir, I know it wouldn't hurt us," T'Ryssa said. "Remember, this same kind of vortex sent me two hundred times as far with no damage, and I was, well, decidedly unshielded at the time."

"Very well. Shields and structural integrity field to maximum. Helm," he said to Joanna Faur at conn, "take us into the vortex."

The ride was bumpy at first but grew progressively smoother as the entity adjusted the vortex. In less than a minute, the ship emerged into normal space and picked up *Rhea* on sensors, still in orbit of the planet T'Ryssa had dubbed Pencilvania.

But it quickly became evident that the *Luna*-class vessel was not in normal space itself. "I'm reading severe time dilation," Elfiki reported from the science station. "The ship is . . . it's in a sort of subspace stasis bubble. The whole pocket of space-time around it has been altered to slow its rate of entropic increase to a crawl. I'd say less than a second has passed for them in the nearly two months since the attack."

Further scans of the ship's interior revealed a grisly picture, one that Beverly Crusher came to the bridge to analyze for the captain. The severe time dilation limited the resolution of the scans; it meant that each hour of sensor sweeps gathered less information than a millisecond of scanning normally would. But analysis of that snapshot revealed evidence that many of the crew were dead and many others critically injured, though it was not possible to distinguish specific individuals. A significant number were apparently frozen in the process of Borg assimilation, although the Borg invaders themselves were gone, presumably sent away by the cluster entity. "I don't understand," Miranda Kadohata said. "Why would it send the Borg away but just . . . freeze the crew like this?"

"Because it didn't know what they wanted," T'Ryssa said with a tone of certainty; Picard realized she was getting another intuition from the cluster entity. "Look at these readings—they're already half assimilated. Farther along than I was, according to the doctors back on Maravel and Earth. I don't think it could've de-Borged them as easily as it did with me. Maybe it could have if it had applied itself . . . but it didn't know if they wanted it. Their minds had already begun to be assimilated. So it couldn't tell whether they'd rather be individuals or drones."

Worf frowned. "Didn't the fact that the rest of the crew were fighting and dying for their lives give it a clue?"

"The drones were fighting for survival too," T'Ryssa said, her voice going flat and her eyes unfocused. She was trying to tap into her rapport with the entity, Picard realized; it was growing easier for her with practice. "It doesn't see the Borg as evil—just a different kind of intelligence, a collective mind rather than a group of individuals. It knew they had boarded the other ship, but the other ship had fired on them first. It has no preference—all it wants for either side is to let them live the kind of life they want to live, safe and secure. But with *Rhea*'s crew, it just couldn't tell which side they belonged on. So it . . . put them on hold until it could get more information."

"Tell it they wish to be on *our* side," Worf said.

"No, wait," Picard said. "If it released them now, the assimilation of the crew would continue."

"That's right," Beverly put in. "Not to mention that many of the crew are on the verge of death. If released, they could have only moments left. If there were any hope of saving them, we'd have to be ready to operate on a massive number of casualties at a moment's notice. And we couldn't do that if some of the crew were turning into Borg drones and trying to kill or assimilate us."

Miranda Kadohata furrowed her brow at the scan results. "It looks like at least some of these life readings are strong and normal. Not everyone had been attacked yet. Why didn't the entity at least send them home?"

"I think . . ." Chen frowned, examining her insights. "I think it had to put them all in stasis at once to keep the worst cases from dying. It couldn't subdivide spacetime on a small enough scale to save some and suspend the rest. And to some extent, I think it saw the whole ship as a single entity anyway. I . . . was alone on the planet by the time it saved me," she finished, lowering her head.

Worf grew thoughtful. "Would it be possible to board the *Rhea* using subspace isolation fields," he asked La Forge, "the way you did when the *Enterprise*-D and a Romulan ship were caught in a temporal fragmentation? Treat their wounds while they are still in temporal suspension?"

Picard recalled the incident from eleven years ago: aliens from outside normal spacetime had inhabited the Romulan vessel's forced-singularity engine core, destabilizing it and causing a fragmentation of spacetime into pockets where time flowed at wildly different rates. It had been a bizarre experience using an isolation field to board the frozen vessels and move around within them.

But Geordi shook his head after working the engineering console for a moment. "I don't know, Commander . . . the way the cluster entity is playing around with the structure of subspace, I can't predict how an isolation field might react. It could collapse as soon as we beamed into that time pocket, just like the warp field collapses when we hit a discontinuity. Until we have a better understanding of just what the entity is doing to the laws of physics around here, I'd have to advise against trying it."

Picard stared at the frozen starship on the viewscreen. "Very well. For now, at least, they are about as safe as they can be under the circumstances. We might as well let them remain that way while we work on a more permanent solution." He looked to T'Ryssa. "Unless you think the cluster entity might suddenly change its mind about their disposition."

She nodded. "I'll make sure it doesn't, sir. These are my friends, my—well, frankly, a lot of them don't like me much, but they're my crew. And I'm not going to let them down."

CHRISTOPHER L. BENNETT

• • •

Geordi La Forge had come to the Riding Club to unwind after a long day, but he wasn't having much luck at it. Maybe it was because the time-suspended *Rhea* was visible out the lounge windows. Or maybe it was because T'Ryssa Chen was sitting by herself and staring out at it as she cradled an untouched drink. Geordi was doing his best not to look at either of them, not wanting to dwell on the subject right now.

Naturally, Guinan noted his unease. "If you don't relax soon," she told him from across the bar, "I'm going to have to ask you to move to a corner table, out of the way somewhere. I don't want you scaring off customers."

"I'm sorry, Guinan. It's just . . . I've been trying all day to come up with a way to help *Rhea*'s crew. And I've got nothing to show for it."

Guinan's hairless brows drew together. "From what I hear, they aren't in any immediate danger."

"No, I guess not. But it's just frustrating to have to sit back and do nothing." He sighed. "I don't know why this is getting to me so much. But it is."

"Hmm." Those dark, fathomless eyes grew curious. "I was wondering something, Geordi."

"What's that?"

"*Rhea*. What's she named for?"

"One of the moons of the Sol system. Same as the other *Luna*-class ships."

Guinan pursed her lips and nodded. "And what's the moon named for?"

Geordi blinked. "Um . . . one of the Titans, from Greek mythology. Mother of the Greek gods."

"Oh, yeah, I remember them." She cocked her head, making her broad saucer of a hat wobble. "Didn't she have a daughter named Hera? I guess that explains why the names are so similar."

As Guinan's point sank in, Geordi fell silent for a time. Then he looked over at a certain table by the windows. "You know, maybe I will move to another seat. Thanks, Guinan."

"My pleasure."

He took his drink with him and came up alongside T'Ryssa. "She's a beauty," he said, making her jump. "Sorry—didn't mean to startle you."

"Didn't mean to be startled," she replied, her cheeks flushing. He could see that her blood ran hotter than the human norm, though a bit cool for a Vulcan.

"Mind if I join you?"

"Too late—I think I already came apart." After a moment, she lightened a bit. "Sure, Commander. It's okay."

"We're off duty. Call me Geordi," he said as he sat beside her.

"Geordi, then." She hesitated. "One thing, though. If you're looking for more than just talk—"

*I'm getting that reaction a lot lately,* he thought. "Not to worry. I know about you and Rennan Konya."

"Well, actually, that's kind of . . . on hold. I think. For now. But I'm not looking for someone new just yet—if at all. I think . . . I kind of need to avoid distractions just now. And I don't want to lead anyone on."

"That's fine. I'm just here as a colleague and a friend." *Again.*

She smiled. "Thanks."

He smiled back, then looked out at the ship again. "Like I was saying, those *Luna*-class ships are really something. I envy Captain Riker sometimes."

"To tell you the truth," Trys said, "I think it's a bit of an eyesore. The nacelles are too big and saggy."

"Saggy?"

"Yeah, the way the pylons curve down. It makes the ship look tired and unhappy to me."

He studied her. "You sure it's the ship you're talking about?"

She sighed. "It's just so frustrating. I came all this way to try to find out what happened to them, and now I know, and it just makes me more worried and unsure. I told the captain I wouldn't let them down, but really, what the hell can I do? I've tried to let the entity know to just . . . keep doing what it's doing, but is that enough? Is there any way to really save them?" She sagged. "And what about the ones it's too late to save? I'll still have to live with losing them."

"Hey, there was nothing you could've done to prevent that in any case."

"That's just it. Having to face the fact that sometimes there's just nothing you can do. That life screws with you and you just have to sit there and take it." She shook her head. "Jazz has been trying to teach me about acceptance," she said, using her incongruous nickname for Jasminder Choudhury, "but I don't think my mind can really work that way. I'm not sure I'd want it to. Something like this . . . it's worth getting upset about."

Geordi thought for a moment. "It is, as long as you don't take it too far. Sooner or later you just have to move on, or you'll let it destroy you." He sighed. "In a way, you're lucky. At least you know what happened to them," he said, gesturing out at *Rhea*. "Ten, nearly eleven years ago, my mother's ship disappeared. The *Hera*. We never found out what happened to her. It was so hard for me to accept it at first. I was desperate to believe she was still alive, nearly got myself killed trying to find her. Eventually I just had to accept that she was gone."

Trys cocked a brow. "Just like that? You can't tell me it was that easy."

"No, it isn't. It can be the hardest thing in the world—just accepting something bad the way it is. We all want to find some way we can change things." He looked out at the stars. "A few years back, when we found out that *Voyager* was stuck in the Delta Quadrant and how it had gotten there . . . I started wondering again. The *Hera* vanished about a year before *Voyager* did . . . what if the Caretaker had abducted them, too? We know it happened more than once, with *Equinox* as well as *Voyager*.

"I resented Kathryn Janeway for a while. Once she got back, I wanted to confront her, to ask her why she never searched for other abductees. What if my mother and her crew are still out there in the Delta Quadrant, surviving the same way Janeway's crew did?" He lowered his eyes. "But I never got the chance. And now I never will. I try to tell myself it wouldn't have changed anything anyway. It would've just been a way to feel like I was doing something when I was really just wasting my effort. But that's easier to say than to believe."

She studied him. "So you were a Starfleet brat too, huh?"

"On both sides. My parents tried to keep the family together as much as they could, but they often got posted sectors apart. I got used to not seeing Mom for months at a time. Maybe that's why, even today, I sometimes expect her to just come back one day."

"So your dad usually took care of you?"

Geordi nodded. "He's a science officer—it was easier for him to get a long-term planetside posting and have time to take care of a child with . . . special needs." He gestured at his eyes.

"Hmm. Wasn't an option for me. Mom and Dad divorced when I was a toddler—I never even met him."

"He didn't try to stay in touch with you?"

"Oh, that would've been illogical." She sighed. "Well, it was what Mom wanted, so I guess I can't entirely blame ol' Sylix. What Antigone Chen wants, Antigone Chen gets."

"Sounds like you're angrier at your mother than your father."

"Hey, I lived with her for seventeen years, so there's a lot more baggage there." She furrowed her brow. "Well, except for the times I ran away from home."

"Times?"

"Mm-hmm. Started when I was seven."

Geordi's eyes bugged. "When you were *seven*?"

"I'd heard that's when Vulcan kids have the *kahs-wan* ritual that lets them call themselves adults. I usually don't go in for Vulcanalia, but hey, what kid wouldn't jump at a chance to be declared a grown-up? I knew Mom was unhappy having to settle for ground postings when she wanted to be on starships—they didn't start putting families on ships regularly until a couple years later."

Geordi blinked, realizing that "a couple years later" would've been when the *Galaxy*-class was launched, at which point he was already the same rank T'Ryssa was and a little bit older. *Good grief, I'm forty-five years old. How did that happen?*

"And so Mom wasn't always the cheeriest person to be around, and I felt like she blamed me for holding her career back. So I figured the logical thing was to run away, make my own way in the galaxy, and let her do what she wanted. Hell, it worked for Dad."

"And you actually managed to get away?"

"Yeah, thanks to a Barolian freighter captain who didn't have a problem with signing on a seven-year-old girl as ship's cook."

"Well," Geordi said, searching for some silver lining, "if your mom taught you to cook, things can't have been that bad between you."

"Oh, I'd never had a cooking lesson in my life. The captain didn't care much more about qualifications than he did about ethics. But I did show a definite talent for cuisine in my week aboard that ship, if I do say so myself."

"But your mom found you?"

"Along with a Starfleet security contingent. I don't think the Barolian kept his ship long after that."

"But that must've proved to you that your mother wanted you around."

"It proved that she considered me her responsibility. That's not necessarily the same thing."

Geordi shook his head. "I can't imagine anyone so young being so cynical."

"Well, it wasn't a total loss. I did learn a valuable lesson from the experience."

"Which is?"

"Never use a hypersonic pulse oscillator to mix milk shakes."

She timed it for when he was taking a sip from his drink, and he spluttered with laughter. "Yeah, it was something like that, actually," she said through her giggles.

But before Geordi could think of something to say, the alert klaxon sounded, and the watch commander's voice came over the comm declaring a Yellow Alert and summoning the command crew to the bridge. Geordi hit his combadge. "La Forge here. What's going on?"

*"We've detected a ship on the outer rim of the cluster. It reads as Borg, sir."*

# 6

———

*Enterprise* broke orbit to intercept the Borg ship as close to the cluster's edge, and as far from *Rhea*, as possible. It was slow going due to the subspace discontinuities, but the engineering team was able to recalibrate the engines more quickly than the Borg vessel was apparently able to, judging from the long-range scans. Picard found that somewhat surprising; if it was the *Frankenstein*, or indeed any Borg vessel that had been in contact with it, it should have at least partially adapted to the subspace distortions by now. Not that Picard was ungrateful for the advantage, of course.

The refractive effect of the discontinuities blurred sensor readings, but as they drew closer, Kadohata was able to report, "It's not a cube, sir. Reads as irregular, starship-sized. It looks like the *Frankenstein*—but if so, it's grown some more."

Picard continued to stare at the blurry shape on

the viewer as the two vessels drew nearer by fits and starts over the next hour. Gradually the image became clearer, an angular, asymmetrical construct bearing little resemblance to the Borg architecture Picard knew so well. Yet he realized there was something familiar about its design. "Number One, Mister La Forge," he said, "does that shape remind you of anything?"

Geordi's synthetic eyes widened. "No. It couldn't be."

"So you do see the similarity."

"I do, sir."

"As do I," Worf added. "But I still recommend caution. We do not know what their intentions may be."

"Would someone like to fill in the rest of us, sir?" Elfiki asked.

Instead, Picard said, "Hail them."

"Aye, sir," Choudhury replied, only a slight lift to her brows conveying her surprise. Her brows went up farther when she said, "Receiving a signal."

"On-screen."

The face that manifested on the viewer was at once familiar and strange: a pallid but youthful face with a snub nose and a wide, squared chin, topped by a high, hairless scalp. A number of cybernetic implants encrusted the man's head, most notably a large, angular eyepiece with a multicolored, diffractive starburst pattern in its lens. Other portions of his scalp and jawline bore scars suggesting that other implants had been surgically removed.

*"Captain Picard,"* the man said in a tenor voice, one more roughened by time and hardship than Picard remembered it sounding. *"I did not recognize your vessel, nor did I expect to find you here. Otherwise I would have contacted you before now. My apologies."*

"Hello, Hugh," Picard said. "It's been a long time."

The former drone smiled. *"Nearly a lifetime, as far as I'm concerned. Is Geordi La Forge still with your crew?"*

At Picard's nod, Geordi stepped forward into view. "I'm right here, Hugh. You're looking . . . better."

*"The Liberated have done our best to divest ourselves of our Borg implants, though we have had limited success. But that is something we can discuss later, old friend. We are here on an urgent mission. A Borg ship is on course to attack this cluster."*

"We're aware of it," Picard said with interest. "Our mission is to make sure it does not succeed. Are you aware of what's at stake?"

*"Quantum slipstream propulsion,"* Hugh confirmed. *"Which we must keep the Collective from acquiring at all costs."*

"How did you come by this intelligence?" Worf asked.

*"The ship in question suddenly appeared in orbit of our homeworld approximately two of your months ago. Its drones attempted to assimilate us. We fought them off but were unable to prevent their escape. But our cortical implants let us intercept*

*their interdrone communication. We discovered that they had been teleported from this cluster using an advanced form of quantum slipstream, and that they intended to return and assimilate it."*

T'Ryssa came up alongside Picard. "That answers the question of where the entity sent the *Frankenstein*," she said. "To the nearest population of Borg. It just didn't know the difference between normal Borg and . . . ex-Borg. Unborg."

*"Entity?"* Hugh asked.

"We'll be happy to explain everything, Hugh. Would you like to come aboard the *Enterprise* once we rendezvous? We should formulate a joint plan against our common enemy—and I'm sure we have a great deal of catching up to do," he added with a glance at La Forge.

*"That would be welcome, Captain. But we have limited time to devise our plans. Our vessel, the* Liberator, *is faster than the Borg vessel, but not by much. We have only days. And given the navigation difficulties within this cluster, we may need a considerable head start."*

"Unless we can get the cluster entity to give us another slipstream lift," T'Ryssa said. "I think I'm developing a good enough rapport with it for that."

Hugh pondered. *"If you think that is the case, Captain, then may I bring a small party with me? There is another matter I believe you could assist us with. And . . . there is someone among us who I think would be happy to meet you."*

Picard frowned in puzzlement as Hugh gestured

to someone offscreen. Another ex-drone came into view, a hairless woman, fortyish and apparently human, who looked at him with astonished recognition in her large, dark eyes. *"Captain Picard. I never thought I'd see you again."*

"I'm sorry, have we met before?"

*"Of course, you wouldn't recognize me, not like this . . ."* She came to attention. *"Lieutenant Rebekah Grabowski, sir. I was a member of your crew aboard the* Enterprise-D *for nearly two years . . . until I was taken."*

Picard's jaw dropped. He recognized the name. He remembered all their names, even after fifteen years. "Rebekah Grabowski. You were . . . one of the eighteen. The first eighteen people we ever lost to the Borg."


"It was difficult for us to function at first," Hugh told the senior staff as they sat around the table in the observation lounge. The ex-drone—leader of the Liberated, as he called them—had come aboard along with Rebekah Grabowski, who still looked amazed and delighted to be on a Starfleet ship again, even a different *Enterprise* from the one she'd known. Picard was equally amazed to have her back. He still remembered the day the Borg had carved a cylindrical section out of the ship like a core sample, taking her and seventeen others with it. At the time, he had not known of assimilation and had believed them to have been killed, discarded by a race that, according to Q, had been interested only in technology (more proof, in retrospect, that Q was not a reliable source of information). After his experience as Locutus, he had wondered if perhaps they had survived as drones instead, and prayed that they had not.

But Grabowski had been one of those rare assimilatees capable of accessing the virtual reality called Unimatrix Zero, and she had thus been freed by *Voyager* three years ago—still physically Borg but with her memory and will intact, able to fight in the Borg resistance. How she had come to be part of Hugh's group was yet to be clarified; Hugh first wished to explain how the Liberated had fared in the eleven years since Picard had last seen them.

Hugh had already told the new crew members how Geordi had shown him individuality and how Picard had sent him back to "infect" his fellow drones with that sense of self. He had told how his cube full of incubated drones, with no prior identity or social structure to fall back on, had been lost and directionless, vulnerable to exploitation by Lore, Data's sociopathic prototype, who had organized them into a brutal and fanatical cult. With Lore's defeat by Data and the *Enterprise* crew, Hugh had assumed leadership of the confused ex-drones, hoping to build a new society of functioning individuals.

"Even with the sociological database you left us," Hugh went on, "it was not easy to figure out how to organize a society, to find purpose as individual beings." Picard nodded. He had offered to leave a team of sociologists with the Liberated to help them adjust, but Hugh had insisted that his people needed to achieve independence, to define their own identity. "Eventually we decided to travel to nearby worlds and make contact with other space-going peoples. Not to imitate them blindly, but to explore possibilities—and hopefully to make friends. Our success was . . . limited," he said with a rueful curl to his lip, "since the Borg were known in our home territory and our appearance tended to evoke fear and hostility. That was when we began attempting to remove our implants, to the extent that we could.

"As for the Borg themselves, they ignored us. We were defective drones, cut off from the Collective to protect it from the 'virus' of individuality. Of course, it soon developed defenses against that virus, but it still had no need for us; we had no bio-logical or technological distinctiveness to add to what they already possessed. So they left us alone, and we left them alone—keeping our use of their transwarp network to a minimum."

"A wise strategy, under the circumstances," Worf said.

"Indeed. We managed to achieve fairly amiable relations with some neighboring powers and avoided antagonizing the rest, and lived peacefully enough for about five of your years.

"But then the Borg came under attack from . . . from outside our universe."

Picard nodded. "The war with Species 8472. We are aware of it."

"More intel from *Voyager*?" Grabowski asked. She was well aware of that vessel from its role in liberating the Unimatrix Zero population.

"Indeed. *Voyager* proved instrumental in ending that species' incursions into our galaxy."

"I wish they had done so sooner," Hugh said, "for that war changed everything for us. Species 8472 did not care about the distinction between current Borg and former Borg, and we became caught in the crossfire. They attacked us with virulent biological weapons that our systems could not cope with at first."

"At first?" Geordi asked.

"We devised a limited defense. Our technology was still based on Borg technology. It was too decentralized, too uniform, so any infection of one part could easily spread to the whole. By changing to a more modular design, with isolated systems, we could slow the spread of the bioweapon.

"But by doing so, we made ourselves of interest to the Borg again." Hugh lowered his head. "Some of our ships were . . . reassimilated so that the Borg could obtain our defenses. Many of the Liberated were stripped of the identities they had worked so hard to build, of the names in which they took such pride, and were reduced to mere mindless cogs once again." Grabowski placed her hand on his to commiserate.

"That explains a lot," Miranda Kadohata said to herself.

"In what way?" Hugh asked.

She caught herself. "I'm sorry, I don't mean to be insensitive to your loss. I just realized that you've answered a long-standing mystery. When we first encountered the Borg, their technology was totally decentralized, like you said—no discrete engines or weapons systems or computer cores, just multiple nodes of everything evenly distributed through their cubes. But the Borg vessels in *Voyager*'s reports from the Delta Quadrant did have distinct transwarp cores and computer cores and weapon systems and so forth. It never made sense why they would've changed, when the decentralized design made their cubes so hard to destroy or incapacitate. I guess they figured the threat from Species 8472 trumped all that and redesigned their whole technology base in response. Or rather, they took that design from the Liberated."

Hugh took in her words. "But they were not content to take that alone. The defense they obtained from us only slowed the devastation. By the time the war ended, the Borg population had been severely depleted, and they began assimilating aggressively to replenish their numbers. Suddenly, they wanted us again. We had to go on the defensive. Fortunately, we had a technology rivaling theirs, although our numbers were far less. We have been able to hold our own and to defend our neighbors from assimilation. But the Borg's hunger to reassimilate us remains. After losing so much, they have grown desperate to reclaim every drone they have ever lost." Picard stared, suddenly understanding why the Borg from the supercube had demanded the surrender of himself and Seven of Nine during their rampage, a demand that had seemed out of character at the time.

Hugh smiled at Grabowski. "It was of considerable help when a new resistance force arose within the Collective."

"The region where I and the others were assimilated wasn't too far from the Liberated's homeworld, galactically speaking," Grabowski said. "So the cube I was on when the resistance started wasn't far from their territory. It was natural enough to join forces."

Beverly leaned forward. "And you were the only one of our assimilated crew who was freed in this way?"

"The Zero mutation was very rare," Grabowski told her. "Maybe a little more common among human females than most; there was me, Annika Hansen—you call her Seven of Nine—and Laura Heimbold. She was taken at the Battle of Wolf 359."

Worf frowned. "But that cube was destroyed at Earth."

"Before then, some of the assimilated Starfleet personnel were sent back to the Delta Quadrant in a scout sphere. The cube had only a limited number of slots available for drones to fill, so the extraneous ones were sent elsewhere to avoid putting a drain on cube resources during the battle."

"Bravo," Kadohata said. "You lot are clearing up a bunch of mysteries today."

But Picard's focus was still on the other seventeen of his crew, and so was Grabowski's. "I'm afraid I have no knowledge of what happened to any of the others who were assimilated with me," she said. "I didn't have the chance to find out. I was one of only four Zeros who awoke aboard my cube, and we weren't able to take control of it; we had to take a scout sphere and flee.

"But eventually we managed to connect with other Zeros and organize a resistance. And soon we found out about Hugh's people and managed to track them down." She smirked. "We had some tense moments before we convinced them we were free."

"And you've been working together to fight the Borg ever since?" Geordi asked.

"Mainly in that first year," she said. "Once their transwarp link to this quadrant went down, the resistance was fragmented, our branches cut off from each other. But it was worse for the enemy, since they were without a queen. With help from the Liberated, we've been able to defeat most of the cubes in our region of the galaxy, to stop them from creating a queen and organizing their forces."

"Then we may owe you a debt," Picard said. "Your efforts may explain why the Federation was safe from Borg attacks for two years, and why the attack was not larger when it came."

Grabowski's chest swelled with pride. "I'd like to think that I was still serving the Federation, Captain."

Hugh looked at her for a moment, then addressed the group again. "But we have not only been fighting side by side. We live together as well. We have given them a home."

"That's true," Grabowski said, smiling at him. "Only a few of us were anywhere near our homeworlds, or even had any homeworlds left. We had no hope of ever returning to the lives we'd known." She lowered her head. "Me, I figured my husband would've mourned me and moved on. So I accepted that there was nothing to go back to.

"But Hugh . . . the Liberated . . . gave us a new life, a new home. They welcomed our help in creating a new society, one that incorporated the best from all our cultures."

"The Zeros are ironically named," Hugh said. "Unlike the rest of us, they were not blank slates when they were freed. They have the one thing we lack: history. They have stories, legends, fables, songs from dozens of worlds. I feel they can enrich our culture immensely."

Beverly cocked her head. "But not everyone agrees?"

"My people take much pride in what we have built," Hugh said. "I certainly believe it to be something worthy and precious, but I also believe it is strong and flexible enough to incorporate new ideas, to grow and mature. But there are those among us who wish our way of life to remain uncontaminated by outside ideas. Perhaps they fear that our young, constructed culture cannot stand up against cultures with millennia of tradition and history behind them."

"Although you'd never get them to admit it," Grabowski said with a roll of her eyes—or rather, her eye, since the right one had been replaced by a Borg implant. "They insist that what they've carefully built is superior to the cultural hodgepodges the rest of us have slapped together over history."

"Suffice it to say," Hugh said, "that we are having difficulty meshing into a true community." He turned to Beverly. "But I believe you could help us with that, Doctor Crusher."

Beverly's eyes widened. "Me?"

Hugh moved uneasily before speaking. "Our . . . society . . . is lacking one thing that is fundamental to most others. We cannot procreate."

"Of course," Beverly said, nodding. "Your people were incubated drones—essentially androgynous."

"And the Zeros," Grabowski said, "well, most of us had our reproductive machinery torn out of us and replaced with circuitry, our gametes harvested to be engineered into new incubated drones. Those few of us who retained the organs had our hormones and nervous systems messed with so much that we're . . . no longer capable of sexual response."

Hugh spoke to Beverly again. "When we battled the ship you call *Frankenstein,* our signal intercepts revealed that you had halted the formation of a queen with a hormonal formula that neutralized her sexual development."

"That's right."

"It is a more . . . elegant solution than we were able to employ. We had to sacrifice many lives to destroy the queen in our galactic arm."

"I'm sorry."

"But if you can prevent drones from developing sexually . . . might you not also be able to do the reverse?"

"You mean . . ."

Grabowski nodded and smiled. "Hugh's asking if you can make a man out of him." T'Ryssa giggled until Picard froze her with a glare.

Hugh gave Grabowski a glare himself, but it was an affectionate one. Picard noted that they were holding hands. "We believe that if we can gain the ability to procreate, it will give our society a sense of . . . permanence. A sense that we are not merely a temporary alliance, but a community with a future. A future we can all work together to build, through the raising of our children. By interbreeding between the two groups of the Liberated, between incubated and assimilated populations, we can merge the two groups into a single society with a common destiny."

Beverly nodded. "It's true. Having children can change your whole outlook on life. It makes you feel like part of something bigger than yourself." She threw a look at Picard. "I'm sure I could find a way to help you start your own families."

"Belay that," Picard said. "Hugh, Lieutenant

Grabowski, while I understand your feelings on this issue, any research toward that end will have to wait until we have dealt with the *Frankenstein*. By your own words, it is only days away at best. Our priority must be to prepare a defense. Everything else is secondary."

The two ex-Borg looked at him with wide eyes, one each. "Of course," Hugh said. "It goes without saying that defeating the Borg is our priority. All I seek is a commitment in principle."

"Well, as long as we understand that, I'd like to move on to the matter of our strategy against the *Frankenstein*. The rest can be discussed at a later time."

"Very well," Hugh conceded after trading a look with Grabowski. The conversation shifted to strategic intelligence and battle tactics.

But Beverly was very quiet for the rest of the briefing.

Hugh's estimate of days before the *Frankenstein* arrived proved optimistic. Mere hours after the briefing, while Picard, Worf, and Choudhury were working to implement a set of shielding upgrades provided by Hugh to block Borg transporter beams, the captain began to hear faint echoes in the back of his mind. He paused to listen to the voices, teasing out meaning. "Sir?" Worf asked.

After a moment, Picard turned to Choudhury. "They're coming. Full long-range scan."

Studying his captain carefully, Worf asked, "You sense the Borg's thoughts?"

Picard nodded. "It's faint, but—"

*"Hugh to Picard."*

"Picard here."

*"We are sensing the Borg ship in proximity."*

"Yes, I sense them too."

There was a pause. *"Really? Without a cortical node, how—"*

"Never mind that." The question was not one Picard was comfortable considering. "Report to the bridge, please."

*"My place is on the* Liberator, *Captain."*

Picard considered for an instant, then nodded. "Yes, of course. Your vessel could be of invaluable help in the battle ahead."

Worf turned back to Choudhury. "Lieutenant?"

"I'm picking them up now. They're in System 66, some eight light-years from our position. I don't know how we missed them before."

Picard listened to the voices. The answer did not come in words but in an intuition, something he simply *knew* without being told. "They've assimilated some form of stealth technology. Hard to spot on long-range scans."

Worf grimaced. "So if they have dropped it now, they must need ship's power for another purpose."

"To attack the cluster entity," Picard said. It would have been an easy enough deduction even without the ability to eavesdrop on Borg thoughts. "Helm, set course for System 66, best speed."

Joanna Faur turned to him. "But the discontinuities—"

"Do what you can, Lieutenant. Just in case we can't find another means." He tapped his combadge. "Lieutenant Chen, report to the bridge."

*"Captain, I was just about to call you! I think the* Frankenstein's *back—the entity kind of told me."*

Picard threw Worf a wry look. "We have confirmation of that from multiple sources, Lieutenant. I need you to persuade the cluster entity to take us to its location."

*"I'll try, sir. On my way."*

The thrum of the engines intensified beneath his feet as the ship jumped to warp. Onscreen, he saw the *Liberator* following them. Choudhury reported, "I'm picking up indications of weapons fire, sir, directed at one of the carbon planets in the system. Spectral signature suggests modified Starfleet phasers on full power. Also picking up spectral readings of vaporized carbon and water in massive quantities. I think it's trying to bore down to the diamond mantle."

"They know they can't assimilate the constructs, but they've figured out that the diamond layers house the controlling intelligence," Picard said, not sure how much of it was deduction and how much was direct insight. "They're trying to assimilate the entity itself."

Worf tensed beside him, no doubt frustrated at their inability to take action without the entity's cooperation. Picard could sympathize. Finally, the turbolift doors opened to reveal T'Ryssa Chen—but rather than exiting, she simply stood in the lift, her eyes closed. "Lieutenant!" Worf called.

Chen jumped, looked around, and entered the bridge. "Sorry, I was communing."

Picard quickly filled her in on the situation. "Will the entity take us to the *Frankenstein*?"

"Umm . . . I'm still working on that, sir."

"Does it not understand," Worf asked, "that it is under attack?"

"I'm not sure it does, sir. Its planets get bombarded by asteroids all the time—these are young systems with lots of debris. And that's never a threat to the diamond layers."

"This time it is."

"Even so," Chen said, "that planet is just one small part of its mind. It doesn't see itself as needing rescue."

"Then don't try to convince it of that," Picard said. "Just convince it that we need to be there." He wanted to convince it not to let the Borg gain access to its knowledge, its slipstream ability. But that would be too complicated to convey.

Chen took her seat, closed her eyes, and slowed her breathing. Worf fidgeted as her meditation wore on but remained silent, aware that distracting her would not help. Picard reflected on how much his first officer had matured.

Finally, a vortex manifested before them and the prismatic star streaks of warp gave way to the blue-lit tunnel effect of slipstream. But Choudhury reported, "The *Liberator* has not entered the vortex with us!"

"Hail them."

The signal was fraught with interference from the slipstream. *"Enterprise, why have you entered the vortex without us?"*

"It was not our intention, Hugh. We seem to be at the mercy of the cluster entity. We may have to fight this battle without you."

*"You have the shield upgrades we provided,"* Hugh said after a regretful pause.

"Yes, and your other intelligence. I'm sure it will prove valuable."

*"Then go with our blessing, Captain. We will follow as best we can."*

"Thank you—all of you. Picard out."

The captain turned to Chen, who had come out of her trance. "Can you explain this, Lieutenant?"

"I don't know, sir. Maybe . . . it knows the *Rhea* fought the Borg last time, and maybe it's afraid of another fight breaking out. So it didn't want to give us too much of an advantage."

Picard frowned. "That could prove problematical, given that a fight will most certainly break out."

"If it does not wish us to fight," Worf said, "why take us there at all?"

Chen pondered. "I think it's more interested in watching us and learning about us than telling us what to do. But if it sees us getting too destructive with each other, it might intervene again."

"Then we shall have to act quickly," Picard said.

If they were to find themselves at odds with the entity, its slow reaction time would be their chief advantage.

But they might have others as well. "Picard to La Forge. Are our slipstream countermeasures ready?"

*"I think so, Captain. But we've got no way to test them."* La Forge had been working on a way to disrupt the slipstream effect if the entity tried to displace *Enterprise* from the battle. In theory, it was easy, since creating a stable slipstream vortex in the first place was so difficult. La Forge had likened it to walking a high wire—requiring such careful and precise balance that even a small disruption could cause catastrophic failure. But theory was one thing, practice another.

"Just be ready, Geordi. Picard out."

"We're entering System 66," Faur reported. "The vortex is dissipating—we're at impulse."

It was sooner than expected. "Shields up!" Worf ordered, wasting no time. "All hands to battle stations!"

"Tactical, status on the multivector agent?" Picard asked.

"Eight torpedoes rigged to deliver it, sir," Choudhury replied, sounding as serene as ever. "Ready to fire on your order."

"The Borg are firing on the sixth planet," Kadohata reported.

Picard ordered a visual, and the screen jumped to an image of the planet, a large icy ball orbited by at least two asteroidal moons, as well as a much smaller object from which an intense phaser beam emanated. At the endpoint of the beam, an immense geyser of dust and vapor erupted into the planet's thin atmosphere, spreading outward over the visible hemisphere as an enveloping cloud layer. The winds blew it preferentially eastward, so under its western edge Picard could see a glint of liquid water. "There's a bit of luck," Kadohata said. "The ice is melting, pouring into the borehole they're digging. Vaporizing it is taking up a fair amount of phaser energy, slowing their progress. But not by much, Captain."

"Magnify the vessel," Picard said. The view closed in on the *Frankenstein,* and he could see why T'Ryssa had given it that name. It was a blocky, cluttered mass, the original designs of its assimilated component ships obscured beneath its Borg exterior, but he could still recognize it for the stitched-together agglomeration that it was.

"Uh-oh," Chen said. "It's bigger than it was in *Rhea*'s distress signal. And more cubist."

"Almost our size now," Kadohata said. "I wish the *Liberator* had come through with us."

"We shall have to make do," Picard said. "Move to intercept. Tactical, shields to full, hold fire until I give the order." He glanced at Worf. "I want them to fire first—let the cluster entity see them as the aggressors."

Worf grimaced. "So long as we fire a close second." Picard nodded.

"Can we count on them to attack us?" Kadohata

asked. "I know these new Borg are more aggressive, but drilling to the diamond layer seems like their first priority."

Picard tuned into the chorus only he could hear. There was something different about it this time, something missing. But he had no time to analyze that. He focused on what he needed to know. "They know we're a danger to them. We've beaten their parent cube twice before, and now we've come to finish the job." He spoke with some heat, as though challenging the Borg directly, taunting them to join the fight. Perhaps he was. The link could go both ways.

Indeed, the phaser beam broke off and the *Frankenstein* began thrusting onto an intercept orbit. Other beams raked out and swept across *Enterprise*'s shields, sending a rumble through the deck. "Shields holding," Choudhury reported. "Detecting transporter beams . . . unsuccessful lock. The modifications are effective."

"Hugh is with us after all," Picard said. "Fire torpedo one." *With luck, we can wrap this up before the entity decides to break up the fight.*

But luck proved as unreliable as always. The torpedo bearing the multivector nanoweapon splashed against the vessel's shields. That was unexpected; Borg vessels generally did not bother with shields, since few conventional weapons could destroy them. These Borg showed an alarming capacity to anticipate rather than merely responding.

The hull shook again as more fire raked it.

"Return fire!" Picard ordered. "We must bring their shields down before they bring ours down."

The ship's phasers lashed out at nearly light speed to strike the Borg vessel repeatedly. Choudhury's firing pattern probed for weaknesses in the shield grid, targeting points where sections from different assimilated ships met, which would be the most likely vulnerable points.

But after a few moments, Choudhury shook her head. "Their shields are holding firm, Captain. But I may be able to deal with that, if I may coordinate with conn, sir."

Picard looked at her for a moment, gauging her confidence. She seemed as certain of herself as she did across the poker table. And she was unbeatable there. He nodded. "At your discretion, Lieutenant."

Choudhury addressed Joanna Faur. "Increase velocity by thirty kph, please. I wish to overtake them." Both ships were still moving forward in their orbital paths around the planet, but *Enterprise,* coming in at impulse speed, had been decelerating from a parabolic entry path while the Borg vessel, orbiting at a lower speed and altitude, had been accelerating to match velocity with *Enterprise,* its acceleration causing it to gain altitude from the planet by the laws of orbital mechanics. It was the standard means by which an incoming ship and an orbiting ship matched trajectories, whether to rendezvous or to engage in close combat. But instead of pacing the enemy vessel, Choudhury was moving ahead of it in orbit.

Her reasons for the move became clear when she announced, "Engaging tractor beam." She locked the beam onto the *Frankenstein* and used it to pull the vessel forward, adding to its own forward thrust and accelerating it more than it had intended. But she made no attempt to anchor *Enterprise* with the impulse engines, instead letting the natural transfer of momentum occur: as the enemy went faster and moved outward from the planet, *Enterprise* gave up kinetic energy to it and began to curve inward under the planet's gravitational pull. As the ships passed each other, still a significant distance apart, Choudhury released the tractor beam and cut loose with phasers and torpedoes on its aft section, which had not been exposed to *Enterprise* before and might perhaps be less strongly shielded as a result. Still, the damage was minimal.

Picard realized that Choudhury was using a martial-arts principle, turning an opponent's momentum to one's own advantage. It delayed close-quarters fighting for a few moments as the ships flew farther apart, but the *Frankenstein* had already reversed direction and begun thrusting the other way, decelerating to orbit inward again, back toward *Enterprise.* Choudhury instructed Faur to decelerate further, falling away from it into a still lower orbit. Their course, he noted, was converging on the orbital path of the inner asteroid-moon.

Suddenly there was a gray-white shape blocking his view of the screen—a cluster construct, looking curiously over the action on the bridge. "Lieutenant," he said to Chen with annoyance, "can you do something about that?"

"I'll try, sir." She moved forward and seemed to be *thinking* at it. She attempted to mime moving over to the side, but it did not follow her lead.

"Lieutenant," Worf said, "move it physically out of the way."

Chen looked skeptical and threw a look at the captain, but Picard kept his eyes on his tactical readout, refusing to get involved so as not to undermine his first officer's authority. After a moment, T'Ryssa sighed and gingerly took hold of one of the construct's winglike limbs, attempting to lead it aside. At first it seemed bolted in place, but in time it allowed itself to be moved slowly out of the way.

The Borg vessel was still closing on *Enterprise,* firing as it drew nearer. The Starfleet ship's deceleration into a progressively lower orbit worked against the *Frankenstein,* for in its higher, wider orbit, it would have to go faster to cover the same angular distance as *Enterprise* in the same time interval—but speeding up would take it into a higher orbit, away from its quarry. While if it slowed to fall into a lower orbit, it necessarily fell farther behind the ship it pursued. Orbital mechanics was tricky that way, even with impulse engines. Counterintuitively, the only way it could catch up was to slow down enough to fall into a lower orbit than *Enterprise*; with a smaller orbital circumference, it could gain on its faster quarry like a racehorse on the inside track, and then accelerate to rise up from below and make the rendezvous.

As the Borg ship closed in this way, seeming to follow a wide curve around and behind *Enterprise,* Choudhury had Faur draw in close to the moonlet, a dense, gray body that seemed to be mostly iron, and keep it between the two vessels, shielding *Enterprise* from the Borg's fire.

But then another distraction arose. *"Konya to bridge,"* came the voice of Choudhury's second. *"There are cluster constructs materializing throughout the ship—in engineering, security, fire control. They're not doing anything, but they're getting in the way at a critical time."*

"They seem amenable to being physically escorted out of the way," Picard told him. "Be gentle but firm."

*"That's my specialty, sir. Konya out."* Picard wondered why Chen was smiling, then decided he didn't want to know.

"Is it simply observing or trying to interfere?" Worf asked.

"I think it's on the fence," Chen said. "It's paying close attention to what we do."

"Encourage it to reserve judgment, please," Choudhury said. "For we are about to show our hand."

The tactical display showed that the *Frankenstein* was closing in, its orbit converging with the moonlet that shielded *Enterprise.* At Choudhury's instruction, Faur used the moonlet's gravity to swing the ship around onto a head-on course with the Borg ship. As soon as it came into view, she deployed the tractor beam again, once more exploiting and adding to its own acceleration. One could use the same move against the Borg only a limited number of times, sometimes only once, but there was little they could do to defend against a move that exploited their own momentum. *Enterprise* essentially grabbed them, swung them around, and tossed them into a collision course with the moonlet. The impact created a new crater and sent a fair portion of the moon's loose-packed regolith flying out into space, but only because its gravity was very low. It was not a devastating collision, but it would be enough to strain their shields, inertial dampers, and structural integrity fields. And at that exact moment, when they were at their most vulnerable, Choudhury cut loose with an intense barrage of phasers and torpedoes targeted at their shield emitters.

"Shields down," she reported after a moment, with no hint of triumph or other emotion. "Firing multivector torpedo."

This time, the weapon reached its target. "Contact confirmed. The multivector agent has been deployed."

The enemy ship was already thrusting away from the moonlet's surface, closing on *Enterprise* again. "Helm, evasive," Picard said. "Let's give it a chance to work."

But after a few moments, Choudhury shook her head. "No good. The agent isn't penetrating past the outer layers of the ship. It isn't reaching the drones."

"Plan B," Picard said promptly. "Beam the MVA into the ship's interior."

"Initiating transport." A moment later, she reported, "Transport successful. Reading high levels of the agent throughout the vessel's atmosphere."

"Excellent. Continue evasive."

*Enterprise* thrust into a higher orbit to gain maneuvering room, but the *Frankenstein* still followed and continued to fire, each blow jarring the ship harder. Choudhury retaliated with pinpoint fire against its weapons banks, but their physical shielding and regeneration ability were strong, and before long their deflectors began to regenerate as well. They closed in, still firing, and Choudhury did not attempt her tractor beam trick a third time, instead coordinating with Faur to ensure that the ship kept presenting a changing profile to the enemy so no section of the shields was too badly weakened. Meanwhile, she elevated the intensity of her own fire, concentrating on the section of the ship that had been damaged in its impact with the moonlet. Part of its shielding collapsed and a section of hull blew out, spilling Borg bodies into the void. But new shields promptly materialized over the rupture, blocking further phaser fire.

Picard tuned in to the chorus in his mind, seeking the queen, hoping to feel it when the agent reached her and neutralized her ability to access the Royal Protocol. But he realized he could not find her. There was volition to this subcollective, the timbre of the protocol in its thoughts, but it was decentralized, a background echo rather than a focused presence. *There is no queen! But how*—

"Uhh, Captain," Chen said.

But Kadohata interrupted her. "Slipstream vortex forming!"

"Activate countermeasures!" Picard ordered, reorienting himself. The ship trembled, but a moment later, the vortex dissipated.

"What about the Borg?" Worf asked.

"It's trying to send them away too," Kadohata said. "No—they've scattered the second vortex. I guess nobody's getting ejected from this game."

"We should use the transphasic torpedoes," Worf advised as the ship shuddered from a fierce blow. "We can stop them here and now!"

Picard's every instinct told him to do just that, but his duty told him otherwise. "They're meant for last-ditch emergencies—Nechayev's orders. Besides, I'm reluctant to destroy our only guinea pigs for the MVA."

"The MVA does not work!"

"It should have worked. Something's blocking it." Even with no queen for the hormonal agent to target, the other vectors should have neutralized the Borg by now. "We need to find out what."

The deck fell out from beneath their feet and sparks flew from the consoles. "And how are we to do that when they will not cooperate? Simpler to destroy them now."

"And what if they've spawned other ships, Number One? We need to know we can stop them."

"Captain!" Kadohata cried. As Picard realized that the firing had stopped, the second officer gestured to the screen. It showed a blank field of dark bluish-gray with tinges of red. "We're surrounded in a spherical shell of matter, sir. Made of the same stuff as the cluster constructs." He recognized that what he saw was the standard gray-white material, illuminated only by the light from the ship's nacelles and running lights.

"The Borg ship?" Picard asked.

"Encased in an identical shell."

Chen shrugged. "It won't let us hurt each other, sir."

"The shells are moving," Kadohata reported. The ship trembled as the spherical construct bumped against the forward shields and began pushing. "Taking us away from each other."

Picard sighed. "I suppose this battle is over." He turned to Chen. "Do you have any idea how long it intends to keep us encased?"

She closed her eyes for a moment. "Just until we make it clear that we're giving up. I think if we set course away from here at warp, it'll let us go—as long as it's in the direction away from the *Frankenstein*. And the same goes for the Borg. Though I bet they'll have to get dragged a lot farther before they get the hint."

"Very well. Faur, set course away from the Borg vessel, warp 1."

"Aye, sir. Plotted . . . and laid in."

Picard waited. After a few moments, half of the spherical shell vanished—the half facing away from their enemy. "Move us clear of the shell." As the ship pulled forward on thrusters, Picard ordered, "La Forge, drop shields and beam one of the Borg corpses into the quarantine chamber in sickbay."

*"Acknowledged,"* came Geordi's voice from engineering. A moment later: *"It's aboard, and quarantine is holding."*

"Engage."

The ship jumped to warp, and Worf glowered at the construct that still hovered in a corner of the bridge. "This is humiliating," he said. "To be forced to abandon an unfinished battle, all because of the whim of a powerful being that does not understand the stakes. Now I know how *Dahar* Master Kor felt at Organia."

Picard appreciated the sentiment but questioned the analogy. The conflict centered on Organia had been an unnecessary one, and its deferral had ultimately proved beneficial for the quadrant. But this was a battle that needed to be fought—and won. There was no room for compromise.

But would it be possible to persuade the entity of that before it was too late?

# 7

Worf approached Jasminder Choudhury's quarters with a twofold purpose. His chief goal was to review the battle that had just concluded and discuss tactics for the next one which would surely come. Long-range scans showed that the Borg vessel remained encased within the shell manifested by the cluster entity, its material being replenished by particle synthesis as quickly as the Borg's weapons were able to disintegrate it. They were contained for now, but Worf knew that would not last indefinitely.

His second purpose was to apologize. He had judged the lieutenant too harshly, assuming that her gentle, peaceful style would make her an inadequate combatant. In truth, she had risen to the occasion admirably, not hesitating to use force when necessary and employing quite innovative tactics. Her application of martial-arts principles to starship combat had been surprising and effective. True, to some extent, Starfleet rules of engagement had always followed martial-arts doctrines, favoring the use of minimal necessary force targeted with precision—such as using pinpoint phasers to take out weapons and propulsion systems rather than destroying vessels outright. But Choudhury had taken it a step or two further and had displayed a surprisingly forceful streak for all her delicacy. He had never seen a starship literally thrown into the side of a moon before. He had liked it. It had made a very satisfying splash.

So it came as rather a surprise to him when Choudhury answered the door with tears streaming down her face. Her eyes were puffed up, her cheeks were flushed, and her breathing was shallow; Worf discerned that she had been weeping heavily for some time. "Lieutenant?" he asked uneasily. "Is there something wrong?"

"No, sir, I'm all right. I apologize." Her voice trembled, the emotion startling in someone who was usually so poised and serene. "Please come in, sir. What can I do for you?"

Worf hesitated. "It can wait until morning, Lieutenant. I shall leave you to—"

"Please don't!" She gathered herself. "That is . . . I would welcome having someone to talk to right now. If you wouldn't mind, sir."

He reminded himself that as first officer, it was his responsibility to see to his officers' well-being. If the lieutenant had a problem, it was his place to address it. So he overcame his reluctance and entered her quarters. "What do you wish to speak about, Lieutenant?" he asked, his diplomatic experience helping him keep his voice relaxed and neutral.

"I really just need some company, Commander. It's . . . it was hard for me today. In the battle."

Worf studied her for a moment. "You comported yourself admirably. I was most impressed."

"Thank you, sir, but my performance was not what troubled me." She gestured him to a seat, taking one opposite him. "Being in pitched combat like that, with no hope of negotiation or understanding . . . having no choice but to kill . . . it dredged up old memories I thought I'd tamed."

"The Dominion War?"

She nodded. "It was terrible for me. I lost so many friends and colleagues . . . saw so much death and pain and horror . . . inflicted it myself." More tears flowed from her dark eyes. But she did not choose to elaborate. Instead, after a time, she asked, "Do you know the *Bhagavad Gita,* Mister Worf?"

Worf searched his memory. "I read it in school," he said. "It has been a long time."

"On the battlefield of Kurukshetra, when Arjuna faced the armies of the Kauravas, his kinsmen and former friends, he laid down his bow and told the Blessed Lord Krishna, in the avatar of his friend and charioteer, that he would not fight. Where was the good, he asked, in killing them for the sake of a kingdom?"

Worf nodded. "And Krishna replied that the distinction between life and death was an illusion, and that righteousness for Arjuna lay in following the path of his warrior clan."

"His dharma, yes. But He went on to speak of the importance of action. The Blessed Lord explained that we do not achieve our spiritual goals by avoiding or renouncing action. 'Since everyone, being powerless, is made to act by the disposition of matter,' we cannot help but participate in actions, in interactions with the universe around us. Therefore it is hypocritical to try to avoid action, especially action that is necessary for the proper functioning of things. 'These worlds,' He said, 'would fall into ruin if I did not do my work.'" Worf was impressed. Though she had been born and raised on Deneva, she still revered the culture and values of her ancestors. He could identify with that.

"The key, the Lord said, is to act without attachment, without investment in the consequences of that action. That is, we should act only to preserve the proper order of things, to fulfill our duties to the universe, and derive nothing self-serving from the act.

"What that meant to Arjuna was that it was no sin to kill when it was necessary to kill, so long as he did so without attachment—without being motivated by the fruits of action, such as enjoyment or vengeance."

She sighed. "I have always tried to do my job in

accordance with these words. To engage in forceful actions while abandoning attachment and being even minded in success or failure. I had hoped that by so doing, I could detach myself from pain and guilt as well as from anger and hate. But it is still hard . . . to take a life. To see a life lost.

"You recall our talk about the Borg as hostages? I have not been able to get that thought out of my mind since I saw those bodies. I fired upon hostages, upon victims. I killed drones who were once fellow officers."

"It is a difficult thing," Worf said from experience. "But as officers, they understood that their duty might be to die at any time. I know if I were assimilated, I would be grateful to anyone who freed me with death. Especially if by so doing, they prevented me from being used to kill my comrades-in-arms."

"I try to tell myself that, but it does not make it easier. It does not send the ghosts away." She shook her head. "People think I'm so . . . so much at peace. Unflappable. But I discipline myself so much because I must. Because after what I endured . . . for a time I was unsure I could ever know peace again. I never will, totally, so long as these memories are with me." She sighed. "I prayed every day that I would never need to face anything so brutal again. That I would never need to be so . . . ruthless."

Choudhury looked up at him. "I know this must be difficult for you—a follower of the dharma of

Kahless—to understand. The idea of battle as something . . . painful, horrific, tragic, rather than glorious."

Worf took in a breath, released it. "Then you do not know the teachings of Kahless as well as you think, Lieutenant," he said. For once, his calm surpassed her own.

Her brows lifted. "Please enlighten me."

"It is true that Klingons are a fierce people. War is the unavoidable reality of our lives. But that does not mean we are blind to its horror, its cruelty, its unfairness. Kahless recognized these things, and thus he sought not to glorify war but to harness it, to discipline it. If it was inevitable, then we would embrace it in order to control it. To regulate it with a strict code of honor, so as to minimize its waste and chaos. Instead of striking randomly against women, children, and the elderly, instead of engaging in assassinations and slaughters and casual brutality, we would battle warrior to warrior, directing our violence only at those willing and able to meet it, those prepared to leave this life for *Sto-Vo-Kor* but capable of fighting to defend their lives. That is where glory lies: not in raw destruction for its own sake, not in causing pain and loss, but in living and dying in accordance with our disciplines, with the path of honor defined by Kahless. For it is honor that enables us to act according to our nature as warriors while still maintaining an ordered, just society."

Choudhury's tears had stopped, and she looked

at Worf in fascination. "I have never heard it discussed in those terms before."

Worf looked away, shifting in his seat. "In truth, not all Klingons understand the true teachings of Kahless. For too long, too many of us have sought glory in battle for its own sake, with no regard for the consequences to the innocent or to society as a whole. Fortunately," he finished proudly, "that has begun to change under Chancellor Martok."

The corner of her mouth curled up. "And the empire has you to thank for that."

He dismissed the suggestion. "I also helped place Gowron in power. That was a mistake. They cancel out."

"As you will," she said with a shrug. "But I would love to discuss Klingon honor with you further. It reminds me very much of the dharma of the Kshatriya."

"Arjuna's warrior caste."

"Essentially. The guiding principles are very similar, it seems to me. But you could—" She broke off, looking over his shoulder. "Oh, hello."

Worf spun around, already expecting what he would see: a cluster construct. He growled in the back of his throat. "These things are becoming an increasing nuisance." He glanced back at her. "And I doubt they will respond to greetings."

"It still doesn't hurt to be polite," she replied, rising to face the construct. The more vulnerable face she'd shown him subsided beneath her wonted stillness.

"Polite beings do not intrude uninvited in other people's dwellings."

"All the more reason to teach by example."

He stared, unsure if she was serious or not. "I would be happier with a shield frequency that could block them."

"I'll speak to Geordi about it."

He nodded. "In the meantime, we need to determine the best policy for dealing with these intrusions. Especially if they continue to disrupt ship's business."

Choudhury tilted her head, a motion that the construct languidly followed a moment later. "When faced with a superior force, pushing against it is usually futile. Better to yield to it and redirect it harmlessly."

Worf looked at her. "You mean, do nothing to antagonize them and their superior power will not become a threat."

"Exactly. Just let them be. Work around them."

He was struck by how familiar her words sounded. "I counseled much the same thing during Q's last visit to the *Enterprise*. Rather than challenging him, simply ignore him and wait until he goes away."

"And that was effective, as I recall."

"Up to a point," Worf grumbled.

She smiled at him. "I'm pleased that we have so much in common, Mister Worf."

He stared back, surprised by the realization that she might be right.

• • •

"How can there be no queen?" Beverly asked as she escorted Picard toward sickbay's quarantine chamber. "How are the drones able to focus on a goal without one?"

Picard had spent hours reviewing his impressions of the Borg's mental communication, trying to figure that out. "As near as I can tell, the last queen—Admiral Janeway," he added with reluctance—"modified these drones specifically to be able to function independently. Each one of them has a limited form of the Royal Protocol within it. That's how they were able to survive when the Endgame virus spread through the rest of the local Collective. They were already cut off from it. They were the Janeway queen's ace in the hole, a backup plan if all else failed."

Beverly shook her head. "Janeway was an incredibly resourceful woman. Somehow, that part of her must have survived. It would explain why these Borg have shown the ability to anticipate rather than just react."

"She fought the Borg more than anyone in Starfleet—knew their weaknesses. Assimilating that knowledge has given them a dangerous new edge."

"Well, then it's good that the other top Borg fighter in Starfleet is here to stop them," Beverly said, stroking his arm and smiling.

But the smiles faded when they entered the

quarantine chamber, where the charred body of the recovered Borg drone lay within the containment field. "Her name was Garem Valz," Beverly told him. "Twenty-five years old, Bolian, an enlisted computer analyst aboard the *Einstein*. Two parents, two coparents, and three brothers."

The captain nodded. "I'll compose a message for her family." He sighed. "It would help if I could tell them that her death had some meaning. Has your analysis yielded anything useful?"

"There are multivector nanocells on the surface of the body," said Lieutenant Taurik. The deputy chief engineer had assisted with the analysis, handling the technological side while Beverly handled the physiological. Geordi himself was overseeing repairs to the ship. "But not on the inside."

"It seems," Beverly explained, "that these Borg—maybe all Borg—have built-in immune defenses, I guess you'd have to call them, against both biological and nanotechnological infection. Perhaps they're adaptations to past attacks like Species 8472's biocells and Admiral Janeway's neurolytic pathogen."

Picard's heart sank. "Then the multivector agent is useless?"

"No, Jean-Luc. When we injected it directly into the drone's bloodstream—or rather, its circulatory system, because I wouldn't call that stuff blood, exactly—the agent did precisely what it was designed to do. The Borg's defenses are mainly on the surface. Like our own skin and mucous membranes, they prevent infectious agents from entering the body, but if those agents can penetrate the outer defenses, then they can do their work."

"And not just in a single drone, sir," Taurik said. "Once they upload the Endgame program into a drone, it should be transmitted through the network. Once that drone connects physically to the vessel's distribution systems," the young Vulcan went on, "the nanotech and biological agents will spread as well."

"Still," Picard said, "what you're telling me is that the only way to deliver the weapon is by injecting it directly into a drone."

Taurik hesitated. "As far as we can determine, Captain, yes."

Picard pondered. "Is there a chance we could modify our previous strategy? Use precision transporting to beam it directly inside the drones?"

"Their shielding would prevent it."

"Then it would have to be delivered in person."

The engineer pondered. "Perhaps some kind of remote probe . . ."

"You know these Borg attack on sight. Any person or probe we sent would most likely be destroyed before delivering the agent."

"I'm aware of that, yes, sir."

Picard considered it. A probe would be too limited, too fixed in its programming. Only a person would be adaptable and resilient enough to have a chance of injecting the toxin. "So the only way this could work is as a suicide mission."

Beverly touched his shoulder—briefly, for they

were on duty. "We haven't given up on finding an alternative. We've only been considering the problem for a few hours."

He met her eyes. "Find something. Anything."

"I think our friend has developed a warped sense of humor," T'Ryssa said.

Geordi glared at her. "Look who's talking." She grinned as though it had been a compliment. But Geordi wasn't in the mood for her quips right now. The cluster entity was still sending constructs to pop up in odd places throughout the ship, and the latest thing it had decided to mimic was the warp core itself. Right now, the forward section of *Enterprise*'s cathedrallike engine room was filled with a gray-white, roughly spherical construct/creature mimicking the size and shape of the warp core that stood in the center of the chamber, staring at it with a Cyclopean "eye" that resembled the hatch for the dilithium articulation frame and pulsing gently to itself in time with the core's injector pulses. Which might not have been so bad if not for the tentacles stretching to the floor and ceiling in emulation of the injector conduits. The lower set of tentacles had engulfed the main "pool table" console, making it hard to get any work done. Moreover, Geordi, Taurik, and Hugh—whose ship had caught up with *Enterprise* this morning—had been working at the console, trying to analyze the failure of the multi-vector agent, when the construct had materialized and lowered its tentacles, giving Geordi quite a fright. It seemed the construct wasn't subject to gravity; it didn't need the tentacles for support but was using them only for mimicry.

"So can you talk the entity into getting rid of it?"

"Jazz says we should just let them be. Besides, all I can do is make suggestions. And even those are hard to get across. And anyway, isn't this fascinating? Before, it only mimicked people and ships— and a dragon from my dreams. I wonder what it means that it's now treating the warp core like an individual entity worth mimicking. Is it trying to talk to it?" She smirked. "What if it's answering?"

"As far as I'm concerned, what it means is that I can't get to my workstation."

"Gee, too bad you don't have those newfangled kind of consoles that you can reprogram to work from anywhere."

Geordi glared, knowing as well as she did that reconfigurable consoles had been standard for decades. "I have unsaved files on the main table. Besides, it's just inconvenient."

Hugh warily studied the construct. "These . . . constructs? . . . have begun to appear on my vessel as well. It was a cause of some concern until we realized they were making no hostile moves."

Trys looked at him. "Did you make hostile moves to them?"

"Attempts have been made to incapacitate or destroy them."

"Maybe that's not such a good idea."

"You think it might feel threatened by an attack on a construct?" Geordi asked, crossing a few ideas off his mental list.

"No more than you'd be threatened if I attacked a hair or skin flake you'd shed. But I don't think it'd be a good idea to show it a pattern of hostility. We want it on our side, remember?"

Hugh closed his eyes for a moment. "I have advised my crew."

Geordi stared. "You still have a shared consciousness?"

"Not as such. We can still communicate through our Borg cortical nodes—which cannot be removed without killing us. We can be aware of each other's thoughts, but it's voluntary."

"Can't the Borg tap into your communications?"

"We have altered the encoding. In fact, it usually goes the other way: we are able to tap into their shared thoughts and thus discern their plans, as we did before coming here." Hugh smiled tightly. "The Borg are too dependent on their collective consciousness even to contemplate placing the kinds of limits on communication that would allow effective signal security. Even if you knew your mind could be read, would you be willing to carve it up into isolated cells communicating only by intermittent, encoded transmissions?"

Geordi shuddered. "I see your point."

He glanced at Trys, who was focusing on the construct, apparently trying to communicate with it, or with the entity behind it. Figuring he should leave her to her work, he led Hugh over to a side console, which he began to reconfigure to take over the pool table's functions. As his hands entered the familiar commands, he considered his old friend. "I have to say, Hugh, I'm really impressed with what you've done here. You've grown into quite a leader."

Hugh's smile was warmer, reminding Geordi of the youthful, innocent drone he had rescued all those years ago. "Thank you, Geordi. But I could never have done it without your example."

"No, but you've gone beyond what I could've shown you."

"You do not see yourself as a leader?"

He shook his head. "Not in that way. I'm in charge of the engineering staff, sure, but that's more like coordinating a team."

Hugh studied him. "Do you regret not becoming a commander?"

Geordi sighed. "Well, I did for a while. I've been pretty much where I am now for over fifteen years—I had started to feel like I was in a rut. But an old friend helped me see the light. Captains aren't the only people who count for something. I'm chief engineer on the best ship in the fleet— that *is* being on top as far as an engineer is concerned. Just like being chief medical officer is the top job for a doctor, or chief science officer for a scientist, or whatever. Captains couldn't do anything without the rest of us."

"Then why do you seem dissatisfied?"

Geordi stared at Hugh. For someone who'd been a blank slate only twelve years ago, he'd become pretty perceptive. "I am happy with my career," he said. "But my career is all I have. I look around me . . . the captain and Doctor Crusher are married. Captain Riker and Deanna are married. Worf has a full-grown son. Even you . . . you have Rebekah. You've built a whole community, a whole society."

Hugh tilted his head. "That will go nowhere if Doctor Crusher cannot give us the means to procreate. Our society cannot endure if we cannot have families. Not only will it not survive past our lifetimes, but I doubt it will hold together that long without a common future to build toward." He sighed. "I will need to talk to the captain again. He must be persuaded to let Doctor Crusher assist us."

"I'm sure he will once this all blows over."

"If we survive this," Hugh said. "If we are not destroyed in the next encounter. The sooner we have something to transmit back home, something that can help them procreate even if we are lost, the better."

"Well, I'm sure it'll work out." He fidgeted, trying to get the topic back to something less grim—well, relatively. "Anyway, even without the biological side, you still found someone who wants to start a family with you. Me, I don't know if that's ever going to happen."

"There are plenty of unattached females on this ship." He threw a glance over at T'Ryssa.

"Yeah, but getting them interested in me isn't so easy." His gaze followed Hugh's. *Trys? She's cute, but a bit young for me. And a bit too flaky.*

Suddenly he realized there was a cluster construct blocking his view, one of the classic Noh Angels. Geordi blinked, wondering how they always seemed to materialize without anyone noticing. He'd been looking directly at it this time, but it had still been absent one moment and present the next, without any transition he'd consciously registered, like in a dream. *Some kind of quantum observer effect?*

He stood. "T'Ryssa!"

But she was already coming over, apparently having sensed its arrival despite its soundlessness. "Wow, two in one place. We haven't seen that on board ship before."

Geordi studied the console readouts. "What worries me is that the shields are still up." The bridge had raised them after its big brother had materialized atop the pool table.

"I don't know if shields would make a difference," Trys said. "They're emerging out of the virtual particles that are already present everywhere."

"I know that. But there must be a way to block whatever energy it's sending to make those particles real." He frowned, struck by a thought. "Any idea what it's doing with the antiparticles? You can't make one real without doing the same to the other— it violates conservation of energy," he explained for Hugh's benefit.

Trys's eyes went unfocused for a moment. "I

think it harvests them as a power source. I'm not sure where it keeps them, though."

She looked over at the Noh Angel construct again. "It seems interested in you two. What were you talking about?"

Geordi flushed as Hugh said, "We were discussing family and relationships."

"Hmm."

"Does that mean something to you?" Geordi asked.

"Not yet. Just 'hmm.'" She threw him a look. "Unless it was *my* relationships you were talking about. Then I might have a problem. Or you might. I have enough already."

"No," Hugh said. "In fact, we were speaking of—"

Geordi interrupted him quickly. "We were speaking in the abstract. Just in general terms."

She quirked a brow at them, looking more Vulcan than usual for a moment. "Yeah, right. None of my business."

Hugh looked puzzled but let the subject go, to Geordi's relief. *Sorry, Trys,* he thought. *I'd rather not have one more person gossiping over my lack of a love life.*

Then his eyes went to Hugh and he remembered the obstacles this man had to overcome in pursuit of a normal family. *So what have I got to complain about? And what the hell is holding me back?*

• • •

"We need to talk, Jean-Luc," Beverly said as soon as they entered their quarters that evening. It was the first chance they'd gotten to have a serious, private conversation since the battle, and the fact that he had once again denied Hugh's requests for procreative assistance demanded that they have one. "Your resistance to having children has gone beyond you and me—it's starting to affect your command decisions."

Her husband stared at her. "Do you deny that defeating the Borg is our highest priority?"

"Of course not. We're doing all we can to solve the multivector agent delivery problem. But we have a large medical staff on this vessel. It won't hurt our preparedness any if some of my people work with the Liberated on their fertility problem. If anything, I think it would relieve stress among the crew if we had something positive to work toward, something to give us a break from the tension of having the Borg of Damocles hovering over our heads."

"And you think I tabled this for personal reasons."

"You tell me. It's not like you to shoot down a medical project without even consulting me first. For that matter, it's not like you to make any decision without listening to your crew's input."

"You know my reasons, Beverly. We cannot relax our guard while the Borg remain an imminent threat."

"I know your reasons, Jean-Luc, and I don't buy

them. We've taken on the Borg time after time and won. Five months ago, we beat the biggest Borg ship ever built! The *Frankenstein* is small fry next to that."

"We cannot allow ourselves to underestimate this enemy."

"I know that. But we don't need to make a monster out of it either. We have the best Borg-fighting weapons ever devised. We took them on and we held our own. And now we have allies in the fight, allies who understand the Borg even better than we do and have the technology to match them. Of course we shouldn't let our guard down too far, but isn't it fair to say we're in a reasonably strong position?"

Jean-Luc gazed out the windows, considering her words. "I have asked myself if I've been letting my . . . fear of the Borg color my judgment. I've been speaking to Counselor Hegol about it regularly. But I don't believe that my experience is compromising my decisions here."

Beverly sighed. She went over and took his hands in hers. "The thing is, Jean-Luc . . . I don't think it's the Borg you're afraid of. Not entirely. It feels like you're using them as, as an excuse to avoid taking the plunge and becoming a father." He looked away, offering no reply. It was all the confirmation she needed. "Why, Jean-Luc? Why are you so uncomfortable with the idea of starting a family? It's not like you haven't done it before—in a way. As Kamin, you had two children, raised them to adulthood, even became a grandfather. You've literally had a lifetime of experience with parenting."

He pulled away. "Not my lifetime," he said, pacing with nervous intensity. "Kamin's lifetime. Those memories were not mine. Just a download from an alien probe."

"I don't need a recap, Jean-Luc, I was there. So I know how real it all was for you. My God, you learned how to play the flute in that other life! You retained that skill, a skill developed over subjective *years* of practice, after you recovered. It was no mere download, Jean-Luc. You *lived* that life. You raised Batai and Meribor."

He shook his head. "Kamin raised them. I may have felt as though I was living that life on Kataan, but it was Kamin who lived it, a thousand years before I was born. I thought of myself as Jean-Luc Picard at first, tried to resist the pattern of his life . . . but eventually I stopped fighting it, just let myself be Kamin. And I believe that the events I experienced were the result of Kamin's choices, not mine. I was just along for the ride."

She moved closer to confront him. "How can you be so sure? Did it ever feel to you that you were out of control of your actions? Because you never told me that before."

"No, it—" He faltered. "It felt like I was in control . . . but I do not believe that I could have made those choices as successfully as Kamin did."

"Why not?"

Jean-Luc ambled over to the couch and sat down.

Beverly joined him, placing a hand on his shoulder. "Because, as you are no doubt aware, my romantic relationships have historically tended to go badly. I have never been . . . very good at making wise choices with women, or at dealing with children."

The hand fell from his shoulder. "Is that what you think? Do you expect our marriage to go badly?"

"I'm not saying that," he hastened to reply. "However . . . you'll recall I once experienced an alternate future in which we had been married. And divorced."

A part of Beverly was almost amused. *Simulated lifetimes . . . alternate futures . . . Grandma Felisa never had talks like this with her husband.* But the greater part of her was growing annoyed with her own spouse. "So? A lot of the things you saw in that future have already been changed. Data's dead, Deanna isn't, the *Enterprise*-D was destroyed . . . it's not like our divorce is destined to come to pass. Or do you—"

She broke off. Her first impulse was to feel hurt at his lack of faith in the future of their marriage. But she knew him too well not to see beneath the surface. This, too, was just a mask for something deeper—some vulnerability he was afraid to own up to. "No. This is still about Kamin, isn't it?"

His eyes met hers briefly, furtively. "What do you mean?"

"I still don't see why you're distancing yourself from Kamin's memories. Why you're so unwilling to consider that you, Jean-Luc Picard, could have made the decisions that let you be a successful husband and father for more than forty subjective years. Even if you're right, even if you were just acting out Kamin's script, you still know what went through Kamin's head when he made those choices. You know what it feels like to have a son, a daughter, a grandson. You know what goes into the decisions a parent has to make. You know what it's like to worry about them when they get sick or scrape their knees or go off to college or get engaged . . . and you know that you have to give them their freedom anyway. And you know that it's all worth it," she said, her voice shaking with emotion, "because of how proud they make you feel to be a part of their lives."

"Yes." Jean-Luc was weeping now, his voice rough, and she realized her words were hurting him. "Yes, I know all that, Beverly. I know what it feels like to love my children. But can you imagine what it feels like . . . to wake up . . . and discover between one breath and the next . . . that your children and their children, your own flesh and blood and future . . . that they all *died* a thousand years in the past? That you'll never, ever see them again? Can you imagine, Beverly?"

*I've been a fool,* she told herself as she took him in her arms and let him sob into her shoulder, comforting him as he shook with a grief that he'd kept buried for twelve years. "Batai," he gasped. "Meribor . . . my beautiful girl. I l-loved you s-so much. . . . And little Kamie," he added, shaking his head. "So unfair. My grandson never got to grow up . . . to find out who he would be. I never . . . I never had the chance . . ."

The words stopped coming, and she simply held him for a long time.

Finally, he straightened and composed himself, and Beverly found herself touched that he would entrust her with such a vulnerable moment. "Thank you, Beverly," he said. "I never . . . I never let myself confront this. It was just too much . . . so I buried it away. Tried to convince myself . . . it was another man's life. His family, his loves. That I was just a spectator . . . moved as I might be by a holonovel, but able to step out of it and resume my own life. It helped that, in reality, my own memories were still fresh and immediate, not worn away by the actions of time upon the brain. So I was able to step back into being Jean-Luc Picard fairly quickly, and distancing myself from Kamin's memories made it easier to do that. But more than that, it was . . ." He looked inward, seeing himself in a new light. "It was the only way I could cope with the loss. I couldn't let myself face the reality of that grief."

"But that grief has still been a part of you," Beverly said, understanding. "The thought of having children . . . again . . . it was a reminder of something you couldn't bear to confront."

"It's more than that," he told her. "I thought I was ready. Enough time had passed . . . I'd buried this deeply enough . . . that I thought I was ready to talk about having children. But then the news of the Borg came, and . . ." He shook his head. "How can I risk going through that again? How can I let myself love a son or a daughter when I might have to lose them?"

Beverly closed her eyes tightly, her thoughts brushing against the grief that was always there below the surface, even after nearly a quarter century. *Jack* . . .

She met his eyes again. "Jean-Luc, if there's one thing I've learned, it's that the memories of the family we've lost are something we should embrace, not run away from. Because if you were happy together, then the joyous memories outnumber the sad ones. I lost a husband. I know what that grief is like." He turned away, perhaps still blaming himself for Jack's death, and she put a hand on his head and turned it back toward her. "But I married you *because* of my memories of Jack, not in spite of them. Because I know what it's like to be happily married, to share the wonders of having a child with a man I love. And I knew that was worth having again, no matter the risk."

He clasped her hand in both of his. "I . . . I understand, Beverly. But it's still difficult. Thinking about this . . . it makes me vulnerable. Unsure of myself. Literally—it dredges up memories of another life, another self. I can't deal with that now, Beverly. With the Borg coming, I have to be . . . bloody, bold, and resolute. I have to be a soldier, a commander. I can't afford this vulnerability."

The hell of it was, she understood completely. She cherished seeing this gentler, more fragile side of him; it brought out her every maternal instinct and made her feel truly needed in a way she hadn't been since Wesley had become an ensign. But she also understood that this crew needed its captain strong and focused in the current crisis.

"Then it's settled," she said. "Let's do all we can to defeat the Borg . . . together. And then, once that's done . . ."

He nodded. They were in accord without words. "But in the meantime," he said, "I think the medical department can spare some time and resources for a preliminary investigation of the Liberated's fertility issues. I don't think that will significantly impact our combat preparedness."

Suffused with warmth, she shared it in a kiss. "Aye, aye, Captain."

# 8

———

Guinan's phaser grew warm in her hand as she jerked it around the room, blasting away target after target with unerring aim. The beeps of the scoring system blurred together, the computer seeming to have trouble keeping up with the barrage of blasts.

Too soon, the last colored blip was neutralized and the computer announced, "Round over. Guinan, fifty-three, Choudhury, forty-seven."

"Reset!" Guinan called, panting hard.

"Pause," Jasminder countered, her own breathing heavy but slower. "Let's take a break, okay?"

"I'm not tired."

She felt a warm hand on her shoulder, controlled her impulse to jump. "You're exhausted, Guinan. You just don't feel it yet."

The bartender turned to look at the security chief, recognizing how bedraggled with sweat the human woman was. Choudhury was as fit as any humanoid Guinan had ever met; if she looked that bad, how must Guinan herself look?

She let herself slump to the floor, and Jasminder joined her there with a soft sigh of gratitude. "Sorry. Got carried away."

Jasminder studied her. "Understandable . . . with all those Borg drones closing in on you."

Guinan winced. "After six hundred years, I thought I wouldn't be so obvious anymore."

"Hey. As far as anyone else can tell, you're as cool and enigmatic as ever. But you can't kid a kidder, my friend. I know from cool and enigmatic."

Guinan chuckled at her unwonted slang. Then she grew serious. "Being here . . . facing the Borg again . . . it's been rough. The more time I spend on this ship, the harder it is to let the memories stay in the past." It felt good to have someone she could unload on for a change. "Hell, I didn't even have these memories a hundred years ago. I was off traveling when the Borg destroyed El-Auria. I came back to find . . . a cratered ruin of a world, ash and smoke choking its air. My home, all our great landmarks, gone or destroyed. Nothing left but . . . roads going from noplace to nowhere. I didn't know what had happened, I was afraid everyone was gone. That I was the only one left.

"Then I found the refugees and they told me. I saw records of the attack, images of cubes and drones . . . just those were enough to give me nightmares for the rest of my life. That and the fear, as we made our way out of the Delta Quadrant— migrated from world to world, ship to ship for decades—all the time afraid that the Borg would catch up with us. Never knowing for sure we were beyond their reach."

She took a deep, shuddering breath. "It wasn't until fifteen years ago that I really met the Borg. Every time I've ever actually faced them, it's been aboard an *Enterprise*."

"Are you saying you don't want to be here?" Jasminder asked.

Uneasy at the question, she said, "Well, it hasn't been all bad. There's Hugh."

"Ah, yes. This is the second time you've met him."

"I was there when we first found him. Geordi really connected with him, taught him what it meant to be an individual. He's a special man, Geordi. So tough on himself, but he always sees others for what they could be and helps bring out the best in them." She shook her head. "I only saw one of the monsters from my nightmares, felt betrayed that one of my friends could sympathize with such a . . . a *thing*. Give it a name like some kind of house pet. But then I went to meet him, and I saw . . . an innocent. A boy. He wasn't a monster, just a cog in the machine. It turned me right around."

"Was this before or after Captain Picard was turned around?" Jasminder asked with a knowing smile.

Guinan threw her a look. "Maybe I gave the captain a little advice. Suggested he should meet Hugh, decide for himself. It was Hugh who convinced both of us." She smiled. "It's been great to see him again—see how far he's grown. He was such a follower back then. No mind of his own, no idea what he was. He just mimicked what was around him, and it was lucky for him that he ended up surrounded by individualists. But now, he knows who he is, he knows what he wants, and he's creating a whole civilization based on his vision." She looked out into the darkness of the phaser range. "That's one thing the Borg will *never* understand. The power of one person who truly knows himself."

She turned back to Jasminder, giving a self-effacing smile. "Anyway, this trip was worth it for seeing him again, at least."

The security chief remained unrelenting in her subtle way. "But this isn't where you'd prefer to be right now."

"I'm here because I need to be," she said. "Picard needs me now."

Jasminder nodded, and Guinan reflected on what a fine bartender she would have made. "And if he didn't need you, where would you be?"

"I don't know. Maybe . . . after that last Borg attack . . . I needed him a little too. We've always been there for each other when it really mattered."

"But aside from that, where would you choose?"

She shrugged. "Anywhere. Somewhere I haven't

been. Travel has always been my favorite therapy—even before I was a refugee."

The human woman tilted her head. "Is that why you've had twenty-three husbands in your life? What is that, about two decades per husband?"

"Well, some didn't last nearly that long. But some were keepers." She sighed. "I spent lifetimes with some of them. Catch is, it was their lifetimes, not mine. So I moved on."

"But you had children with them, right? And grandchildren?"

"Of course. Dozens."

"And you enjoyed being a mother?"

Guinan pursed her lips. "It had its ups and downs. I wasn't always the greatest at it. But yes. It meant a lot to me."

"So why did you move on?"

She pondered it. "Because they'd grown up. They had lives of their own to lead. That's the way life's supposed to work—it moves on, and people move with it."

"So you did it for them."

"That's right."

"Hmm. In other words, sometimes the best way to take care of someone is to let him go. Sometimes that's what he needs the most."

She blinked, realizing that Jasminder had just used one of her own trademark conversational gambits on her. "You're saying I shouldn't stick around just because Picard needs me. That I need to let him manage on his own."

The other woman demurred. "I wouldn't presume to make that decision. You should stay as long as you feel it's needed."

Guinan studied her friend, beginning to wonder how much she really was needed with this woman around.


"I was sorry to hear about your husband."

"Thank you, Doctor," said Rebekah Grabowski. Crusher's commiserations were only the latest she had heard since learning that Armin had been killed five years ago in a war with a power called the Dominion. Much might have changed in the past fifteen years—the ship, the crew, the uniforms, the technology—but news still traveled just as fast aboard starships. "But I already mourned him a long time ago. I never expected I'd see him again."

"It must have been hard for you," Crusher said as she continued her scans of Rebekah's reproductive system, or rather the ruins of it left behind by the Borg—and to some extent by the rough, makeshift surgeries and treatments the resistance members had had to perform when her immune system had begun rejecting her implants.

"It was. In a way, normal drones have it easier—their minds, their memories, are completely suppressed. But we Zeros had to cope with knowing. With remembering. And being helpless to do anything about it." She shook her head. "That place . . . Unimatrix Zero . . . I hated it for so long.

They made it look like a paradise, but it was . . . sometimes it felt like the Land of the Lotus-Eaters."

"From the *Odyssey*?"

"Mm-hmm. It was just . . . an escape, a permanent vacation. Nothing more. I couldn't be a scientist, since there was nothing to study, nothing real. Oh, if I'd been a sociologist, maybe, with all those people from all over the galaxy to talk to . . . but what's a biochemist to study when everything around you is made up of dreams and wishes instead of molecules? I couldn't do anything except dwell on what I'd lost and make futile attempts to figure out ways to carry my consciousness into the waking world. They all knew it couldn't work, but they always let newcomers figure it out on their own."

"But you eventually adjusted."

"I had to. I finally resigned myself to the fact that this was my existence from now on, and I had to try to make the best of it. I made friends, took a few lovers . . ." At Crusher's surprised look, she smiled. "It was an unreal place, in more ways than one. We tended to be . . . less inhibited as a result. As though it didn't really matter what we did, because no one but us would ever know. And frankly," she added with a shrug, "there wasn't much else to do."

Crusher gave her a wry look. "Sounds ghastly."

"But it didn't mean we couldn't come to care about certain people more than others. There was someone who became pretty important to me after a while." She pushed aside the memory and moved on. "But then *Voyager* came along and freed us—if you can call it that. To go from feeling like your old self in an idyllic woodland to being a walking junk pile inside a metallic maze while other walking junk piles try to kill you or enslave you again . . ." She shook her head. "At least it was real. But that special someone . . . he was one of the first casualties of the resistance. The queen blew up a whole cube just to silence him and a couple of others like him."

"I'm sorry."

"Yeah, well, let's just say it made me strongly motivated to carry on the fight. When Hugh and the other Liberated showed up to help, it was a godsend. Not only did he give us new allies, but a new home, too. And not a fake Eden like U-Zero. It's a beautiful planet, but we have to work the land, mine the earth, earn our survival."

The doctor chuckled. "I don't remember you being such a pioneer type, Rebekah. I recall some notations in your medical file about needing to get out of your lab and get some exercise and fresh air."

"Well, living in U-Zero for over a decade can change your outlook on a life of leisure. Plus, it keeps us strong for fighting the Borg. Even cut off from the Delta Quadrant, the remaining ones in this quadrant are still a serious threat."

"As we discovered." Crusher checked some readings. "Well, you're definitely in excellent health, all things considered. Pioneer life seems to agree with you."

"And what about . . ."

"I believe we can regenerate your reproductive system. We can also do some cosmetic work, if you like—restimulate hair growth and give you a prosthetic eye that matches your real one."

*To have hair again!* Rebekah had always taken pride in her curly brown locks. Still, she hesitated. "I don't know, Doc. I'll have to talk it over with Hugh, with the others. We've de-Borged ourselves as much as we were able, but still . . . I'm not sure I want to set myself apart from the others, not unilaterally. They're my people now."

Crusher held up her hands. "I'm just saying it's doable. No pressure."

Rebekah relaxed—but still caught herself stroking her bald scalp in contemplation.

"So you and Hugh have become close, huh?"

"Yes. We intend to have children together, once we're able to. *If* we're able to."

"It shouldn't be too hard. Hugh's sexual differentiation wasn't entirely suppressed—clearly his jawline and his vocal cords have been shaped by testosterone."

Rebekah nodded. "The Borg want their incubated drones to be physically strong, so they feed most of them enough testosterone to make them develop masculine build and musculature, while still suppressing their sexual development."

Beverly absorbed the information with interest but stayed on topic. "So I think the raw ingredients are there; it's just a matter of stimulating them."

"Still, I don't want to get my hopes up."

"I understand. You can get dressed now."

As Rebekah donned her functional jumpsuit, Crusher went on, "It's quite a coincidence, isn't it? You and Hugh ending up together?"

"Because we were both on the *Enterprise*?" The doctor nodded, and Rebekah envied the way her red-gold tresses bobbed and shimmered as she did so. "I think that's what brought us together, really. That shared experience. I was able to tell him more about the people who'd given him his freedom, about the society that had produced that idea of individual rights, and the things we'd done with them. And . . . and he was able to give me a glimpse into the world I'd lost. To tell me how my ship and my crew had made out after I . . . was taken from them." She laid a hand on the bulkhead.

Crusher studied her. "You miss Starfleet, don't you?"

Rebekah pulled her hand away. "Just a little nostalgia. It's nice to see these displays again." She gestured at the big black wall panel with its curving, colorful graphics. "Nice to have coffee again, and pierogi and strawberry ice cream. And to see holonovels again. I've already downloaded the later seasons of *The Boomer Diaries* into my personal database."

"They weren't that good, as I recall," Crusher said. "The storylines got increasingly contrived. It got harder to maintain that same sense of isolation the deeper they got into the warp-5 era."

"Still, I've been wondering for years if Vallejo and Dirani ever got together."

"Okay, I won't spoil it."

She chuckled, amazed to be sharing such mundane conversation with another human being once again. Then she grew wistful. "Well, just as well they stopped making them. That's one less thing to miss back home."

Crusher spoke tentatively. "You still have a daughter back there, you know."

Rebekah didn't meet her eyes. "It's been fifteen years. Most of her life. Ruthie's an adult now. She's gotten by just fine without me." She cleared her throat. "And I have commitments to the Liberated. I'll be raising a new family, over a thousand parsecs away from her. Better just to let it be a clean break. No point in . . . in dredging things up, reminding her of what she lost, when I can't stay." She blinked; her eye was stinging. "I have commitments now."

But the doctor was no longer looking at her. Her gaze was off to the side. Rebekah turned and jumped at the sight of a gray-white, vaguely humanoid creature that had somehow arrived in sickbay without making a sound. "Is . . . is this one of your crew?" she asked, not wanting to be rude.

"It's one of the cluster entity's constructs," Crusher said. Rebekah had heard that these things had begun manifesting on the *Liberator*, but this was the first one she'd seen herself. "They've been popping up all over," the doctor went on. "And I think I'm starting to notice a pattern."

Beverly's perception of a pattern was embarrassingly confirmed for her and Picard that night, when a construct intruded on the couple during sex, startling them badly. Before long, other members of the crew came forward with reports that constructs were materializing as spectators or mimics during their own acts of intimacy. Other than that, the constructs increasingly seemed to be manifesting during conversations about love and family, the medical team's researches into ex-Borg fertility, and the like.

"The entity's trying to understand procreation," T'Ryssa Chen summed it up in a briefing for the senior staff. "It's figured out that we're capable of creating new organisms that are extensions of ourselves, and I think it's waiting to see if we're going to make it happen."

"You mean it thinks that having children is like the way it creates its constructs?" Kadohata asked.

T'Ryssa nodded. "Mm-hmm. See, it can interpret our thoughts and actions somewhat better than I can with its—since I don't have a brain the size of eight hundred planets. But we're still very alien to it, so its understanding is vague. It's met beings like us before, but I guess they never stayed long enough for family and parenting to come up.

"Anyway, it doesn't yet understand that

humanoid children aren't just extensions of their parents the way its constructs are extensions of it. It gets that we're individuals, able to think and act independently, but I don't think it entirely grasps that we aren't all just facets of some single bigger thing. That's an idea that's more natural to it, easier to understand."

Picard frowned. "This concerns me greatly, Lieutenant. For that is the most fundamental difference between us and the Borg."

"I've been trying to tell it about the Borg, Captain, really. I've . . . I've let it relive my memories of the Borg attack on my away team over and over," she said, her expression bleak. "With my nightmares, that kind of happens anyway. And it understands that we're afraid of the Borg. I'm just not sure it agrees with our reasons." Her hands lifted from the table, waving uncertainly for a moment. "You know how I made the analogy that it sees us like neighborhood cats? I like cats, but when I see one running in panic from a little rain, I don't suddenly believe I need to do the same."

"Then we must consider the possibility," Worf said, "of having to battle the entity as well as the Borg."

"If you were a cat, Commander, could you do more than inflict a few minor scratches on a Klingon?"

Worf puffed up proudly. "I have learned never to underestimate the fighting prowess of a feline." Picard smiled in spite of himself. Klingons reflexively recoiled from small, furry, adorable creatures, but since reluctantly inheriting Data's cat, Spot, Worf had gained a new appreciation for the predatory prowess and independence of the species. He and Spot were now inseparable, in their own aloof and undemonstrative way.

"I have to agree with T'Ryssa," Choudhury said. "The idea of battling the cluster entity is not a realistic one to pursue—especially given the fact that it is observing us at all times," she added pointedly. "We must persuade it to side with us over the Borg. I take heart from the fact that it hasn't sided with them yet. It may understand a collective consciousness better than a species of individuals, but so far it has done nothing to indicate a preference either way. And given the newfound belligerence of these Borg, I suspect that if it had allied with them, we would have found ourselves under attack by now."

T'Ryssa said, "It might help if I understood the Borg better. Got more insight into their beliefs, their culture."

"The Borg have no culture," Picard stated. "Only ruthless pragmatism."

"Are you sure, sir? I mean, look at their ships. All those cubes. Why use cubes?"

"For efficiency," Picard said, considering it self-evident.

"But a cube isn't the most efficient shape."

"She's right, sir," Kadohata put in. "The most efficient geometric shape is the sphere. It requires the least material to encase a given volume, the least power to shield it, the shortest maximum distance between any two interior locations."

"Right," T'Ryssa went on. "So if they were really into efficiency, their ships would be spherical."

"The Borg do use spheres," Worf said.

"But only for small ships, where the difference in efficiency isn't as great. It should be the other way around. I mean, damn, look at that last supercube you fought. That thing was big enough to get pulled toward a spheroid shape by its own gravity. The structural field energy needed to resist that would've been enormous—and for what? It was a monumental waste of power. That thing had to be the most inefficient starship ever built."

"Well," Kadohata said, "our scans showed it actually had a spherical core structure but with a relatively hollow cubic shell. So the energy to maintain it wouldn't have been so great."

"But then why make the cubic shell at all? The only reason is as a statement of their power and purpose. Rigid, machine order imposed on nature, straight lines instead of curves. It's a symbol of the created perfection they aspire to. Maybe it has something like a religious significance to them."

"Don't go overboard in your speculations, Lieutenant," Picard advised. "There is no 'them.' There is a single collective will following an imperative to expand."

"Okay, now there is. But they had to come from somewhere. I think maybe what we see in them now might be a reflection of the culture and beliefs of the people they evolved from. Like, maybe there is no reason why the central coordinating node has to be a female drone. Maybe it's just tradition. Maybe their ancestors were matriarchal and that assumption got fed into the original program."

"Lieutenant, I was one of them. If any of this were true, I think I would be aware of it."

"Unless the knowledge was lost. They may not even know where they came from. Like you say, they're slaves to the program. And they're driven to go forward. Why would they even look into their past? I bet there's a ton about the Borg's origins that even they don't know."

Picard had to admit she had a point. As a student of archaeology, he knew that every culture had things in its past that it forgot or deliberately buried. And he had to respect T'Ryssa's imagination and insight in raising these questions. "Even so," he said, "none of this is useful to us now in communicating with the cluster entity."

"It could be, sir," Choudhury said. "If we could communicate to the entity that the Borg started out as individuals like us who were turned into something else, it could help them understand that this was done to them against their will. That they were harmed by their assimilation. Since it seems to care about protecting other beings from harm, that could help convince it."

Picard reflected on the irony of the situation. It was really rather refreshing to encounter an advanced, incredibly powerful alien being that, for once, actually seemed to share the Federation's core values of compassion and regard for the lives and rights of other beings. It was regrettable that in this particular context, the innocence and fundamental *decency* of this creature put it at odds with *Enterprise*'s mission. He sincerely hoped it would be possible to persuade it that they shared the same essential goals.

He nodded. "Make the attempt, Lieutenant Chen, along the lines Lieutenant Choudhury suggests. Or along whatever additional lines of reasoning you deem productive. It is urgent that we convince the cluster entity to see the truth about the Borg. Not only for our own protection"—he held her eyes, sharing a moment of understanding with her—"but because it does not deserve what they will do to it if we fail."

When the computer told Miranda Kadohata that T'Ryssa Chen was in Holodeck 1, she resisted her initial impulse to suspect that the lieutenant was goofing off when she should be on the job. T'Ryssa had actually done a fairly good job of working with the cluster entity, perhaps as good a job as anyone could expect under the circumstances, and her commitment to the mission seemed quite clear. So Miranda reserved judgment and went to the holodeck herself to see what T'Ryssa was doing.

She found the lieutenant surrounded by various simulated families and children of various species at different stages of development, as well as a pregnant woman, a nesting Aurelian, and a clinically explicit simulation of a four-member Andorian bond group in the act of procreation. All the simulations were being observed by cluster constructs, which had taken on variant forms to mimic what they saw (if "saw" was the word). T'Ryssa was watching the Andorian foursome with some interest but started and flushed green when she saw Miranda. "Commander! Umm . . . look, this isn't what it looks like . . ."

"It looks like you're trying to teach the cluster entity about the humanoid—and other—life cycle. Right?"

"Oh. Well, I guess it is what it looks like. I, um, figured the holodeck would be something it could relate to, since it's so much like what it does with constructs. Instead of just thinking something at it, I think it and create a physical representation of it."

"And has that helped improve its understanding?"

"I think so. It certainly seems to be getting more involved in the, er, conversation." She gestured around her at the various spectating constructs. "I started out with just one simulation, but it seemed to have trouble focusing on that, and it occurred to me that it could probably multitask like crazy. So I gave it multiple inputs at once. That might be closer to how it normally takes in information."

Miranda nodded. "I have to say, that's very perceptive. But didn't the captain assign you to talk to it about the Borg?"

The younger woman bristled. "I am, Commander. Sort of. I mean, I started out trying to, but I still couldn't get it to understand the whole individuality thing. I needed to go back to basics, try to define what an individual *is*. It's still having trouble with the idea that we aren't just extensions of our parents. It's confused—it sees that we inherit things from our parents, that we're sort of a continuation of them, but I don't think it gets that we can be that and still have a unique . . . essence, identity, of our own."

Miranda looked askance at the simulations. "Word of advice, Lieutenant. You won't convince it of that by showing it sex-ed holos. It's not the physical side it needs to understand, it's the personal. The *experience* of growing up human—or whatever. What it feels like to be a child. How a parent and a child relate to each other. That's what you need to share with it."

"I've tried that," T'Ryssa said, looking away.

"Have you? Have you really shared that experience with them, those feelings, or have you just stuck with generalities?"

"Look, what do you want from me?" T'Ryssa cried. "I don't exactly have a model family experience to share with it. What the hell do you want me to tell it? That a father is some name you hear about occasionally but never actually meet? Some guy who dumps some green-blooded chromosomes into you and saddles you with a lifetime of expectations about being logical and controlled and perfect but can't be bothered to stick around and tell you what any of that means? You want me to tell it that a mother is someone who takes care of you out of a sense of duty but makes you feel guilty and unwelcome because you're holding her back from the career she'd rather have?"

Miranda was stunned by her outburst of pain and anger, and puzzled that it was directed at her. Trying to be understanding, she said, "I'm sure your mother loves you, Trys—"

"Of course *you'd* side with her! Hell, you're living her dream! Drop a couple of kids, then leave them with Daddy while you go gallivanting around the galaxy doing important science stuff! You've got it made!"

Bristling, Miranda came nose to nose with the girl, not caring that the constructs were observing them now, and said, "For your information, young lady, I love my babies more than anything! The months I spent with them on maternity leave were the happiest times of my life."

*"Then why did you leave them?!"*

Miranda stared. The pain and rage in her voice were too great, too personal, for that to be what she was really asking. Suddenly T'Ryssa's rebellious, hostile attitude toward her made sense.

"I remind you of her, don't I?" she asked softly after a moment. Trys just looked away. "Or maybe of both of them. At least she stayed with you."

"And she hated it." It was a sullen murmur.

"I doubt that very much, love. I'm sure she was torn between her family and her career. I know what that's like. But she never left you."

"She never exactly did much to make me sure she wouldn't."

"Because your dad left you, you thought she would too?"

T'Ryssa sighed. "Sometimes I wish it had been the other way around. Maybe we would both have been happier if Sylix had taken me in the divorce and Mom had been free to go off exploring. Although then I guess I'd have grown up like a good little Vulcan and wouldn't have felt anything."

Miranda clasped her shoulder. "I'm sure she'd have missed you terribly."

"As much as she missed her career when she had to stay with me?"

"I don't know." Miranda shook her head. "Lord knows, I couldn't tell you which I'd miss more. I love Vicenzo and the kids desperately—but I couldn't live without the work, being out here making new discoveries. That's part of who I am, and anyone who's part of my life just has to accept that."

Trys glared. "But your kids didn't have a choice in the matter."

Miranda winced. "I guess they didn't. But I talk to them every chance I get. And I thank God they have Vicenzo."

"Lucky them."

Miranda blinked away tears, and Trys reacted with surprise. "Don't ever think this choice was easy for me, T'Ryssa. I'm happy being here, doing this work, but I'm terribly unhappy every day I'm away from my family. They're part of me. Try all you want to convince the cluster that children and parents are separate from each other. I could never convince it of that, because I don't believe it. I'm not complete without them."

Trys studied her. "So what if it were the other way around? What if you'd stayed with them?"

She sighed. "I think the mix of happy and unhappy would be about the same. There's no easy way to choose." Miranda found herself noticing how the light caught T'Ryssa's hair. It wasn't so different from Aoki's—that beautiful silky hair that she was so determined to cover up. Could it be because that hair reminded her of her mother's? Did she resent her mother for leaving her? Miranda knew she'd be composing a very long letter to her daughter tonight. "Just because your mum wasn't happy all the time, Trys, doesn't mean she wasn't happy to have you in her life. If I'm anything like her at all, then I know that's true. And I know she never would've left you."

Trys was blinking away tears of her own now and hesitantly accepted a hug from Miranda, gradually relaxing into it. When she pulled away afterward, she chuckled. "Damn. Who knew I had such major abandonment issues? I thought I was the one who ran away from people."

"Maybe you wanted to beat them to it. Be the abandoner instead of the abandonee, so you could have some control."

Clearing her throat, Trys said, "Speaking of control, I guess I've been taking some things out on you that you didn't deserve." She blinked. "Um, the control part is about you being in command over me."

"I got it."

"Not one of my better segues."

"I said I got it." They shared a tentative laugh.

"Anyway, I'll try to be less insubordinate."

Miranda looked at her askance. "You'll 'try.'"

"Well," T'Ryssa said with a shrug, "let's not expect miracles."

*Liberator*
Stardate 57895

As Hugh completed a maintenance check on his regeneration alcove, he gazed wistfully at the alcove next to his, where Rebekah spent her downtime alongside him. He hoped that, soon, he would be able to lie beside her in a different context. He hoped that Doctor Crusher could enable him to become a husband to her, to replace the one she had lost.

He shook himself, realizing it was nearly time for the communal meal. He headed out for the dining hall, passing through the command bay en route. There, he found Lyton, his executive officer, bent over a console with Telos, a cybernetics specialist. "Come," he said. "It is mealtime."

"You go without us, Hugh," Lyton said. "We are in the middle of that analysis of the Borg's nano-defenses."

"Is it in a critical stage?"

"No, but—"

"Then attend the meal with us."

Lyton came around the console to face him. "Why? It is only the Zeros who need to eat every day." He grimaced. "And those foods they brought back from the *Enterprise* . . . all those colors and textures . . . disgusting." Lyton was one of those incubated ex-drones who felt the processed nutrient mash they occasionally ingested was far more palatable than the solid foods that other humanoids needed to masticate and break down the hard way.

"You know it is not about the food, Lyton. If we are to survive as a united culture, the incubated must share communal mealtime with the assimilated. Just as they share the Speaking of Names with us, even though many of them have no stories to tell of their own naming."

"We are already united in the fight. Why indulge in these trappings?"

"Because there must be more to living than the fight. Because the Liberated need a future, or our liberation was for nothing. We need a society, a shared heritage to pass down."

"Then let it be two different heritages. Or more, as many as there are species among the Zeros. Why not? Unity is the Borg way. Should we not embrace individuality?"

"Not to the point that it isolates us from one another. Our differences are in no danger of disappearing—what we need are more commonalities to balance them. Otherwise we will fragment and our community will not survive.

"Now, come. Both of you. Let us share mealtime with our friends and enjoy each other's diversity."

Lyton and Telos reluctantly suspended their analysis and followed Hugh, but they contributed little to the evening's conversation—except to note that Rebekah had failed to show up for the meal, despite being one of those who actually ate. Hugh masked his annoyance at her for undermining him in that way—at least until he could confront her about it alone.

But when she finally beamed back from *Enterprise* and he went to meet her, he found her seemingly in shock, as pale as a drone but with her eyes puffed from crying. "What has happened?" he asked.

"I . . . I got a communique from the Federation. It was . . . it was Ruth."

Hugh's throat constricted. "Your . . . your daughter."

"Yes." She smiled, though her eyes still glistened. "She's all grown up now—in college, studying to be a doctor. She's dating a nice Jewish girl . . . oh, she's just so beautiful! Everything I could've dreamed of." Rebekah blinked away tears. "When she learned . . . that she wasn't an orphan anymore, she told me that after the shock wore off, she felt such joy. It was hard for her to lose her father . . . after losing me too," she added with difficulty. Hugh took her in his arms, and she held him close for a while.

When she looked up at him again, she seemed almost guilty. "She . . . she really wants to see me again. To have me back in her life."

Hugh pulled back a little. "And . . . you wish the same, don't you?"

She clasped his hand. "Hugh, I love you. I'm committed to you, to the Liberated. This is my home now, you know that." He nodded. "But to see my Ruthie again . . . I can't help but be tempted to go, just for a little while. Maybe I could just . . . visit. Spend some time with her, catch up with all the years I lost. And then I'd come back, and we could start our family."

"You would postpone our family plans?" Hugh asked, his voice tightly controlled.

"There aren't a lot of ships going to the Federation from here. It would make the most sense to go with *Enterprise*." She stroked his cheek. "You could come with me."

"You know that's not possible. I have a whole community to lead. The longer I'm away from the homeworld, the more fragile the situation will become.

"And how would it look to the other assimilateds?" Hugh went on. "The ones who can't go back to their homes and families? Or the ones who are already teetering on the edge of trying, even if it takes decades to return home? Even a temporary visit might destabilize an already delicate situation." *And what if you found your old life preferable to your new one with us? With me?*

Rebekah sighed. "You're right. I know that. But it's my little girl."

He held her hands. "We have all led lives of great sacrifice and hardship. But take heart, Rebekah. Soon, you and I will have new children. A new family. Concentrate on that."

She gave him a smile, though it was not wholehearted. "I do. Really. But you can't just interchange people like that. Someone who's your own flesh and blood, someone you took care of every day for five years . . . you just can't understand yet what that means. You can't understand what I've lost."

Her words were like a physical blow. He had never so strongly felt the divide between the incubated and the assimilated—not with her. Ever since she had boarded the *Enterprise,* he had felt a distance growing between them. She had accepted his offer of a new life when she had had nothing else, but could he really compete with the chance to reclaim her old life?

And could he blame her if she chose to return to that life? It was a chance that few of the Zeros would ever have, a rare and precious opportunity. How could he begrudge her that?

Was it right to ask her to make the sacrifice, rather than taking the burden upon himself?

But how could the community survive if the intended mate of its leader set a precedent by leaving?

# 9

---

"Lieutenant, you are out of uniform!" Worf bellowed as T'Ryssa Chen barged out of the bridge turbolift in her uniform undershirt and slacks, in her stocking feet, and carrying her gray-shouldered jacket in one hand.

"Less so than I was a minute ago, sir," she said, panting. "The folks on deck 5 got an eyeful. Sorry, Captain, but it's urgent."

"Then please get to the point," Picard said.

"The entity," she said between breaths. "Told me in a dream . . . *Frankenstein*'s loose, sir."

"The constructs are no longer confining them?"

"They've adapted. They're drilling again."

"In the same location?"

"Yes, sir," she said, slipping on her jacket.

"And you still haven't convinced the entity to prevent it?"

She leaned on the back of her seat, still out of breath. "I don't think it wants to, sir. It's curious. Maybe it sees this as a new form of communication, and it wants to try it out."

"Well, we can't fault it for curiosity," Kadohata said.

"How about giving us a slipstream vortex?" Picard asked.

"It's not sure it wants us there. We'll just get into another fight."

"Conn, how long to System 66 at best speed?"

"If the distortion zones haven't changed, sir," the relief flight controller answered, "four hours."

"Contact the *Liberator* at once. At least this time we can fight together."


Minutes later, both ships were at warp and Picard had assembled the senior staff for a precombat briefing, with Hugh on the observation-lounge screen, monitoring from the bridge of the *Liberator.*

"How long until they penetrate to the diamond layers?" Picard asked Dina Elfiki.

"Hard to say exactly, but we'll be cutting it close. I'd say our best hope is that it takes them time to absorb the slipstream knowledge once they access the computational layers."

"And that the entity itself does not turn against us," Worf added. "If one of its component planets is assimilated, will the rest follow suit?"

"I doubt it," T'Ryssa said. "Its parts can work synchronously by quantum entanglement, but as we've seen, they can also operate in isolation. It's one being, but it has multiple facets to its personality that sometimes think independently of each other. If one part of it became Borg and tried to destroy us, it'd be outvoted by the rest."

"But the entity would still be likely to prevent us from destroying the Borg."

"Eventually. But dealing with the assimilation would probably be one hell of a distraction from what we're doing. Even if it wouldn't be immediately endangered by it, it would still be really curious and confused. I'd say we'd have a good chance if we acted quickly."

*"But with what weapon?"* Hugh asked. *"We are still no closer to finding a safe delivery method for the multivector agent."*

"We've had no more luck on our end," Beverly said. "The only way to be sure would be for someone to go over there and inject it directly into a drone. If he could avoid being slaughtered long enough to do so."

*"Even then, we could not be certain,"* Hugh said. *"These Borg are more cautious, more defensive, than the ones we have battled in the past. They have been defeated too many times and have adapted by*

*raising their guard, anticipating threats. Even if a drone were successfully injected with the agent, they would be aware of that and would destroy the drone before it could interface with the system."*

The crew absorbed that, and after a moment, Hugh spoke again. *"There is only one way to be sure. Rebekah told me of a human myth—the Trojan horse?"*

Picard stared. "Allow someone to be assimilated . . ."

Beverly finished his thought. "With the agent already in his bloodstream?"

*"Exactly."*

"But that would still be a suicide mission!" the doctor insisted.

*"Yes. But one that could actually work."*

"Would it?" Worf asked. "As you say, the Borg would be alert to an infection."

*"What if it could be concealed somehow? Something that would mask it long enough to allow it to spread through the vessel's systems before it activates?"*

"A timed-release delivery system?" Beverly asked. "Yes, I could make that work." She raised her head with new optimism. "Maybe that would even allow us to retrieve whoever we sent—beam him back and deassimilate him."

Picard shook his head. "That would not be an option here. Once assimilated, his life signs would be difficult to distinguish. And a transponder implant would be a giveaway. Besides, we'd be in pitched battle, with shields raised. I'm sorry, Doctor. This will be a one-way trip."

Her eyes widened as she understood what she saw in his. "You're planning to go yourself!"

"I would not ask this of anyone else," he declared, to the crew's dismay.

"Captain, I must protest!" Worf cried.

"As must I," said Choudhury.

Beverly's question was simple. "Why you?"

But he could hear the layers of meaning beneath it, and he tried to convey his feelings in his eyes as he met hers. Aloud, he said, "I am the logical choice. No one here knows the Borg better than I."

*"I do,"* said Hugh. *"I should be the one to go. They might kill you on sight. I can already pass as a drone, with minimal modification. That could give me the edge I need to ensure the agent is delivered."*

"Out of the question. You have a responsibility to lead your people and to help ensure their procreation."

*"Do you not have the same responsibilities, Captain?"*

"There are far more captains where I came from, Hugh."

*"And what of your other responsibility?"* Hugh asked with some heat. *"You are the last of your line, unless you survive to perpetuate it. That is why it must be me. Only that way can we both do what must be done to ensure the future of our families."*

"Hugh," he answered tensely, "I appreciate your concern. But I cannot—" He faltered as his eyes met

Beverly's again. "I cannot allow personal considerations to interfere with my duties. You are right, most any one of us would probably be killed on sight. But that is why it must be me. The Borg . . ." He repressed a shudder. "They have . . . a proprietary interest in me. When the progenitors of these Borg attacked the Federation months ago, they sought to reclaim me. They want me back. They always have.

"You spoke of the Trojan horse, Hugh. The reason it was a horse was that this animal was sacred to the Trojans, a symbol of their patron god. It was the one offering they could not refuse. That was the only reason the ploy worked. If there is to be a Trojan horse here, it must be me.

"No matter the cost." He met his wife's eyes again, seeing pain and anger but acceptance and trust as well. She understood why he needed to do this. And he loved her more than ever for it.

*My love, I'm so sorry.*


As the crew prepared to carry out Picard's orders and prepare for the coming battle, the captain himself engaged in what had become a sort of prebattle ritual for him in recent years: walking the corridors of the ship, observing the crew in their preparations, letting them see their captain and be aware that he was with them, thinking of them, believing in them. Perhaps, as he had told Data so many years ago, he could not walk disguised among his troops and gauge their mood like King Henry V, but he felt it was better to walk openly among them and let them see him as a man existing on the same level as themselves, a partner in the harsh times ahead.

"Are you crazy, Picard?"

However, there were limits. He turned to face Guinan, his expression warning her to mind her tone when speaking to him in a public corridor with crew walking by. Her voice was not raised or openly angry, but its sternness was evident and the choice of words was most unlike her. "I take it you've heard of my intention."

"Word gets around when the captain declares his intention to commit suicide."

"Guinan, this is not the place."

"Then find a place. We are having this conversation *now*."

He was angry at her for undermining his authority in public, but he understood how exceptional it was for Guinan to do anything of the kind. He could not talk her out of this—nor could he deny that her words were always worth listening to.

Stiffly, he led her to a nearby geology lab, currently shut down to save power for defensive systems. The lights came up when they entered, but only to half level. He said, "If you know what I plan to do, then you must be aware of my reasons. This is something that must be done."

"Yes, but not by you."

"I am the best choice."

"No. You're not. Not anymore."

He frowned. "What does that mean?"

"'I now pronounce you husband and wife.' Ring a bell?"

It was a moment before he responded. "Whatever else I may be, I am still captain of the *Enterprise*. I cannot let other factors compromise my command judgment."

"Like hell you can't. Yes, I understand the responsibilities of a starship captain. But you need to get used to the fact that you have other responsibilities now. Responsibilities to that woman you promised your life and soul to."

"And it's her I'm doing this to protect!"

"She doesn't *need* a protector, Picard! She needs a husband! She needs someone who's willing to live for her, not just die for her."

She lowered her voice and stepped closer. "Haven't you figured it out yet? Don't you know why I got married twenty-three times? Why I've got children scattered across three quadrants? Because it *matters*. Family isn't some incidental thing that takes a backseat to war and politics. Family is where everything else begins. Sure, captains protect the future, but families create it. Without husbands and wives having children and teaching them what matters, there's no future to protect.

"So don't you tell me that being a husband, being a potential father, matters less than being a Starfleet officer. You know it's not true. If you had to send another officer on a suicide mission, and you had to choose between one who had a family and one who didn't, you can't tell me it wouldn't be a factor."

Her words reached him, but they were not enough to sway him. "What is my alternative, Guinan? To let Hugh sacrifice himself? He's an aspiring father too. And he's young, strong, a leader for his whole people. How is he a better choice than I am?

"Besides, it wouldn't work. The Borg would recognize him as an intruder, an enemy. They want me back. That's my edge."

"Don't make the mistake of thinking the Borg care about you as an individual, *Locutus*." Picard winced at the name. "It isn't personal. It never is. They want you back because you're a piece of their property that they misplaced. Because they can't stand to let anything escape their control. They want Hugh back for the same reason—they've been fighting to get him back for over six years. And the harder he's fought them, the more he's defied their control and bloodied their nose, the more determined it's made them to get him back. He's just as qualified to be the irresistible bait as you—maybe more qualified."

Picard shook his head. "We are responsible for Hugh. You and I, Guinan, we helped make him into the man he is. I will not throw his life away simply to save my own, and I can't believe that you—the one who convinced me of his worth as an individual—would ask me to do so."

"I wouldn't ask that of you, if that was what

happening here," Guinan said. "But it isn't. This isn't a choice between you and him."

Characteristically, she let the cryptic statement stand for him to ponder. But its meaning remained elusive. "I know of no other candidates."

"The point is, you shouldn't be a candidate at all. A captain isn't supposed to sacrifice himself to begin with. According to regulations, a mission like this should be Worf's job, or Choudhury's. It's their duty, not yours."

"You're not suggesting—"

"No. I'm saying it's false to treat this as a choice between you and our Liberated friend. Hugh is not a member of your crew. He's a free agent, and he's volunteered to do this. I don't want to see him sacrifice himself, but . . ." She paused. "But he's all grown up now, and he has the right to make his own decisions. It's not your place or mine to tell him what he can't do.

"So your decision to throw your life away, it's not about Hugh. You're doing this for your own reasons."

He spoke in measured tones. "And what do you believe those reasons are?"

"Why else do people kill themselves? Because they're more afraid of living. Because they don't want to face the choices they'd have to make, the responsibilities they'd have to shoulder, if they kept on going."

He stared at her for a long moment. "You're saying I'm so afraid of becoming a father that I've become suicidal?"

"I'm not saying you want to kill yourself. I'm saying that when you look at your future, all you let yourself see is the potential for pain and loss. You see the Borg destroying what you hold dear. You see yourself reliving the grief of losing a child."

His gaze sharpened. "Beverly would not have told you . . ."

She threw him a look. "How long have we known each other?" He blushed a bit, conceding her point. "You just can't let your guard down and be happy with what you have. You're so afraid of losing it that you're making it a self-fulfilling prophecy—throwing it away yourself before anyone else has the chance to ruin it for you. If a man believes he's going to die tomorrow, he'll usually find a way to make it happen."

Picard frowned, for it sounded like a quotation. "Where have I heard that before?"

"Probably Will Riker mentioned it. I said it to him—a day or so before he rescued you from the Borg." She angled her head. "As I recall, he found a way *not* to let it happen. For you or your crew."

Picard's gaze wandered over the rock samples in the lab's display cases, vague, elusive shapes that he was unable to discern clearly in the darkness. "Beverly and I have had a long talk about my fears. I've faced them."

"No, you haven't. You've only recognized they're there for you to face. You won't begin facing them until you conceive your first child."

"I want to. I do. I'm not just doing this to run away from that. Beverly understands. She accepts my command judgment. If she thought it were compromised, she would . . ."

"She knows your command judgment is fine. It's your judgment as a husband that's the problem. You're putting that aside to go on being Captain Picard, pure and simple. And you know what? She understands that. She loves you for who you are and she knows she can't change you. So she's keeping up a brave, stoic front even though she's dying inside. After all, she knows what it's like to be a Starfleet widow," Guinan went on relentlessly. "She knew the risks when she said 'I do.' She's strong. She survived once, she'll survive a second time."

"Stop it!"

Her fierce expression gave way to a gentle smile. "There you go. You know this isn't fair to her. You know she deserves better."

"Yes, she does," Picard gasped. "But how do I know I can give it to her?"

"Just stop second-guessing yourself. You can be so happy together if you just relax and let it happen." She touched his arm. "You married her because you finally realized you belonged together. All you have to do is remember what you already figured out.

"And *let her in,* Picard. *Let* her matter to you in

the decisions you make. She's part of you now—
she has a right to be part of your choices. Even the
ones you make by yourself."

He looked at the rock samples, but all he saw
was the petrified look in Beverly's eyes when he
announced his decision. The look of a woman
walling in her emotions and hopes, fortifying herself against loss. His eyes squeezed shut, tears
stinging them.

In time, he turned to Guinan, smiling wistfully.
"What would I do without you, Guinan?"

She looked him over. "You don't need me,
Picard. You have a family now."

He sighed. "In time, perhaps."

"No. Now. Look around you." She glided over to
the door. "You asked me to come along because
you thought you needed me to help this crew
mesh. And I helped out once or twice. But they
hardly needed me." She smiled. "I've enjoyed the
visit, but I feel like it'll be time for me to move on
soon."

He came forward and clasped her shoulders.
"Whether we need you or not . . . we will still miss
you."

"Don't worry," she said. "I promise to come visit
when the baby's born."


"I can't let you do this."

Hugh brushed the tears from Rebekah's eyes,
hoping her pain and anger were not so great that

they would trigger a shutdown of her cortical node. Hoping he was right that they would not be. "It is my choice, Rebekah. I do it for my people. And I do it for you."

"For me? How is this a good thing for me, you idiot?"

He chuckled. Around them in sickbay, the medical and engineering officers preparing to infuse him with the multivector agent paused briefly, then resumed their work. "Because you have a daughter in the Federation who loves you and needs you. I know you were torn between your love for her and your obligations to me. I'm solving that dilemma for you. Now you can go back to her and stay there."

Rebekah sighed and shook her head, her eyes lifting to the ceiling as though expecting to find guidance there. He regretted that he'd never gotten around to asking her why she did that. "You really are a fool if you think what I feel for you is only obligation. Just because our hormones are screwed up doesn't mean I can't love you."

"And I love you. Which is why I must set you free. Just as I can set my people free from the further threat of the Borg by delivering this weapon."

"But how will we unify our society without you to show the way?"

He clasped her hand. "I am not Lore, Rebekah. I have led my people, but I do not wish them dependent upon me. I have always striven to create a system that could function just as well without me—to make myself as irrelevant as possible. If you will pardon the word." She gave a tearful laugh despite herself.

"I have done my part. I brought us here to Doctor Crusher, and she has nearly solved our procreation problem. Lyton and the rest will bring that knowledge home, and that will be my legacy. That, and what I do here today. By doing this, I show them that the future of our people is worth any sacrifice. That our personal desires and differences, as precious as they are to our individuality, do not override our commitment to ensure the continuation of the Liberated."

She took his hands. "I don't want to lose you."

Hugh met her eyes and sighed. "You would not have stayed anyway. And I do not blame you for that. This simply facilitates the choice. Go home . . . and give your daughter my love."

Rebekah broke into sobs, turning away. Nurse Mimouni came over and escorted her into the next room as Geordi and Doctor Crusher came over. "I will want to see her again before . . ."

Crusher nodded, understanding. "Of course. We . . . we're ready whenever you are." The look in her eyes was complex, at once thanking him for taking on the burden that would otherwise have been her mate's and apologizing for playing a role in his sacrifice.

He smiled. "It is all right, Doctor. I am ready."

"Hugh," Geordi said. "You can still change your mind. We can find another way. Maybe . . . maybe a hologram. We have a prototype mobile emitter . . ."

Hugh shook his head. "You know the Borg would not be fooled. They will aggress against any intruder . . . unless it is one they feel compelled to reassimilate." He had recognized how naïve his initial proposal in the briefing had been. These Borg's numbers were small, their technology different from his own; there was no way he could pass among them without being recognized as an intruder. There would be no attempt at disguise—not of his identity, at least.

Geordi remained dejected. "It's just . . . it feels wrong to let you do this. This is what we wanted to do to you a dozen years ago—make you a Trojan horse for a virus to destroy the Borg. Hell, it's even a modified form of the same virus. It's like . . . like everything we did, everything you learned, was all for nothing."

Hugh looked at him in amazement. "Geordi, that could not be less true! You gave me life. Thanks to you, and to Doctor Crusher, and to the captain and Guinan, I have had a dozen years of life as an individual. It may seem a brief time to you, but it has been an entire lifetime to me, a life that has been rich and well lived.

"And don't forget—you *did* send me back to infect the Borg with a virus—the virus of independent thought. That infection overtook a whole cube and gave birth to an entire society of free humanoids. It was the first of many blows struck against the Borg, and now we will strike another, perhaps the greatest blow of all. It was the right thing to do then, and it is the right thing now." He clasped Geordi's hand. "And it is fitting, my friend, that we strike that blow together, one last time."

Geordi returned the handclasp and gave Hugh a tight, sad smile. "You're a hell of a man, Hugh. It's been an honor knowing you."

"Thank you, Geordi. For my name . . . for my life . . . for everything."

# 10

———

*Enterprise* and *Liberator* arrived in System 66 only to find that they might already be too late. "The borehole has reached the diamond mantle," Kadohata reported in a hushed voice. "I'm reading Borg signatures at the base. They've begun to assimilate the entity."

"Just this part of it," T'Ryssa said. "And they haven't taken it over yet. I would've known." She did not sound especially confident, though.

"Still, we must act fast," Picard said. "Picard to *Liberator*. Are you ready?"

*"Ready, Captain,"* said Hugh, now back aboard his own ship. *"Let us put an end to them."*

Hugh's image vanished from the viewer, and Picard breathed, "Make it so."

From then on, he was all business. "Conn, intercept course. Ready on phasers and quantum torpedoes. Transphasic torpedoes on standby."

But then the ship shuddered. "Report!"

"Forward motion falling off, Captain," Faur said. "Impulse engines are on full, but it's like we're fighting some kind of gradient. We're not going anywhere."

"The entity," Worf said.

"It's altering local spacetime," Elfiki confirmed. "Putting an asymptotic gradient between us and the Borg." Picard understood the principle: there was nothing between them and the Borg except empty space, but traveling through that small amount of space would require as much energy as traveling to the edge of the universe.

"The *Liberator*?" Picard asked.

"It's stuck right along with us."

"Reverse course, try to get around it."

But they found the same obstruction in all directions, a spherical enclosure. "Can we warp past it?"

"It's like the discontinuities, only affecting normal space, too," Elfiki said. "We can't get through it. Neither will a phaser beam, sir, if you're wondering."

"What about a transphasic torpedo?"

Choudhury answered that one. "The torpedo itself does not exist in multiple phase states, only the compression pulse it generates. The torpedo would detonate against the barrier, not penetrate it intact."

"Geordi, can you generate a subspace field to counter the effect?"

"Maybe—given a few days to study it. I'm sorry, Captain."

Picard turned to T'Ryssa. "Then it is up to you, Lieutenant. You must convince the entity to let us pass."

His words broke her out of her concentration, so he knew what she would say. "I've already been trying, Captain. But it knows we intend to destroy the Borg if we can. It isn't going to let us hurt each other."

"You must make it understand how many other lives will be lost if it does not."

"I've been trying! Captain, I've been trying for days. I just can't convince it to stand by and let the Borg die. I don't know what more I can do." She looked up at him pleadingly, wordlessly seeking his forgiveness for letting him down.

But he wasn't about to give up on her. "Maybe there is something you can do, T'Ryssa." Her eyes widened at his use of her first name. "You can help me communicate directly with the cluster entity. Speak to it myself."

She shook her head, pulling away. "No. No, you don't get it, I can't mind-meld, I never learned."

"Lieutenant." His stern tone froze her. "You have the ability within you. It is not atrophied, merely untried. It is the birthright of all Vulcans."

"But I'm not—"

"Yes, you are. Whatever else you may be, your Vulcan side is part of you too. And we need it now, T'Ryssa. I need it. Your friends aboard this ship, your friends aboard the *Rhea*—we all need you to be a Vulcan for us now."

She quashed her protests, straightening at the reminder of her obligations. But she was still suffused with doubt. "What if I can't do it? I don't even know where to begin, sir."

"You've been in communication with the entity for more than a week."

"But it's doing that, not me."

"No. You both are. You can reach me the same way you reach it."

"Are you sure, sir?"

He gave her a fatherly smile. "I have . . . some experience with melding." Indeed, his mind-meld with Ambassador Sarek had been exceptionally intimate and extended as such melds went. In a sense, a part of Sarek was still within him, and he called on it now for guidance. "I will help you."

She took a shuddering breath and nodded. "I'll tr— I'll do it, sir."

"You have the bridge, Mister Worf," he said as he guided T'Ryssa into his ready room.


It was not easy to initiate a meld when only one partner had the telepathy and only the other knew how to use it. But Picard coached T'Ryssa as best he could, instructing her how to place her hands to make contact with the primary nerve clusters in his head, and guiding her to relax and open her mind. The mental preparations for melding were not very different from the meditative techniques T'Ryssa had already learned from Choudhury, so she took to them more easily than she had feared. Picard had been thinking of calling in Lieutenant Taurik to coach her if her initial attempt failed, but he felt it was important to let her do this on her own. And before long, he sensed her presence in his mind, a vivid flame burning too hot for its own good. He felt her surprise at hearing his own thoughts, the shock of it threatening to break the tenuous link. *Calm,* he sent to her. *This is how it is supposed to be. Let it happen.*

She schooled herself to acceptance, letting the connection solidify, but he still sensed her distaste. *I feel invaded. No offense, sir . . . this is just so wrong.* But he felt the other thought echoing beneath it. *So Vulcan.*

With that thought came an image, a shadowy Vulcan figure towering over him/her, observing him/her with a cold, unforgiving gaze—a vague memory of her father, or an image constructed over the years? But the image quickly receded, faded into a related but more comforting image. A human father figure, just as stern and demanding, but in a way that felt warming and safe. A man in gray and black with a smooth, shining head.

*Me . . . a father?*

"Okay, okay," T'Ryssa said. He turned, seeing her standing next to him, hearing her as though she spoke. She blushed and kicked at an imaginary pebble with her imaginary foot. "So you're a daddy figure to me, big deal. Let's not get all Freudian about it."

"I don't know what to say." To see himself as if from a daughter's eyes . . . not only as a father but as a *good* one . . .

"Oh, don't go mushy on me, Captain! I need you to guide me through this, remember?" She frowned. "And who the hell is Meribor? And why am I blond?"

He shook it off, saw T'Ryssa again. "Never mind. We must contact the entity, we have no time to waste."

"Oh, that! It's already here." She gestured behind him.

He turned and found himself facing a large gray-white wall. Except the wall was curved and textured, and rose and fell as if . . . *breathing*.

Picard stepped back to get a fuller view of the creature in his path. It was an enormous dragon—or rather a *long,* in the Chinese tradition. "And it's a very long *long*," he heard T'Ryssa say, but he ignored her. Still, she was right—its sinuous body wrapped all around them, enclosing them. It was a beautiful creature, with a head more lupine than reptilian. Two long, whiplike whiskers extended from its snout, undulating around them as though tasting their scent. Multiple backswept horns framed its head in a starburst pattern. Along its back was a deep azure mane that rippled and flowed like storm clouds. Its eyes glinted like diamonds in the light of a young blue giant, as did the claws of the vast, four-taloned feet on which it crouched.

"This is the entity?" he asked.

"It's my current mental image of it."

"Does it choose the image, or do you?"

"My subconscious does, pretty much. It's like a dream. My mind trying to interpret the inputs, matching them with familiar images."

Picard recalled that Benjamin Sisko's reports of his encounters with the inhabitants of the Bajoran wormhole had detailed a similar effect: visitors to their continuum had seen its occupants as people they knew in scenes from their memories, their brains struggling to impose some familiar order on profoundly alien inputs. But at least those aliens had been able to communicate in a way the humanoid brain could understand as speech. From T'Ryssa's reports, all her communication with the entity was nonverbal.

"Will it at least be able to understand me?" he asked.

"What matters is the ideas, not how you convey them." Her voice had taken on a new power and formality, and perhaps a touch of a European accent like his own. As he turned to her again, he found her image had changed once more. Now she was attired in green and brown leather, the sort of garb he hadn't seen since Q had sent him and his crew to a mythical Sherwood Forest. She bore a quiver over her shoulder and leaned nonchalantly on a longbow. There was a rakish confidence in her stance that he hadn't seen in her since entering this illusion. He noticed that her hair was swept back behind her ears, their elegant points openly displayed. He realized that in her fantasy image of herself, she was half elf, not half Vulcan. Here, as an elven ranger, she wore her pointed ears proudly. "Talking is how you frame ideas best, Captain. So talk."

He moved forward to face the elegant head that was larger than he was. The diamond eyes watched him patiently. "I am Captain Jean-Luc Picard, representing the United Federation of Planets. It is urgent that I speak with you. Do you understand me?"

The dragon simply looked at him. Nothing changed. "It already knows what you are, Captain," said Trys the elf, "and the labels mean nothing to it. It knows you're eager to communicate, or you wouldn't be here. Get to the point." She was more poised and confident here than he'd ever seen her. This was her realm, after all. He realized there was grass beneath their feet, great sequoialike trees visible over the dragon's billowing mane.

"You must allow us to pass . . ." He faltered. "What do I call it?" It was awkward for him to address a being respectfully when he had no title to apply to it.

Trys cocked her head. "Try Qing Long. The Azure Dragon of the East. We're in its tail, after all." She gestured up, and he realized she wasn't referring to their present position in the illusion. Above him was a night sky as seen from Earth, centered on NGC 6281. In the Western tradition, that cluster was in the constellation Scorpius, but in Chinese astronomical terms, it was in the Tail mansion of the Azure Dragon. Perhaps, he realized, T'Ryssa's awareness of that fact had influenced her perception of the entity here.

He turned his gaze back to the dragon. "You must allow us to pass, Qing Long. I understand and respect the compassion that leads you to protect the Borg—the collective mind that seeks to join with you." In his imagination, he perceived a cluster of Borg drones on the other side of Qing Long's body, trying to abscond with an egg from its nest. In this mental realm, he could see it even though it was behind the dragon from his line of sight. Qing Long's whole body seemed to grow cloudy, translucent, without losing any of its solidity.

"And it is that compassion that I appeal to now. If you do not allow us to prevent the Borg from gaining your knowledge, then they will corrupt that knowledge. They will use it to destroy other beings throughout the galaxy." Beyond Qing Long, a plague of black nanotechnology spread out from the nest at lightning speed. The forest withered and died. Only within the Azure Dragon's compass did the grass remain green and healthy. "I know you would not wish to be responsible for such a tragedy. You must prevent them from joining with you, Qing Long. It is the only way."

Still eerily silent, the great dragon moved its head closer to Picard, transfixing him with its diamantine eyes. In those eyes, he saw a vision—a vision that soon engulfed him. He had no body, no physical location, but he saw a ship in space, illuminated by the light of a hundred blue suns. He saw it land upon a reddish-brown world with tarry black seas and a dense, smoggy atmosphere, disgorging small moving things that wandered about its surface, investigating. He felt confusion at this unknown, dealt with the unprecedented the only way he knew how: by embracing it. The entity (for that was whose memory he now shared) had burned with curiosity, eager to learn what it had encountered and what it meant. It had sensed emanations from them, had altered the nature of spacetime in their vicinity to amplify those emanations.

But it had not understood something. Their bodies as well as their telepathic minds had reacted to the change in the laws of physics. It had learned to sense their thoughts, and what it had sensed had been agony, terror, the slow dissolution of the mind and will as their bodies gradually disintegrated. The entity's first contact with other life-forms had been its first contact with death, with pain, with loss. It had felt the pain of those it had killed, and had known guilt and remorse.

And it had resolved never to feel those things again. From then on, it had been cautious and delicate in its infrequent interactions with other life-forms. It had patiently allowed them to seek ways to communicate with it. It had offered no protest when they had given up and left. When they had attempted to do harm, it had tenderly carried them out of reach.

And it had resolved never to be responsible for taking life again. It could not bear the pain.

Picard could not help but understand. When you spent most of your existence alone with your thoughts, how could you bear to live with guilt? When visitors were a rare and precious gift, how could you bear to do them harm?

He lowered his gaze from the piercing blue stars and found himself looking at Qing Long again, the elven Trys beside him. "I understand your commitment to peace," he told the dragon. "I revere it. But that is why you must prevent the Borg from escaping with the knowledge they are acquiring from you. If you permit their escape, you will be culpable for death on a scale even you cannot imagine. I know you do not want that."

The Azure Dragon glanced at the galaxy that floated beside Picard, a galaxy that was dimming under the creeping shadow of assimilation. Picard looked in Qing Long's eyes, seeing the galaxy reflected in one, himself in the other. "It doesn't acknowledge the difference," Trys said. "It's one, and it's legion. Numbers don't have meaning to it. It can't see trillions as being more than dozens."

The reflection of Picard spoke. *"I refuse to let arithmetic decide questions like that!"* They were his own words, spoken years ago in rejection of the idea that Wesley Crusher's death was justified for the good of a greater number. How could he now argue the opposite?

But how could he not?

"You do not understand, Qing Long. The entities you wish to protect . . . they have already been lost. They are trapped in a horror far worse than the one you showed me." He shared his memories of assimilation, of watching helplessly as the Borg used his knowledge to slaughter thousands of fellow officers at Wolf 359. "I know that they would gladly give their lives to prevent the horror they will otherwise be forced to unleash—and to free themselves from the ordeal they now endure."

Qing Long's whiskers multiplied in number, and now there was a Noh Angel at the tip of each one, floating in midair and gazing upon him, surrounding him. "Numbers again," the she-elf said. "The one and the many are the same. It knows the parts aren't what they were, but that doesn't change the right of the whole to exist."

Picard stared at the dragon, struggling to think of some way to reach it. What argument could he offer that it *would* understand? What concepts, what values, did it share with humanoids? Compassion was a nonstarter. Curiosity? Curiosity . . .

He looked at T'Ryssa, remembering how she had looked at him. "Children. Procreation—the entity is fascinated by it. Why?"

The elf pondered the question. "Because it senses there's something different about it. Something more than a self creating extensions of itself.

Some way that the many and the one are *not* the same."

He turned back to the dragon. "You're right about that, Qing Long. Our children . . . they are so much more than extensions of ourselves. They take what we give them and add to it. Transform it into something unique and new." He looked to either side, and there was Batai, there was Meribor. He gazed at them, and for the first time in eleven years was able to contemplate them without pain, for their presence here meant that they would always be a part of him.

"Yes, they are a part of me," he told Qing Long, sensing its confusion. "But they were so much more. They became their own people, lived lives that were full and unique, if all too brief. They created new lives of their own, and if given the chance, those new lives would have carried on the cycle in their turn.

"That is procreation. It is the fundamental process of life itself—always growing, always changing. Always giving birth to something new that the universe has never seen before. You yourself were born of processes that, so far as we know, have never created life before. But life always expands, always grows. Its very nature is the process of *becoming.* Of going beyond previous limits and fulfilling new potentials. That is life.

"And that is why the Borg are *not* life. The Collective does not procreate. It does not spawn new life or new possibilities. All it does is to absorb other lives into a stagnant, uniform mass. It strips away everything that makes them unique. And it takes away their ability to give birth to new life, new uniqueness.

"The Borg are antilife, Qing Long. They are anathema to everything you and I believe in. If they win, there will be no more birth. No more parents. No more families."

The dragon shifted uncomfortably, its claws kneading the grass. Its body grew cloudy again, thinning to fog but remaining a barrier around them. A taloned foot on the far side of its body reached toward the drones that stood there, but froze in place, unable to contract around them. "Resistance is futile," one of them said in Locutus's voice.

"It can't do it," Trys said, leaning forward on her longbow. "It understands what's at stake . . . it just can't bring itself to strike. Despite what the Borg are, it still can't deny them their right to be."

"Then let us do it," he pleaded. "Release our vessels from confinement, allow us to engage the Borg."

Qing Long's head shook convulsively as it struggled with doubt. Its whiskers—back to two now—lashed through the air, their cloudy substance passing unfelt through Picard and Trys. "It's not working," he muttered.

T'Ryssa's eyes darted around. She leaned in close to him. "Can I try something, sir?"

"If you think it will help."

She stepped forward. "Hey, Qingy! C'mere." Picard still saw Trys the elf, but in voice and manner she was now the T'Ryssa he knew. She gestured with a hand, and the dragon lowered its head to listen. It was smaller now, and she was able to drape an arm over its neck and lean in to whisper in its deerlike ear. "You know . . . you won't really be destroying anything if you let this happen." The head moved uneasily. "No, really! Listen. You see those guys?" Picard followed her gesture to see Hugh, Rebekah Grabowski, and Seven of Nine standing in a cluster. This being T'Ryssa's mind, of course, it wasn't as simple as that; Rebekah was looking on in annoyance as Hugh ogled Seven's caricatured figure. "They're what happens when you hurt the Borg. Bring down the Collective, and you free . . . mm, more than a few drones." She cleared her throat. "Numbers don't matter, right? You'll free a lot of them, that's what matters.

"And once they're free, they'll be able to procreate again. But they'll still be Borg. They'll still carry the knowledge and identity of the Collective with them—just like children carry on the knowledge and genes of their parents. And the free drones will be able to take that knowledge and add to it, evolve it into something new. And they can pass that on to their children so it can grow and evolve even further.

"Think of it, Qingy! All those different freed drones, from all those different cultures. Spreading out all over the galaxy." She swept her arm, and the darkness over Picard's miniature galaxy broke up and coalesced into branching streams that flowed and collided, erupting at the points of contact into prismatic bursts of fireworks, flowers, balloons. "Imagine all the different forms the knowledge and culture of the Borg will evolve into!"

Picard ran his hand over his pate. *Good Lord, what have I unleashed?*

"So you've got it all wrong, my friend," T'Ryssa went on in oily tones. "We don't want to *destroy* the Collective. We just want to help it . . . you know . . . undergo mitosis. Yeah, that's it! You wouldn't be hurting the Borg, you'd be helping them reproduce! Giving them the wonderful gift of procreation. And all you have to do is step back and let us do our thing. Okay?"

Picard stared at her in dismay. This was her great negotiating strategy? To wheedle and deceive? To attempt to trick the entity into compliance? Perhaps he'd misjudged her fantasy image—not so much an elf as an imp.

But the dragon was even smaller now and rising to its feet. Nuzzling T'Ryssa with its head like a friendly horse, it locked eyes with Picard in acknowledgment before launching itself into the air and flying skyward. It continued to circle the vicinity, its sinuous body rippling through the air like a banner blown loose in the wind, but it no longer obstructed them.

Picard folded his arms and gazed sternly at T'Ryssa, but the she-elf spread her arms and said, "Hey, it worked, didn't it?"

He sighed. "As a rule, Lieutenant, I don't approve

of bald-faced lying as a negotiating strategy." He spoke softly and kept his attention focused on her, hoping to ensure privacy.

"Hey, I didn't lie, exactly," T'Ryssa insisted. "There's . . . well, a *degree* of truth to what I said." He kept staring. "Look, it's too alien to understand humanoid concepts of truth." He stared some more. "Which . . . aren't really absolute anyway. So I . . ." She glared at him. "Look, you were interpreting the truth too! Saying whatever you thought would persuade it best."

Picard shook his head. "We will need to talk about the difference between persuasive speaking and manipulation. But in the meantime, I cannot argue with results. We have a battle to fight, so we really must get back to reality."

"Okay." She looked around. "Um . . . where's the door?"

"Wait," he said, glancing skyward. "Before we leave, I have one more request for the Azure Dragon."

# 11

—

When Picard and T'Ryssa returned to the bridge, they found the barrier still in the process of dissipating; it was taking longer in reality than it had in their dreamscape. But it had given the Borg time to respond to their presence. "The *Frankenstein* is on the other side of the barrier," Worf reported, "ready to attack once it becomes passable."

"Then we shall have to attack first," the captain said. "Picard to *Liberator*. Stand by."

*"Acknowledged,"* came Hugh's voice.

Looking for an edge, Picard turned to his science officer. "Lieutenant, what would happen, theoretically, if we fired a quantum torpedo at the spatial barrier now?"

"There's still a substantial gradient. It wouldn't penetrate."

"I'm aware of that. What *would* it do?"

Elfiki thought for a second. "It would thrust forward without getting very far. Like trying to climb an ever-steeper slope."

"But what happens when that slope flattens out?"

Her dark eyes widened. "All that built-up potential energy becomes kinetic all at once!" She turned to her console. "Give me a moment, I'll compute the best timing and send it to tactical."

"Make it so, Lieutenant," he said, resolving to cite her efficiency in his formal report. "Good work."

"It'll be tricky," she demurred. "If our estimate of the rate of collapse is off—"

"The more unpredictable, the better, if we hope to take the Borg by surprise."

"Computing their probable evasive patterns," Choudhury reported. "Calculating optimal torpedo spread."

"Barrier collapse accelerating," Elfiki warned.

Choudhury stared intently at her readout for a second and hit the firing button, not waiting to recompute. "Torpedoes away."

On-screen, four quantum torpedoes shot out and slowed as their micro-impulse thrusters strained against the invisible potential barrier. Beyond, the *Frankenstein* had already begun an evasive course change, based on the torpedoes' expected trajectories. But the spatial distortion threw off those calculations. A moment later, the torpedoes began to gain ground again, then shot forward with remarkable speed as the barrier finally collapsed. Picard blinked and thereby missed the impact of two torpedoes with the Borg ship, striking it before it had time to dodge. Choudhury's instincts had proved sound, which was no more than Picard had expected. The torpedoes' added kinetic energy gave them an extra kick. The other two torpedoes missed—naturally, for they had been fired to cover the other most likely evasive path—and went flying far out of range before they could decelerate and double back.

But Picard wasted no time absorbing the result. "Both ships, continuous fire!" Together, *Enterprise* and *Liberator* hammered at the weakened section of *Frankenstein*'s shields until the vessel flipped over to shelter it. The two allied ships arced around the Borg in a pincer maneuver, trying to come at it from both sides. Out here, in interplanetary space, the mechanics of planetary orbit did not hamper their trajectories.

Of course, space was still three-dimensional, so the Borg could easily enough escape the pincer maneuver by thrusting perpendicular to the plane shared by its attackers, keeping its weakened shield section away from both of them as they peppered its other side with phaser and disruptor fire.

But then, just as Choudhury had planned it, those two prodigal torpedoes caught up with the battle and slammed right into the weakened section of the shields. The pincer movement had been a ploy; by arcing slightly "above" the *Frankenstein* relative to the plane of the system, they had ensured it would thrust "down" in the direction that would allow the torpedoes to catch up with it. Picard gave a grim smile. "Your chess game is improving, Lieutenant."

"Thanks to your tutelage, Captain."

Worf glowered, no doubt reminded that he was still losing to her at poker on a weekly basis. "Just so long as we do not do *too* well in this battle. We only want to make it look convincing."

"No worries on that account, sir," Choudhury said. "The targeted section had time to regenerate. Damage is minimal." The ship rocked. "And as expected, they've focused on *Enterprise* as the immediate threat. This is going to get rough."

The *Frankenstein* thrust hard toward *Enterprise*, firing continuously at it while directing a more limited barrage at the *Liberator* to keep it at bay, forcing distance between the ships. Or trying to. The *Liberator* continued to close relentlessly, its pilot ignoring the pounding it was taking.

But *Enterprise* was getting it much harder. Faur evaded as best she could, swerving and rotating the ship to spread out the impact on the shields as before. But there was a limit to how far she could manage that. The *Frankenstein* was thrusting continuously, accelerating toward *Enterprise* on full impulse, forcing the Starfleet vessel to keep thrusting as well to maintain distance from it. That meant the ship essentially had to keep its aft (and its impulse engine vents) toward the enemy, unable to fly backward as it could if coasting on momentum or traveling at thruster speeds. As such, the rear half of the shield envelope took a greater pounding. "Aft shields down to fifty-eight per-cent," Choudhury warned after a particularly shud-dering blow.

"Redirect power aft," Picard ordered. If the shields fell too far, the Borg transporters would be able to penetrate them. "Maximum cover fire."

But the tail end of the ship continued to take a pounding as the battling vessels thrust farther and faster out from the ecliptic plane. The Borg's own forward shields absorbed *Enterprise*'s fire, but held stronger, continuing to adapt to the conditions they faced. Picard had to admit there were aspects of Borg technology whose inclusion in Starfleet's repertoire would be welcome. "Aft shields down to forty-seven percent!" Choudhury called.

That was when the *Liberator* made its move. Still closing in relentlessly, it gave an extra burst of impulse to put it on a trajectory that took it between *Enterprise* and the Borg ship, then vec-tored reverse thrust to hold it there, bodily shield-ing the Starfleet vessel. The *Frankenstein* pounded it nonstop, altering its vector to veer around the obstruction, but *Liberator*'s pilot matched its every move, ensuring that his ship continued to take a pounding. Its shields flickered, failing; phaser beams and plasma bolts tore through its armored skin and blasted gouts of debris and incandescent atmosphere into space.

"Picard to Hugh!" the captain called. "Do you require assistance?"

Hugh's image appeared on the viewscreen. The

ex-drone looked battered but unbowed as sparks erupted all around him. *"Negative,* Enterprise! *Save yourselves!* Liberator *will hold them off! I swear as leader of the Liberated that we will never succumb to the Borg again!"*

As his image dissolved in static, Kadohata winced. "Ooh, he overplayed it a mite, don't you think?"

"Let's just hope they haven't assimilated any drama critics," T'Ryssa replied.

As the *Liberator*'s impulse engines failed, the ship "fell behind"—still moving forward at a steady velocity, of course, but no longer accelerating to match *Enterprise*'s increasing speed. *Here's where we see if they take the bait,* Picard thought, gripping the arms of his seat.

Indeed, the *Frankenstein* stopped accelerating and paced the crippled *Liberator.* "Detecting transporter activity," Kadohata reported grimly.

Picard nodded. "Farewell, Hugh," he whispered. "And thank you."


*Liberator*


Hugh stood to meet the drones as they materialized before him. They were not like the Borg he remembered—their implants were sleeker and more silvery, their movements more fluid, their eyes more alert. They had advanced in ways that the rest of the Collective could not be allowed to share. More than ever, Hugh resolved that this must end now.

"You're too late," he told them as their lively eyes darted around the empty bridge. "My people have escaped to *Enterprise*."

One of the drones faced him. "No transporter activity was detected."

He shook his head. "Borg have so little imagination."

"Imagination is irrelevant. Interrogation is also irrelevant." Hugh gasped as the assimilation tubules pierced his flesh. "Third of Five. Secondary Processor of Peripheral Matrix One Zero One One. Welcome home."

Hugh wanted to scream but strove to discipline his thoughts. In moments, his mind would be accessible to them. He needed to close it to them, keep them from discovering the secret he carried. Doctor Crusher had modified his neurochemistry to mimic that of Rebekah and the other Zeros, allowing him to dissociate his awareness, partitioning his recent memories into a corner of his brain that the Borg would be unable to read. It might be unnecessary; as a rule, the Borg paid little attention to the thoughts and memories of those they assimilated. But with these shrewder Borg, it paid to take precautions.

And it meant that, in a way, Rebekah would still be with him at the end.

Detached, the remaining part of his awareness watched as the Borg transported him back aboard their ship. Nanotechnological growths were already sprouting across his body, newer, sleeker implants than before. But the drones led him to a surgical alcove to perform more macroscopic alterations. His partitioned mind did not hear their thoughts, but he expected that they would begin to upgrade his outdated implants.

But none of that mattered now. As they plugged him into the alcove, he became connected with the system. The Trojan horse was through the gates. Now it was only a matter of time.

He only hoped it would not be too much time.


*Enterprise*


As much as Picard hated leaving Hugh to face his fate alone, doing so was the only way to make his sacrifice worthwhile. So as soon as the *Liberator* fell to the Borg, *Enterprise,* with the remaining Liberated aboard as they had been since before the battle began, made a warp microjump to bring it close to the sixth planet. The ship emerged from warp still carrying the realspace momentum it had picked up in the pursuit, threatening to hurtle past the planet, so Faur spun the ship around and thrust at maximum impulse to brake into orbit.

"Take us in over the borehole," Picard ordered, "as low as you can." It was an easy mark to aim for, since a plume of dust and vapor still rose from the recently completed excavation, now wrapped around a vast swath of the planet by upper-atmospheric winds. The borehole itself was the bull's-eye of a vast crater in the icy crust of the planet, a crater that sparkled, for much of the graphite mantle beneath the ice had been fused to diamond by the heat of the Borg drilling beam.

As soon as the ship was in position, Picard turned to his right and nodded to Choudhury. "Fire."

Two quantum torpedoes spat from *Enterprise* and plummeted down the shaft toward the Borg emplacement at its base. Beside Picard, T'Ryssa winced in anticipation; she had assured him that the entity would not be significantly harmed by the destruction of a small portion of its brain, certainly no more so than it already had by the assimilation process, but even she could not be sure whether this would cause the entity pain.

But it proved a moot point. "Detonations!" Choudhury called. "Too soon!" Moments later, a tongue of plasma shot out of the borehole, the backfire from the torpedoes' detonation.

"Report!"

"A barrier materialized in the shaft," Kadohata said after a moment. "It's made of construct material," she went on in a heavy voice. "Particle-synthesized."

"Oh, no," T'Ryssa said. "They're getting its knowledge!"

"Concentrate, Lieutenant," Picard reminded her. "Make sure the entity is standing by." She nodded and regained her inner focus.

But Worf's attention remained on the immediate crisis. "This must end before they obtain slip-stream!"

"*Frankenstein* incoming!" Choudhury called, and a second later the ship rocked as phaser fire strafed the shields.

"Return fire! Evasive action!" But *Enterprise*'s phasers splashed against particle-synthesized ablative armor that regenerated continuously, just as the cluster entity's containment shell had done.

Picard cursed his mission parameters as more Borg fire blasted the shields. The multivector agent was of limited use as a tactical weapon; the time it required to infiltrate the Borg's systems made it most effective as a long-term stealth weapon, one with a latency period of days or weeks to allow it to spread as far as possible before it struck. Perhaps one day, if Starfleet's slipstream experiments bore fruit, a ship could deliver the MVA to the Delta Quadrant and take down the Borg once and for all. But in a case like this, the efficacy of this so-called ultimate weapon was more limited. Beverly had calibrated the time-release agent with a short fuse, so to speak—just long enough to spread through the *Frankenstein* and then begin doing its work. But in the interim, Picard had no choice but to prolong the battle and wait. It would be easier just to fire a transphasic torpedo and have done with it; indeed, if he had done so six days ago, Hugh would not have needed to sacrifice himself now.

But then, he reminded himself, the weapon that

might finally bring down the Borg in the long term would never have been tested. The circumstances of that test may have been far from ideal, but in the long run, the test had to proceed, no matter the cost.

The ship rocked again, sparks flying from the consoles. "Dorsal shields at thirty-eight percent," Choudhury said.

*We have Third of Five,* the Borg chorus spoke in Picard's mind. *Now we come for Locutus.*

Picard shot to his feet and drew his phaser, knowing what was coming. With a familiar hissing whine, three drones materialized around him, one directly before him and two to the sides. He had his phaser against the first one's head before it was fully materialized and fired instantly, not giving it time to raise its personal shield. *Thanks for the warning,* he told the voices in his head as the drone, now lacking a head of its own, fell to the deck.

Worf had reacted almost as quickly, placing himself between the captain and the drone to starboard and reaching back to draw his *mek'leth,* the ornate short sword he had tucked in his baldric in anticipation of just such an occurrence. He swung at the drone, but it blocked the sword with an armored forearm and deployed a blade of its own from the other, slashing across Worf's chest; only the metal baldric saved him.

At the same time, the drone on Picard's left strode toward him, its own shields deflecting his phaser fire. He was backed up against Worf, sur-

rounded by consoles and chairs. *Bad bridge design,*
Picard decided as the drone loomed . . .

As a rule, Rennan Konya hated violence. He had
gone into security because he had believed that his
unique brand of "body empathy" and the edge it
gave him in unarmed combat could serve a purpose
by letting him protect people in need. He had
understood that his job would sometimes require
the use of force, even lethal force, but he had
hoped his abilities would help him defuse most situations before they got that far.

And that had often been the case. By sensing
hostile moves the moment they began to be made,
he had often been able to preempt them. By judging
his opponents' body state, he had been able to
judge exactly where and how to strike to incapacitate them with minimal injury. And though he
lacked the full telepathy of most Betazoids, his
ability to read emotions and the gist of surface
thoughts had often tipped him off to danger or
helped him make a connection with someone who
didn't need to be an enemy.

But then there were times like this. Times when
there was no choice but to harden his heart and try
with all his might to end the lives of other sentient
beings. The first time had been four years ago
aboard the *da Vinci,* when a mission in pursuit of a
rogue Vorta had pitted his security team against her
Jem'Hadar enforcer. The genetically engineered

warrior had proved remarkably resistant to phaser fire, and Konya had been left with no alternative than to deliver a lethal phaser barrage to save his shipmates. He had remained stoic about it then, trying to absorb the cold detachment of his battle-hardened chief, Domenica Corsi. And he had told himself afterward that Jem'Hadar had short lives anyway, that they were little more than killing machines bred as cannon fodder. But he had had nightmares about it for years. Weak telepathy or no, he had felt the Jem'Hadar soldier die; he knew it had been more than a machine.

Battling the Borg now, as the team he led struggled to keep them from taking over main engineering, was at once easier and harder. He felt next to nothing from these drones; despite their lively, alert behavior in battle, despite the awareness and purpose that seemed to shine from their eyes, their minds were a blank to him, and he could get only a limited somatic sense from them. (He was still trying to sort out a new name for his ability. For years he had called it "proprioception," until Bart Faulwell, *da Vinci*'s resident linguist, had finally grown tired of it, taken him privately aside, and explained to him that the "proprio-" prefix meant "one's own"; his power was to tap into *others'* proprioception, their awareness of their own bodily position and motion. So much for his favorite fancy word.) It made it easier to detach himself, to see them as enemies rather than people and shoot to kill. But intellectually, he knew that many of these

Borg had once been fellow Starfleet personnel, that all of them were hostages, as Chief Choudhury would say. It tore at him that he couldn't find a way to incapacitate or restrain them safely. His Betazoid senses told him they were walking corpses, but those senses were highly limited; who knew what he might be missing?

Nearby, Lieutenant Taurik interposed himself between a drone and the console that controlled the annular force field around the warp core. The drone slashed at him and he fell, injured. Ensign Vogel dove into the fray and wrestled with the drone, ultimately driving its own arm blade into its neck, but not before sustaining serious, life-threatening injury himself. Konya winced, trying to shut out his perception of their pain, and realized there was something he could do after all. The somatosensory cortex of the brain, the part responsible for proprioception, was also responsible for nociception, the awareness of pain. Concentrating, he sent sharp spikes of pain through their somatosensory cortices, causing them both a momentary flash of agony but temporarily overloading their pain reception and leaving them numb—as much to protect himself as to help them. In Vogel's case, it was enough to make him lose consciousness a few moments sooner than otherwise.

*I wonder,* Konya thought. *How would Borg drones react to a surge of pain?* No doubt their senses were dulled, the input suppressed; but if his ability could let him "hack" past that suppression and reactivate their pain reception, what would it do? Best case, it could cause them incapacitating but physically harmless pain and drop them where they stood. He doubted he'd get that lucky, but at least it might cause some mental static and interfere with their cybernetic control.

*Oh, who am I kidding?* He was no science officer. He might as well just try it. Concentrating on the nearest drone, he tried to perform his usual pain-spike trick, but with a slower buildup, to keep the cortex from overloading. Chief Corsi had tried to get him to develop this trick as a form of mental attack, but he had resisted; not only did he find it borderline sadistic, but he would've felt every bit of the pain that he inflicted. That had been the deal breaker; even Corsi wasn't enough of a martinet to order him to throw himself on his own bed of nails. But here, it would be worth the pain to himself and might even help the person who'd been turned into this drone.

But all that happened was that the drone paused and jerked around slightly, as though distracted by a minor irritation. Still, Konya hoped there might be a less visible effect. He fired his phaser rifle at the drone. Its shield went up, but it was weaker than usual. He poured on the fire while intensifying his concentration. Finally, the shield flickered and the phaser beam tore through the drone, felling it.

Konya sagged, as much from fatigue and shared pain as regret at failing to save a hostage. The mental exertion had taken a lot out of him, and for very little gain.

But that left the physical. Even with little proprio—body empathy—whatever from these drones, he still had an intuitive understanding of how the humanoid body moved and reacted. Surely he could find these drones' weak points without needing to feel them from the inside. It would just be like fighting blindfolded, relying on his other senses.

Sure, he would probably get killed in the process. But he'd known that the moment the Borg had materialized in engineering. What mattered was that he did what he could to protect his crew.

Although, as he charged into the fray, he wondered if Trys would miss him much. He knew he would miss her a great deal.

As one drone closed on Picard, Choudhury fired on the one Worf was battling, but its shields were in place. She vaulted over her console and kicked it in the head, snapping it forward. Worf got a grip on its head and twisted, finishing the job.

Unfortunately, their battle blocked Picard's retreat from the other drone. But suddenly, T'Ryssa leaped onto its back and held on, kicking futilely at its legs and pulling at its arms. For whatever reason, the Borg's personal shields deflected only energy or particle beams, not solid matter; that was one limitation these upgraded Borg had not overcome. Still, the drone's strength was too great for T'Ryssa to overcome. So she quickly changed tactics, clamping her hands over its eyes. "Hey, tin man!" she cried. "Your mama was a fembot!"

Picard took the opportunity to act, tackling the blinded drone in the abdomen. Combined with T'Ryssa's weight on its back, that was enough to knock it off its feet. Trys hit the deck first, though, yelping in pain, and the yelp modulated to a curt shriek as the drone's head landed in her lap. But she recovered quickly. "Hey, buy me dinner first!" she protested and wrapped her legs around its neck, trying to pin it in place. The drone's assimilation tubules shot from its fists, and Picard, lying atop its body, grabbed its wrists and held them against the deck with all his might. But it threw him off with a convulsive move of its legs and torso, and when Picard brought his head around again, he could only watch in horror as the tubules plunged into T'Ryssa's calf. "Aww, *shit*! Not again!" she gasped as more drones materialized around the bridge.

"The hell with this," Picard said. "Target transphasic torpedoes on the *Frankenstein* and fire!"

"No, wait!" Kadohata cried. He turned to stare at her in shock, but she was gesturing toward the Borg. Indeed, the drones were beginning to stagger and move aimlessly. One by one, they sagged and fell to the deck. "The MVA must be working! We did it!"

But there was no time for celebration. Picard

moved to T'Ryssa's side. "Lieutenant, are you still with us?"

She was panting hard, eyes unfocused as though listening, waiting. "I . . . I think so, sir."

"It's time. Tell the entity." She looked at him in confusion. He hated to do it to the terrified child, but he put on his command voice and barked, "Now, Lieutenant! *Now!*"

T'Ryssa jerked as though slapped, but then she nodded and closed her eyes. Picard glanced up at the screen, where the *Frankenstein* drifted, rotating slowly before the backdrop of the damaged ice planet. Even with the advance warning T'Ryssa had given it, would the cluster entity react quickly enough?

Moments later, an alarm sounded on the ops console. "Slipstream incursion," Kadohata reported. Then, a second later, with surprise and relief, "It's *Rhea!*"

"Picard to Crusher," he called. "Go on Operation *Rhea*."

"Acknowleged," Beverly said. "All right, people, we've got incoming!" The entire medical staff mobilized at once, following the plan she had drilled into them over the past week. *Rhea*'s crew had been frozen in midbattle and midassimilation; saving them would require split-second timing and surgery on a major scale. Fortunately, this *Enterprise* had been equipped with combat in mind and

thus had a massive triage center adjacent to sickbay, large enough to receive over a hundred casualties at a time. Cargo Bay 4 was also standing by to
receive additional casualties as needed. "Bridge,
confirm, the MVA worked?"

*"Affirmative on MVA,"* Jean-Luc's voice replied.
Beverly was relieved. The plan, of course, had been
contingent on the multivector agent doing its job.
Picard had discussed his intentions with her before
the battle; presumably at this very moment, the
cluster entity had delivered the *Luna*-class starship
to the vicinity and released it from stasis, so that
the Borg drones and nanoprobes now aboard it
would be instantly affected by the Endgame virus
the MVA was propagating through the Collective's
interlink network. They wouldn't be affected by the
hormonal agent or the anti-Borg nanites, of course,
but just the computer virus should be enough to
shut them down, ensuring that the medical team
would not be under attack from the very people
they were trying to save. The plan had been that
the rescue effort would not be undertaken unless the
MVA had been deployed and the virus activated,
but under the circumstances, Beverly had felt it
prudent to make sure. She just prayed that the necessary lag time to ensure the Endgame virus had its
effect would not cost them the precious seconds
they needed to save someone's life.

Moments later, transporter chimes filled the
room as Kadohata on the bridge ran a program that
locked onto every remaining sentient life-form on

*Rhea,* even the faintest, and beamed the ones showing signs of injury or assimilation to the triage center or the cargo bay. Her team immediately moved
in to identify the priority patients. *"We have
injured crew of our own as well, Doctor,"* Picard
said. *"They're on their way to you."*

"Acknowledged." They would be triaged alongside the *Rhea* survivors and treated in accordance
with the severity of their injuries.

*"We also have inactive drones. Estimate eight
living."*

"As long as they're stable, they can wait." She
would do what she could for them in their turn,
but a fair percentage of *Rhea*'s crew was spilling
blood on the sickbay deck at the moment.

She, Doctor Tropp, and the others proceeded
efficiently, having been hardened to such massive
operations during the Dominion War. They had
good help, too; the entire medical staff of the *Liberator* was here to assist, eager to deprive the Borg of
any more victims. Beverly also knew she could rely
on sickbay's Emergency Medical Hologram, which
could work faster and more exactingly than any of
them. The latest model was even likable, taking the
form of a soft-spoken young woman with straw-
blond hair, a gentle, slightly sad face, and none of
the arrogance or quirks of the earlier models. When
she'd "met" the new model, Beverly had been
pleased that Doctor Zimmerman, the head of the
EMH design team, had finally been persuaded to

enter the third millennium and acknowledge that there was such a thing as a female doctor. But she'd been more impressed by the EMH Mark IX's surgical abilities—not to mention her capacity to duplicate herself and perform more than one surgery at a time. That function put a strain on computer resources, limiting the amount of selves available to "Nina" (as the Mark IX had been nicknamed) at any given time. But Beverly hoped matters had calmed down enough outside that extra processor time could be allocated to sickbay.

Because it would be a long time before things calmed down in here.


"*Rhea* survivors are all aboard, sir," Kadohata reported.

Picard nodded. "Grand."

"Umm . . . what about me, sir?" T'Ryssa asked.

"Do you feel any ill effects?" he asked, looking over her paternally.

"Well, I think I'm gonna throw up . . . but that's probably not nanoprobe related."

He smiled. "Look at it this way. You're probably the only person ever to be injected with Borg nanoprobes and be spared assimilation *twice.* Another record for you to commemorate."

She looked up at him with gratitude. "I still haven't gotten the plaque for the first one."

"Noted."

"Sir!" Choudhury called. "Energy buildup on the *Frankenstein.* Its containment is failing—core breach is imminent."

He turned to the viewer. "Can we lock onto Hugh? Or any of the drones aboard?"

"No, sir," Kadohata said. "No detectable life signs."

Picard closed his eyes briefly. *More of our own we must lose. Let them be the last.* "Conn, take us to a safe distance."

The *Frankenstein*—the ship that had once been the science vessel *Einstein,* and maybe half a dozen alien ships besides—receded from view, and then the planet itself began to shrink away. Moments later, a brilliant white flare shone briefly over the planet's surface, reflected thousands of times over in the diamond-flecked crater that had been burned in the planet.

Picard stared at the brief, bright star as it faded away and spoke in a whisper. "Farewell, Hugh. Your sacrifice will not be forgotten."

# 12

---

Trys had gotten off easy in the guilt department. For two months, she had lived in dread that Ensign Janyl, the Tormandar crewwoman assigned to the console duty that should have been her own, had been killed by the Borg. But now it turned out that Janyl had barely sustained a scratch; if anything, her assignment to a low-priority station had protected her, making her section one of the last the Borg had reached. Trys had still apologized profusely, but Janyl had assured her it was just as well their positions had not been reversed; her Lyentha faith would have compelled her to submit to a lengthy period of fasting and purification rituals if she had been the one to be seen unclothed in public.

But all was not entirely well. Dawn Blair had

been badly injured while protecting the three children who were part of *Rhea*'s complement. Her heart had actually stopped, and if not for the split-second timing and efficient work of Doctor Crusher's team, she would have gone from clinically to permanently dead. As it was, she remained in critical condition, though Crusher was confident that she would pull through. And all three children were safe and well, thanks to her courage.

Overall, nearly a third of *Rhea*'s crew—just over a hundred people—had been killed by the Borg before the entity had frozen the ship. Roughly eighty more had been saved from serious or life-threatening injuries in the marathon surgical session, and another sixty-odd, whom the Borg had judged worthy of assimilation for whatever reason, were stabilized and waiting to have their implants removed. Ironically, though, many of them would require bionic organs to replace ones that had been damaged or lost.

Captain Bazel was one of those in the last category. As with many of the others, the "half-grown" status of many of the Borg implants in his body left them unable to take over the functions of the organs they had shoved aside and damaged. But his Saurian anatomy gave him enough redundancy to remain marginally functional despite that. So while T'Ryssa sat vigil by Commander Blair's bedside, she overheard (those darn Vulcan ears) Bazel insisting, over Crusher's objections, on getting out of bed and making the rounds of sickbay to instill confidence in his crew. After making his slow but steady way across sickbay, greeting and encouraging the patients who were conscious, he eventually reached Blair's bedside and spoke to T'Ryssa. "I wanted to thank you for the fine job you did, Lieutenant Chen. You didn't give up on us. And it's thanks to you that we're alive right now."

She felt her cheeks flush. "I wouldn't go that far, sir. If I hadn't brought the *Enterprise* here, you'd just still be in stasis."

"Which would have just been suspended death, not life. The entity would never have made its choice without your skills at communication." He tilted his head to study her. "I must admit, we underestimated you on *Rhea*, Lieutenant. We should have done more to encourage your potential. And there's still time to remedy that. Once *Rhea* is repaired and back in service, I'd like you back."

T'Ryssa stared, speechless. But before she could answer, a new voice came. "Trying to poach my crew again, you old dinosaur?" It was Picard, who'd just entered the room. "You haven't changed in thirty years."

The two captains shared a laugh. "You have. Didn't you have hair once? And not so many wrinkles."

"At least I accept my mortality, Bazel. You have yet to learn that even you aren't indestructible."

"Fah. If you were in my place, you'd insist on letting your crew see you on your feet."

"Perhaps I would. But you are on my ship, and

I'm married to your doctor. I'd say that entitles me to pull rank."

"Married, eh? That explains the wrinkles."

"Bite your tongue. Your crew has seen you; now get back to bed."

"I still have a question pending an answer from the lieutenant. Her rapport with the cluster entity would be of great value in our studies." The entity had volunteered to send the badly damaged *Rhea* and her crew back home via slipstream once they were both declared well enough for the journey. But Bazel was determined to bring the ship back again when it was ready, in order to continue studying the entity itself and its slipstream, particle-synthesis, and subspace-modification abilities. The knowledge that had already been gathered would no doubt be of use in Starfleet's slipstream experiments, even though there was no drive per se to bring back to the Federation.

Picard took his arm. "She doesn't have to decide now, Captain. Mister La Forge still needs a few days to batten down *Rhea*'s hatches for the slipstream journey."

"Excuse me," T'Ryssa said. "Sirs, I already know what my answer will be." She faced Bazel. "I appreciate the offer, Captain. It's really nice to hear it from you. And I have enjoyed getting to know the entity. But you have stronger telepaths than me in the crew." Unlike *Enterprise*'s telepaths, those aboard *Rhea* had been scanned and studied by the entity in as much detail as Trys had, if not more, so it would be able to connect with them as well. "And ol' Qingy deserves the chance to get to know more people than just me."

She shifted her weight uneasily. "Besides, I think staying on *Rhea* would bring me too many reminders of . . . you know. Now that I know you're safe . . . most of you . . . I think it's time to move on to the next thing."

*Still running away?* she asked herself. But she promptly answered, *No. This time I have something to run toward.* She glanced over toward another bed, where Rennan Konya was recovering from the injuries he'd sustained in the defense of engineering. *Maybe more than one thing,* she thought, remembering how afraid she'd been when she'd first heard that he'd been injured.

She turned to Picard. "Captain, I'd like to stay aboard the *Enterprise* as your contact specialist. If you'll have me."

The captain studied her with an aloof gaze for a moment, then let her off the hook and smiled. "Lieutenant, I would very much have regretted it had you made any other decision."

Her eyes widened. "Really?"

"Oh, I admit, your approach to diplomacy is somewhat . . . unorthodox. But your instincts have proved sound. Now, I'm not about to let you go on any contact mission without close supervision yet. You still have a lot to learn, particularly about the difference between negotiation and flimflammery."

She giggled. "Is that really a word?"

Picard harrumphed, and she subsided. "Not to mention about when to keep your thoughts to yourself. But . . . perhaps . . . there are things I can learn from you as well." His mouth quirked up again, just a bit. "Like how to let myself enjoy life a bit more. The capacity for humor in difficult times is a valuable thing indeed.

"In any case, you have meshed well with the crew. I have no interest in tampering with a proven rapport." He extended a hand. "T'Ryssa, you are welcome to stay with this crew for as long as you wish. So long as you behave yourself."

She shook his hand with reverence. "I won't let you down, sir." He nodded and began to escort Bazel back to his bed. But a devilish grin overtook Trys's features and she added, "Well—no more than a little. I have my reputation to uphold."

Picard paused, sighed, and shook his head. Turning to Bazel, he said, "I should've let you have her while I had the chance."

The entity had offered to give *Enterprise* a slipstream ride home as well, but Picard had declined. Of the eight *Frankenstein* drones to survive aboard *Enterprise,* half were from the *Einstein* crew, the other half from ships assimilated en route to the cluster—including one Mabrae and three of unknown species. Right now, they were still in the early stages of recovery, needing weeks more in sickbay to be restored to a semblance of their original conditions, and had not yet recovered to full consciousness or individual awareness. Once they were able to identify their places of origin, Picard intended to backtrack the *Frankenstein*'s course and return them to their respective peoples.

"I can't say I'm disappointed," Rebekah Grabowski told Picard when he met her in sickbay to share the news. She was beginning to look more like her old self again, for Doctor Tropp had restimulated her hair follicles and her curly nut-brown tresses were beginning to grow back. "The Liberated can certainly use more blood, but I'm not about to try to assimilate anyone who doesn't want to join. If they can go back to their own peoples, more power to them. We'll manage."

Picard stared, surprised by her choice of words. "We?"

His former crewwoman nodded. "I've been wrestling with this decision. I'm dying to see my daughter again . . . and Hugh sacrificed himself thinking that it would set me free to go home. I've been asking myself if I'd be betraying both of them by staying with the Liberated. But without Hugh, they need a leader. There's still a chance there could be other offshoots of the *Frankenstein* out there—we need to be ready to take them on."

"I doubt it," Picard said. "It's the nature of the Borg to consolidate. As far as I could discern from their thoughts, they had only absorbed other ships, not spawned any."

"We got the same impression," she told him.

"But it is wise never to underestimate the Borg."

"I suppose not," Picard said after a moment's pause.

"Besides, the Liberated need to survive as a culture, not just an army. They need someone to keep Hugh's dream alive, to help the factions bond into a united society that celebrates its differences instead of being divided by them." She shrugged. "Who better than a citizen of the Federation?"

Picard looked on her with pride. "Who indeed?"

"So I figure I'd be letting both Hugh and Ruthie down more if I didn't stay with the Liberated." She patted her belly and looked over at Beverly, who was nearby checking up on the recovering drones. "Besides, Doctor Crusher's ready to start regenerating my reproductive system . . . and she's perfected her hormonal formula to let the incubated drones procreate. I'm needed to start a new family now." Beverly looked up and smiled at them. Rebekah smiled back, a bit wistfully. "She even saved samples of Hugh's genetic material. He wanted so much to have a child with me. I owe it to him to see that it happens." She blinked away tears.

Picard clasped her shoulder. "Far be it from me to obstruct a member of my crew from starting a family," he said. "You have done the *Enterprise* proud, Lieutenant Grabowski."

"Thank you, sir. It was a privilege to be back." She took a deep breath, let it out. "Permission to disembark, Captain?"

He smiled. "Permission granted . . . *Captain*." After all, she commanded the *Liberator* now.

Blushing a bit, Rebekah gave him an old-fashioned salute, which he returned. Then she pivoted smartly and strode out the door. Picard's gaze lingered there for a long moment.

He turned at the sound of a throat clearing. T'Ryssa stood there—or rather, bounced there, as though barely able to contain her excitement about something. A cluster construct hovered beside her, a sight Picard had gotten used to by now, although this construct had taken a form resembling the Chinese dragon of their mind-meld vision, a graceful serpentine shape with multiple pairs of small delta wings along its length. Somehow the construct seemed to convey excitement as well. "Yes, Lieutenant?"

"Great news, sir. Looks like Rebekah's not the only one who'll be having a baby."

For a split second, Picard wondered if T'Ryssa was about to say she'd been careless with her contraceptive boosters. But he doubted that was what she meant. His eyes went to the construct. "The entity?"

She nodded exuberantly, a grin threatening to split her face. "Recent events have inspired it. It finally sank in that the Borg would've destroyed what it was. It started thinking about mortality and realized the stars that make up the cluster are short-lived, as stars go. And what with all of us talking and thinking about making babies . . . Well, I think it wants to tell you itself."

The serpentine construct had coiled up in midair and was beginning to transform. Soon it had become a hundred-odd small orbs that hovered in the shape of the cluster. Each orb was circled by a miniature of the dragon-shaped construct. Slowly, they converged and shrank as though receding into the distance—or rather, Picard realized, like a simulation being reduced in scale. Indeed, in moments, other similar clumps began to materialize at the edges of sickbay, seeming to come in through the walls, floor, and ceiling. Beverly gazed at the sight in fascination, coming over to stand alongside Picard. "The other open clusters nearby," she interpreted.

"That's right," Trys said. "Its neighbors. But not alive like it. Not yet."

Now, some of the tiny dragonets were splitting off from the original cluster, wending their way across to the neighboring clusters. Upon arrival, each dragonet began to duplicate itself around the various component orbs of each cluster, and soon many of them were swirling with life. "I think it's going to use slipstream to send pieces of its diamond mantle to other clusters—those that have carbon planets, anyway."

The corner of his mouth quirked up. "You mean . . . it intends to give them a piece of its mind?"

T'Ryssa gaped. "Sir, *you* made a pun?"

He glared back. "I'll have you know, Lieutenant,

that wordplay is a respected literary tradition. Shakespeare himself was famous for it."

"Thereby hangs a tale, I bet, sir."

Picard refused to take the bait, but silently reflected on how apt it was that she would quote Othello's clown. "About the cluster, Lieutenant."

"Right, sir. There's so much we still haven't figured out about how its semiconductor layers work, but apparently they're based on a kind of neural-net circuit that can seed itself, transform a diamond layer into more of the same kind of circuit. That's how it managed to spread across the entire cluster when it was first born."

Picard gazed at the simulation in wonder. "And now it intends to do it again."

"Thanks to you, sir," Trys said. "You convinced it that something that doesn't reproduce, doesn't create something new and different out of itself, isn't contributing to life. So it wants in. It wants to be part of that. To create beings that are like itself, but different, individual. And to make sure its legacy lives on." She sighed. "It'll probably take centuries—millennia, even. So we won't get to meet its kids."

"But our own progeny will," he assured her. He watched the simulated clusters for a moment longer, enthralled and delighted by what they represented. "Extraordinary. We were sent out here on a mission of destruction, and yet, in the process, we helped contribute to the birth of a whole new species."

"And the survival of another," Beverly added. "Thanks to the Liberated, I can feel that something good has come out of all these Borg horrors."

"New life," Picard murmured. "That's what our voyages are supposed to be about."

Faltering, clearing his throat, he said, "Thank you, Lieutenant. Dismissed." T'Ryssa left sickbay, but the now–re-formed cluster dragon remained to watch Picard and Beverly. He nodded at it awkwardly and led Beverly into her office, the door closing behind them. At last they were alone. Hesitantly, he turned to his wife and took her hand. "Um, along those lines, Beverly . . ."

"Yes, Jean-Luc?"

"Lately, well, given recent events . . ." He sighed and went on with self-deprecating irony. "Frankly, it seems as though the universe is trying to tell me something. So I may as well just give in to it already." He could tell she understood that he was joking, but few wives let their husbands off so easily; she cocked an eyebrow and crossed her arms at him until he sighed and grew serious again. "I've been a slave to my fears for too long, Beverly. I won't let them keep me from living my life any longer."

He clasped her hands. "I'm ready, my love. I believe that, together, we can overcome any challenge life gives us."

She smiled and pulled him into an embrace. "We'll see if that resolve holds up to diaper duty."

# GREATER THAN THE SUM

*U.S.S. Enterprise*
Outskirts of Mabrae space
Stardate 57983

Picard and Beverly strolled through the Riding Club, enjoying the camaraderie and cheer of the festivities around them. Guinan's holiday party had drawn more attendance than had been usual back in the Ten-Forward days, even among those from species and cultures to whom Christmas or the Earth winter solstice held little meaning. After all, the party doubled as a send-off for Guinan herself. Tomorrow, she would be accompanying Tared, the Mabrae they had liberated from Borg assimilation, when he beamed over to the Mabrae vessel that would take him home. The young humanoid had struggled with his recovery over the past month; in addition to dealing with the horrors of his assimilation and the things he had been forced to do as a drone, and with the grief of losing his family aboard the scout ship the *Frankenstein* had assimilated, he'd also had to face the trauma of being without the epiphytic plants that had grown on his body and been, in his mind, a part of himself. Guinan had taken him under her wing and helped him through it, and now that he, the last of their four non-Starfleet drones to be repatriated, was about to return home at last, the El-Aurian had decided that now would be a good time to take her leave. "The Mabrae are an interesting people," she'd said by way of explanation. "Besides, with their expertise in plant cultivation, they must have all sorts of interesting beverages. I'm always on the lookout for new recipes."

In the meantime, however, she was as dedicated a hostess as ever, making sure the partygoers kept their spirits up. Not that they required much help in that department. The past month had been an invigorating time, a much-needed tonic after the crew's latest ordeals with the Borg. Once the alien ex-drones had recovered enough to identify their homeworlds, the cluster entity had given *Enterprise* enough of a slipstream "push" to get them close to the nearest one, which was also the only one advanced enough to cope with the ex-drone's medical treatment without Starfleet assistance. After that, the ship had taken its time journeying the rest of the way back, not only to give Beverly time to oversee the other drones' recovery, but also to do some real exploration of the sectors they had raced through on the way out. In the past few weeks, they had made several first contacts, and the crew was invigorated by the return to good old exploration for its own sake.

T'Ryssa, of course, was the liveliest of all. She'd come in costume as an elf, more the traditional Santa Claus variety than the prouder, nobler creature he'd seen in her mind, and was hanging off Rennan Konya's shoulder and acting far more intoxicated on synthehol than she probably was, relishing the excuse to cast discipline aside. Miranda Kadohata was right there giggling and whooping it up alongside her, much of their mirth directed at the very surly Father Christmas who stood between them, stiffly rebuffing Jasminder Choudhury's invitations to dance. Worf was no doubt still upset about losing that bet to her; honor compelled him to live up to the terms and endure the red suit and padded belly, but he did not have to enjoy it. Jasminder soon gave up and took Geordi out on the dance floor, with T'Ryssa and Rennan following.

But all of them smiled and offered greetings as the Picard couple came near. Well, Worf didn't smile, but his scowl softened considerably at the sight of them. Even he could see, Picard reflected, that Beverly had that glow about her.

Clasping his wife's hand more tightly, he gazed down at her belly, still amazed after two weeks at the idea that a part of himself was growing inside her. A part of himself—but something greater than himself, a life with potential he could not as yet imagine.

*A baby,* he thought for the ten thousandth time. *Our baby.* His mind was reeling with the possibilities. *Will you follow in your father's footsteps as an explorer, or your mother's as a healer? Will you decide to return to the good Earth and keep the winery alive? Or will you find some new path all your own?*

Even the more immediate decisions still left him dizzy. What name would be worthy of his first true offspring? His preference changed hourly. Thank goodness there were eight and a half more months to decide. Though he suspected that time would go by in an eyeblink.

Beverly squeezed his hand back and smiled. "What are you thinking?"

"Oh . . ." He shrugged, for words were so inadequate. "About family," he said, looking around at his happy crew. Then he laid his hand on her belly. "About new life. *Our* new life."

"I think that calls for a toast," Beverly said more loudly, catching the attention of the group. Guinan was magically there, providing them with glasses of eggnog (fortunately, synthehol was safe for pregnant women to consume). "Will you do the honors?" Beverly asked her husband.

Picard raised his glass, the others following suit. "To new life," he intoned. "To family. And to a bright future for all our children."

# EPILOGUE

*U.S.S. Bhutto*
Beta Columbae star system
Stardate 58011


Zelik Leybenzon hated peacetime.

Well, no, that wasn't exactly right. It wasn't as though he wanted the Federation to be in a constant state of war, or wanted innocents to be killed. More proper to say that he didn't fit into peacetime very well. He was a soldier to the core, and the one thing he was really good at, the one thing that made him feel a complete man, was charging out onto a battlefield and doing the dirty, violent things that mainstream Federation society frowned upon so that they wouldn't have to. And it was a big Federation, with borders abutting literally hundreds of other powers. Even when most of its population was secure in the bland, numbing embrace of peace, there would always be places on the fringe where someone was making trouble and needed to be put down. That was where Zelik Leybenzon needed to be.

Unfortunately, Starfleet did not agree. He had known the risk when he had transferred off the *Enterprise.* He had been told—first by Admiral Haden, then by Commander Worf—that giving up a posting aboard the flagship of the fleet, rejecting the one real break he'd ever gotten in his tenuous career as an officer, would effectively end any chance of that career advancing further. He had understood it would also make it very unlikely that Starfleet would be inclined to take his preferences in mind when it came to selecting his next posting.

But being aware of it in theory hadn't made it any easier to cope with the tedium. For three months now, he had been the security chief of the *Bhutto,* a *Saber*-class patrol vessel assigned to patrol the Barolian system's stellar magnetopause— the zone where Beta Columbae's magnetic field gave way to the interstellar medium beyond, considered by starfarer tradition to be the border of the system's "territorial waters." Barolia was a center of trade and shipping in the Columba sector of the Federation, not too far from Klingon and Romulan territories, but not particularly close to them either. It attracted its share of smugglers and pirates, and its role as a trading hub made it a world of moderate strategic importance. The *Bhutto* was far from a prestigious assignment, but Leybenzon had hoped that his posting there would let him see a decent amount of action.

Unfortunately, things had been fairly quiet on the Barolian system's borders lately. Relations with the Klingons had improved since President Bacco's summit meeting last month, so the Defense Fleet was cracking down harder on Empire-based smugglers. Meanwhile, the fragmentation of Romulan territory had made it a fertile ground for smugglers and criminals of all sorts, but most of the illicit traders and thieves were occupied with smuggling food and supplies out of the so-called Imperial Romulan State, the splinter regime that had captured the Romulans' main farming worlds in order to starve out the opposition. And with the self-styled Empress Donatra wishing to maintain good relations with the Federation, and none of the other Romulan factions strong enough to do much of anything, there was no action to speak of on the espionage front either.

Leybenzon had thus been left with no major battles to fight, just routine police work, inspecting cargo holds and confiscating the odd bit of contraband. The most exciting encounter they'd had in the past three weeks was with a local freighter captain who'd resisted arrest and held a weapon on Leybenzon's team for a good twenty seconds before being stunned from behind; he'd been caught employing child labor and had shouted something about not wanting to lose his license a second time. Leybenzon drove his team relentlessly in daily training, but there was little happening to train them *for,* and many were growing restless. He reminded them that it was a soldier's duty to hurry up and wait, but privately, even he could do with a little more hurrying.

So when *Bhutto*'s red alert klaxon went off just as he'd bunked down for the night, Leybenzon leaped out of bed with enthusiasm, hoping that this time there would finally be a battle worth fighting.

When he arrived on the bridge, he was reminded that fate tended to answer one's prayers in the cruelest way possible. There was more than a battle going on; from the chaotic images on *Bhutto*'s main viewscreen, the screams and pleas for rescue coming in on all its comm channels, it was clear that an outright invasion was taking place. More than an invasion: a slaughter. The enemy showed no mercy, exhibited no agenda save wanton destruction. Barolia, a world of more than a billion inhabitants, was being systematically cleansed of life. The orbital defenses had been blown away in seconds, but a few escaping ships managed to send images of the vessel raining death down upon a peaceful world.

It was a cube.

Leybenzon shared the shock felt by the rest of the bridge crew as they absorbed the sights and sounds of the massacre. But he felt something else too, something he would not share with any of his fellow officers, for they would never understand.

He felt joy.

Not for the deaths, of course. He felt pure rage at the deaths. But he allowed himself a moment of sheer, self-centered joy that he finally had a real war to fight again. All he wanted out of life was to fight and die in defense of the Federation. Now he would once more have his chance.

*Bhutto*'s captain, a grizzled Andorian named ch'Regda, briefed his crew for the impending battle as the ship raced in from the magnetopause to engage the Borg. "There is a weapon," ch'Regda said. "The multivector nano-agent recently used by Captain Picard of *Enterprise* against the former *U.S.S. Einstein*. Not an ideal tactical weapon; it won't let us save what's left of Barolia. But if we can infect this cube with the nano-agent, given sufficient latency, it could spread through the entire Collective and end them as a threat once and for all."

Leybenzon reflected on the irony. It was his refusal to participate on the mission to test that weapon that had led to his current posting. As a result, he was now in a position to use that same weapon to strike the decisive blow against the Borg. So much for a backwater assignment.

"Wouldn't the Borg already know about the weapon, though?" asked Margark, the Benzite first officer.

"Apparently those Borg were out of contact with the rest of the Collective," ch'Regda told her. "The catch is, there's no reliable way to deliver the agent short of infecting your own bloodstream with it and allowing yourself to be assimilated. It would be a suicide mission."

"That," Leybenzon said, "is not an issue. Infect me with the agent. I will deliver it to the Borg personally."

Margark stared at him. "What makes you think the Borg would assimilate you rather than just kill you?" she asked.

"In their attack on *Rhea,* they assimilated the tactical officer, no doubt to gain military intelligence. If I make it clear I am the commanding security officer, a man with knowledge of Starfleet deployment and procedures in this sector, they should judge me a strategic asset worth acquiring."

He didn't know if that made sense. He didn't care. This was his job, his purpose. Fighting bad guys was all he was built for. If now was the time that he died for the Federation, so be it. Especially if it meant that this lowly grunt managed to save the Federation in the process. That would show Picard, Aenni, and the other officer types who'd looked down on him. They might not respect the grunts, but it was the grunts they depended on to save their flabby asses.

And if the Borg didn't assimilate him, if they tried to kill him instead, then he would fight until he managed to inject one of them with the agent. If these were the regular Borg, they'd have no idea what to expect, wouldn't guard against the threat until it was too late. Sure, he'd read Picard's reports, his crew's conclusions that no one could survive long enough against the newly bellicose Borg to inject the agent. But officers were always underestimating the ability of the enlisted troops in the field. He would deliver that agent, all right, one way or another.


Borg cube
In orbit of Barolia
Twelve minutes later


Zelik Leybenzon lay helpless on the deck, his back broken, watching his own blood pour out onto the cold metal grating beneath him, dripping through it to the decks below. Around him lay the remains of his security team, all volunteers, all injected with the agent and ready to die gloriously for the Federation along with him—Stolovitsky, Chi'iot, Leung, Vallasa. They had died, all right, but all their glory had spilled out onto the deck.

Leybenzon had led them boldly and openly. He had barked orders at every step, making it clear he was the commanding security officer. He had kept his comm channel open and spoken to the captain about available ships for backup, establishing the extent of his strategic knowledge. But no attempt had been made to assimilate him. The drones had come at him with cold, relentless lethality, maybe slower than the "evolved" drones from the *Einstein* and the supercube, but just as driven to destruction.

He and his people had readied their backup hypos and fought with all their skill and passion, but not one had managed to deliver an injection before being slain.

Now, his own hypo lay on the grating just centimeters from his hand. Summoning every last bit of will, Leybenzon forced his hand to move toward it, slowly, tremulously. Numb fingers brushed against it and knocked it farther away.

A drone strode over, knelt, and picked up the hypo. It carried it over to a wall alcove, tapped an adjacent console, and initiated a scan before wandering off to its next task. It had performed the action with surreal casualness, totally unaware of the importance of what it had just done.

No.

Of what Leybenzon had just done.

He had delivered it right into their hands.

He had been so hungry for battle, for purpose, for a renewed sense of pride, that he had marched into the fray without properly evaluating his enemy. As a result, he had committed what might be the greatest tactical blunder in history. And there next to him on the floor, his open tricorder warbled, transmitting the fruits of his hubris to the *Bhutto* so everyone would know who had doomed them.

Maybe he had wanted to die. Maybe he hadn't felt there was a life for him in a peaceful society like the Federation, not after the crucible of the Dominion War. He could accept that.

But he might have just killed the entire Federation along with him.

*U.S.S. Enterprise*
Outskirts of Antares Nebula
Stardate 58013

Picard was speechless for a long time after viewing the images from the Borg attack on Barolia—and the nearly simultaneous attack on Acamar, five sectors away. Two entire worlds eradicated in the span of an hour. It was a while before even Admiral Nechayev could speak, and she had seen the images already. *"We have no idea where they came from, Captain. There was no sign of any quantum slip-stream vortices, transwarp conduits, wormholes . . . we even scanned for Iconian gateway signatures, time warps, or portals from parallel realities, and there was nothing. Whatever they've found, it's something new. But it's letting them come in force . . . in waves. And they've already assimilated our 'ultimate weapon.' All that trouble you went to, and it's useless to us now, thanks to one bungled, reckless operation."*

*Of course,* Picard thought, his soul heavy with the inevitability of it. Every time they thought they'd beaten the Borg, the Collective had come back with a new trick. Every time they got complacent about the Borg's lack of ingenuity or adaptability, the Collective proved them wrong. How could he have let himself forget that, even for a moment?

But the admiral had said "waves." "Has there been a second attack?" he asked.

*"Not yet. But there will be."* She looked away for a moment, troubled by what she was about to say. *"The Borg sent us a communiqué just before they vanished back to wherever they came from."* Nechayev let out a sharp, sighing breath and went on. *"It said: 'We are the Borg. You will be annihilated. Your biological and technological distinctiveness have become irrelevant. Resistance is futile . . . but welcome.' "*

Picard shuddered. Nechayev had been right in that first briefing months ago; the Borg now considered the Federation too great a threat to tolerate. But no one had expected what was contained in those last two words. All the past actions of the Borg, all their assaults and atrocities against the Federation— they had never been personal. If Starfleet's string of victories over the Borg had made the cold, dispassionate Collective feel threatened enough to react like this—to *dare* Starfleet to do its worst—then the Federation was about to face a fury the likes of which it had never known.

But if these were the Borg from the Delta Quadrant, they would still know nothing of the victories over the supercube and the *Frankenstein.* If all this was just retribution for *Voyager*'s strikes on their transwarp network and Unicomplex three years ago, then how much more relentless would the

Borg become once they learned the fates of their errant children?

It didn't matter. The past was irrelevant. All that mattered was protecting the future.

He glanced over at Beverly, who sat beside him. Glanced down at her womb. *The future.*

*"You are ordered to report back to Federation space at maximum possible speed, Captain Picard. The* Enterprise *is the only ship we have that's currently equipped with transphasic torpedoes. That last-ditch emergency we were saving them for is here."*

Picard didn't wait for pleasantries. "Lieutenant Faur, increase to warp 9.5. Mister La Forge, get down to those engines, get every last bit of speed you can squeeze out of them. Faur, increase speed as it becomes available."

"Aye, sir." Geordi was already in the lift.

*"Thank you, Captain,"* Nechayev said. *"I think I speak for us all when I say I'll feel better once* Enterprise *is home. Nechayev out."*

Over at the auxiliary science station, T'Ryssa was crying. Beverly had tears in her eyes as well, but she held his gaze evenly, sharing her strength with him. He opened his mouth, wanting to order her to leave the ship at the nearest friendly port. The life she carried within her was too precious to risk. *She* was too precious.

But in the same moment, he knew she would never leave. And Nechayev's orders left him no time to drop her off in any case. Whatever they faced, they would be facing it together.

But his eyes still darted down to her womb, and he knew she could see the fear and guilt in them.

She leaned in and spoke softly, for his ears only. "Do you regret it?"

He wasn't sure what to say. He loved this child so much . . . the thought of conceiving a child only to put it in danger was unconscionable. But in that very thought came his answer. "No," he told her. "I wouldn't change it for the galaxy." He clasped her hand in both of his. "And I swear to you—I will protect our child no matter what it takes."

But at the core of his conviction was a hollowness. He had no idea whether he could keep his oath in the struggle ahead. Two cubes had annihilated two entire worlds. The Borg had thousands of cubes. And they would commit them all to the destruction of the Federation.

So how could he possibly protect his family?

# ACKNOWLEDGMENTS

---

Thanks to Margaret Clark for inviting me to tell this chapter in the post-*Nemesis* adventures of the crew of the *Enterprise*-E. This book relies heavily on concepts laid out by the authors of earlier installments in this and related novel series, particularly Christie Golden (*Homecoming/The Farther Shore*), Michael Jan Friedman (*Death in Winter*), J. M. Dillard (*Resistance*), Keith R. A. DeCandido (*Articles of the Federation, Q&A*), Peter David (*Before Dishonor*), and David Mack (the upcoming *Destiny* trilogy). In particular, Jasminder Choudhury and Dina Elfiki are joint creations of Dave and myself. Keith and Dave were both valuable sounding boards in the writing of this novel, as was Kirsten Beyer, who helped me greatly in sorting out my ideas about the Borg. Thanks also to Rick Sternbach for a spot of technical advice where needed.

This story also relies on concepts from a number

# ACKNOWLEDGMENTS

of *Star Trek: The Next Generation* episodes, espe cially "Q Who" by Maurice Hurley, "The Best o Both Worlds" by Michael Piller, "I, Borg" by Rene Echevarria, "The Inner Light" by Morgan Gende and Peter Allan Fields, and "Descent" by Jeri Tay lor, Ronald D. Moore, and René Echevarria; the movie *Star Trek: First Contact* by Rick Berman Ronald D. Moore, and Brannon Braga; and *Sta Trek: Voyager* episodes including "Hope and Fear" and "Timeless" by Rick Berman, Brannon Braga and Joe Menosky, "Unimatrix Zero" by Mike Suss man, Brannon Braga, and Joe Menosky, and "Endgame" by Rick Berman, Brannon Braga, Ken neth Biller, and Robert Doherty.

My depictions of the cluster entity's variou: manifestations owe much to the *anime* creations o Hayao Miyazaki and Chiaki J. Konaka. As for the star cluster itself, NGC 6281 is real and can be seer with binoculars or a telescope in the constellation Scorpius, about two and a half degrees east of M Scorpii. My research made use of the WEBDA data base, operated at the Institute for Astronomy of the University of Vienna, at www.univie.ac.at/webda/ The cluster is too far away for accurate distance measurements, so my description of the relative distances of its various component stars is specula tive. Thanks also to *An Atlas of the Universe* a www.atlasoftheuniverse.com for helping me find the cluster in the first place. I'm also indebted to the paper "Extrasolar Carbon Planets" by Marc J Kuchner and S. Seager. Carbon planets probably would have diamond mantles, but the idea that semiconductive layers in those mantles could produce a natural computer is entirely my own and is admittedly one of my more implausible notions.

For Hindu and Buddhist lore and quotations, I'm indebted to Ainslie T. Embree, ed., *Sources of Indian Tradition,* 2d ed., Vol. 1 (Columbia University Press, 1988).

Special thanks go to Xuân Stanek, without whom T'Ryssa Chen would never have existed. I created the character who became T'Ryssa for a unique and sadly short-lived role-playing game she ran with me in late 1996, putting a *Star Trek* character in a *Dungeons and Dragons* world. I'm pleased that the character has found new life, and she does so with Xuân's blessing.

# ABOUT THE AUTHOR

Christopher L. Bennett, a man barely alive, was rocketed to Earth from a dying planet. Searching for a distant star, the weather started getting rough, and the tiny ship was tossed where no man has gone before. He was in a coma for six years, in a dimension not of sight and sound, but of mind. Pressured to prove his theories or lose funding, an accidental overdose of gamma radiation altered his body chemistry. Now he can control the horizontal and the vertical, and is not a number but a free man. He also watches far too much television.

Meanwhile, Christopher has authored the critically acclaimed novels *Star Trek: Ex Machina, Star Trek: Titan: Orion's Hounds,* and *Star Trek: The Next Generation: The Buried Age,* as well as the eBooks *Star Trek: S.C.E. #29: Aftermath* and *Star Trek: Mere Anarchy Book 4: The Darkness Drops Again,* and stories in all four *Star Trek* anniversary anthologies to date as well as the *Mirror Universe:*

# ABOUT THE AUTHOR

*Shards and Shadows* anthology. His short novel *Places of Exile,* depicting an alternate history for the *Voyager* crew, was recently published in the *Star Trek: Myriad Universes* anthology. Outside of ST, Christopher has authored two Marvel Comics novels, *X-Men: Watchers on the Walls* and *Spider-Man: Drowned in Thunder.*

# STAR TREK®
## Destiny

# Gods of Night

## David Mack

Available October 2008

It had been nearly three months since the *Enterprise* crew had succeeded in its mission to hunt down and destroy the Borg-assimilated Federation science vessel *U.S.S. Einstein*. At the end of that mission, Beverly had sensed and taken advantage of an opportunity to cajole Picard into the most hopeful undertaking of his life: starting a family with her.

There had been no denying that, on some level, he had wanted this for a long time. The need had been awakened in him nearly ten years earlier, when his older brother, Robert, and young nephew, René, had been killed in a tragic fire at the family's vineyard home in Labarre, France.

Beverly's reason for wanting a family was just as poignant to Picard. Her only son, Wesley—whom she had treasured as the last surviving remnant of her late husband, Jack Crusher—had evolved many years earlier into a Traveler, a wondrous being capable of moving freely through time and space . . . but he also was no longer fully human. The more that Wesley had grown into his powers as a Traveler, the less frequently he had returned to visit with Beverly. He had appeared at their hastily arranged, low-key wedding a few months earlier, but there was no telling when he might return—if he ever did.

After the *Einstein* had been destroyed, Picard thought they had earned a chance to seize their dream. After all, the *Voyager* had destroyed the Borg's transwarp hub to Federation space a few years earlier. The *Enterprise* and her crew had stopped the most fearsome Borg cube ever encountered. And the last rogue Borg element in Federation space seemed to have been eliminated.

For a moment, Picard had dared to hope. He and Beverly had started their family. And less than a month later, the Borg began their blitzkrieg into Federation space.

*You should've known. You've always known.*